Want and Need

C.J. LAURENCE

DEDICATION
For Michele.
You know why
XXX

Chapter One

H E CAPTIVATED ME ENTIRELY. His entire essence called to me, leaving me as helpless as a moth hypnotised by a glimmer of light. My body hummed in delight from his divine touch. The delicious strokes of pleasure from between my legs left me revelling in new levels of joy. His lust-filled gaze trailed down my heaving chest, sending shivers running through me. I found myself transfixed on his arms, the taut, defined muscles straining from the hard grip he had on my thighs. That image alone almost released me from his sensual assault.

He plunged himself in and out of me, faster, deeper, each urgent thrust pushing breathless gasps from me. With his chiselled cheeks and burning blue eyes, he brought me to my sweet edge in seconds. I collapsed back on his desk, panting and swimming in an ocean of decadence.

He glued his lips to mine and groaned, letting his pleasure vibrate right through him. He stilled for a few seconds, then collapsed on top of me. His laboured breaths resonated with me as I struggled to catch my own breath.

He pulled away, and as he sorted his clothes out, I propped myself up on my elbows, biting my lip with a seductive bat of my lashes.

"So," he said, a cheeky grin tweaking the corners of his mouth as he glanced back up at me. "How do you think your appraisal went, Kyra?"

I flashed him a wicked smile. "I think it could have been better."

He raised an eyebrow. "Really?" he said, smirking. "I look forward to seeing your notes on improvement."

He moved back towards me with a mischievous grin, those succulent lips of his inching their way towards my neck. Like prey to a vampire, I succumbed and gave him all the access he required. I couldn't help the moan of desire escaping me as he grazed kisses across my skin...

"Kyra. Hello, Kyra. Anybody home?"

I startled, my cheeks heating up in an instant as I saw him smiling down at me from the edge of my desk.

"Yes, sorry."

"You were away with the fairies there, weren't you? Anything good?" He darted his tongue over his lips, that one simple action making my heart rate spike in an instant. "Can you please type these letters and give them back for me to sign?"

I nodded and made a grab for the papers, trying my best to hide my flustered state. With a sly smirk, he sauntered back to his office, the definitive click of the closing door piercing through the deafening silence.

Running a shaky hand through my dark hair, I breathed a sigh of relief. Oh my god. I need to pack this in.

He happened to be my boss and a new director in our company.

Young, athletic, and smoking hot married with an air of confidence to mesmerise any female within a ten-mile radius, in the past two weeks he'd been at my company he hadn't left my thoughts for more than five minutes.

He carried himself like a Greek god, looked like a Greek god, and I had no doubt he was, in fact, a Greek god. If his body was anything like his edible face, I knew I'd be lost to him.

His name was Paul Connors and, as far as I knew, he had no significant other—purely based on a lack of wedding ring, no cute family pictures in his office, and no mysterious phone calls that I'd so far noticed.

I'd convinced myself he flirted with me, but I couldn't be sure if my overactive imagination happened to be playing tricks on me. I worked as the PA to all the directors in the company, but he gave me the most work. The director he'd replaced hardly gave me any.

Calming my rosy cheeks along with my imagination, I completed his work within an hour. Knocking on his office door, I held my breath and waited for that honey laden voice to coat me in its sugary sweetness and invite me in.

As effortless as silk falling from a blade, his voice slid across the room. "Come in."

I opened the door and walked through, careful to avoid direct eye contact for as long as possible so I wouldn't keep picturing him naked or in a white toga with me feeding him grapes whilst stroking his bicep.

"Shut the door, Kyra, please. I think we need a little chat. Please have a seat."

The clunk of the door as I closed it seemed to be the catalyst for the atmosphere beginning to crackle with tension. Each step I took towards the soft blue chair facing his desk seemed to be like an ominous walk of death. I placed the letters on his desk, my heart pounding so loudly against my ribs he had to have heard it.

"Thank you." He picked up his tumbler glass and sipped some of his water. I couldn't help but focus on his red lips, wishing they were wrapped around parts of my body instead of that glass. He set the glass back down and with sparkling eyes, asked, "Are you ok, Kyra? You seem very distracted of late. Is there anything you would like to discuss?"

Watching glee and amusement dance through his eyes, I resisted the urge to squirm in my seat and focused on a painting on the wall behind him. The scorching burn of my cheeks complemented my now sweating palms.

"Um, no, I'm fine, thank you. I have a tendency to daydream now and again. I'm sorry, I'll try to stop it."

"It's fine, we all do it," he said, waving a hand through the air dismissively. He flashed me a dazzling smile causing more heat to gather in every part of me. "So long as there are no problems that are distracting you?"

I shook my head and pressed my lips together to stop myself from speaking. Could I say that my problem was him and the nymphomaniac he seemed to be turning me into? I'd never been affected by a guy quite like this. This was my normal lust dialled up a hundred levels. I didn't know what to do with myself. Maybe it was just because I seemed to be having a dry spell at the moment.

Yep, that was definitely it. I hadn't had sex for six months and this guy simply sent my hormones haywire. That was it, nothing more. The feelings would fade in time. Maybe, hopefully, by the time I had my next period and my ovaries stopped twitching.

"Well," he said. "My door is always open if you need to talk about any problems you may have. And I do mean any problems."

My heart skipped a beat. His emphasis on the word 'any' struck a chord inside me. Did he know I had a crush on him? A smile escaped onto my lips as the words danced on the end of my tongue, desperate to tell him that he was my problem.

I could picture it already—me telling him that he was my problem and him replying that he would give me a big problem. I would look suggestively at his trousers and bite my lip whilst peeking up at him from under my lashes, then he would get up from his seat and walk to me, tugging me from my chair to my feet. Pulling me into his body, he would run a hand through my hair and plant his lips on mine...

"And there you go again," he said, chuckling. "Are you smiling about anything nice?"

His voice snapped me back to reality, but still melting me like butter under a hot knife. I crossed my legs, cleared my throat, and mumbled an apology, trying to think of anything other than him to calm my raging hormones. I lowered my eyes in shame, that at thirty years old, I couldn't control myself any better than a teenager with front row seats at a One Direction concert.

"You know," he said, lowering his voice to a husky whisper. "I would love to know what you daydream about."

His blasé statement combined with his seductive tone of voice caught my attention and like a deer caught in headlights, I couldn't do much except breathe out, "What?"

"Well," he said, talking in a normal tone again. "Maybe it's something that would benefit the company."

My heart raced like a stampede of wild horses. "No," I replied, shaking my head. "Sorry to disappoint."

His svelte mouth creased into an innocent smile. "I'll let you get back to work. I heard old Andrews shouting for his papers earlier."

He stood and gestured towards the door. I jumped up and turned my back on him, rushing for the escape I so desperately needed, as if my life depended on it.

Only I didn't realise he'd followed me to the door.

Like some cliché movie moment, we both grabbed the handle at the same time. I startled, my breath catching in my throat. I snatched my hand back, hoping he hadn't noticed the slight sheen to my skin. The unexpected contact only threatened to turn that sheen into a full on nervous sweat.

He took a step towards me, invading my personal space just a little too much for a professional relationship. "Just to clarify," he whispered, leaning into me, his lips brushing against my ear. "You never disappoint me, Kyra."

I gasped as he lingered next to me, his breath skimming over my skin. Goosebumps shot up all over me and a shiver ran down my spine. As he pulled away, our eyes locked together allowing me to see the mischief skipping through his eyes. I couldn't help but wonder if this mischievousness carried into the bedroom.

He opened the door, signalling for me to exit. "Back to work, Kyra."

Chapter Two

ALL WEEKEND I THOUGHT of nothing but what Paul had said, finally convincing myself I was reading far more into it than I should be. Putting aside the hierarchy at work issue, a guy like him would never be interested in a woman like me anyway. I vaguely wondered if he had a line of women following him everywhere. It really wouldn't surprise me.

Like lines from detention, I repeated to myself I would control my daydreams about him. It wasn't healthy—or normal.

Monday morning soon came around and as I stepped into the office, I couldn't help but breathe a sigh of relief when I realised no one else had arrived yet.

My company building had three storeys, and of course, being just my luck, I happened to work on the top floor.

The elevator opened out into a long corridor with a mahogany door at the end. Through this door was an open plan room.

On the right-hand side of the room sat a long line of nine dark tinted glass offices, one for each of the directors. Soft coloured grey blinds from floor to ceiling allowed them their privacy when they wanted it, although they all had them closed most of the time anyway.

On the left-hand side of the room was a wall adorned with fancy artwork, then at the end, a sharp corner that led down to the kitchen. I sat with my back against the far wall, facing the door, enabling me a clear view of anyone who walked in, plus the visitors seating area in front of me.

The plush grey sofas for the visitors needed plumping, and the country house magazines strewn all over the glass table needed tidying. I hummed to myself as I fussed over everything, making it all 'just so'. My thoughts trailed off to Paul for just a second and I became all fingers and thumbs as my temperature crept up again. This man was not healthy for my mind or my ovaries.

The magazines fell from my hands, scattering across the soft beige carpet. I cursed under my breath and bent down, clearing up my mess as I mentally chastised myself. Standing back up, I turned around, screaming as I met Paul's handsome face inches from my own.

"Oh my God! You gave me a heart attack." The adrenaline pulsing through my veins made me lightheaded. I couldn't quite work out if it was shock or nerves. I put a hand over my chest, hoping it would somehow stop my heart from trying to beat out of my chest. "I didn't hear the door. Sorry."

"Good morning," he said, giving me a warm smile. "Sorry for scaring you."

"Good morning. No problem, I think I'm still alive. I didn't think anyone was in yet."

"Sorry to disappoint," he replied, giving me a cheeky wink.

The tension between us was now becoming impossible to ignore. I felt as if I could reach out and pluck it like a strained elastic band. Every passing second heightened the atmosphere to new levels of intensity. I didn't know what to do except escape this awkward situation so I offered him a cup of coffee.

"That would be lovely, thank you." As he moved behind me, en-route to his office, he whispered in my ear, "And I would love to be your God."

Shock rendered me motionless for several seconds. By the time I whipped around to face him, he was already closing his office door.

I didn't imagine that.

Did I?

Maybe I didn't have an overactive imagination after all.

In a complete daze, I wandered down to the kitchen and made his coffee. As I raced through all the recent happenings, I realised with a heart-warming, nerve inducing swell he was definitely hitting on me. He had to be.

I took his coffee to him, surprised to see we were still on our own. My gut began to churn as I wondered exactly why that was.

"Thank you." He smiled and cleared his throat. "Just you and me today, Kyra."

My heart stopped dead, anticipation lodging in my throat. Just the two of us in this space for eight hours? My stomach clenched. "Oh. Ok. I haven't been informed of anything to alter the movements diary."

"Andrews and Chapman have a delayed flight back from New York—no doubt you will have an email from them both. Michaels is off sick, and Harris is on holiday as you know. Nicholls, Tate, and Atkins are in the meeting in Devon with Mr. Collins. That leaves just me. And you."

"Ok." I thought over my options for a split second before a naughty thought skimmed its way past my lips. "I guess I'm all yours, then," I said, as innocently as possible with a slight shrug of my shoulders.

He raised his eyebrows, seemingly stunned by my response. I grasped my opportunity with both hands and left him to chew over it as I sashayed my way out of his office.

Two can play that game, mate. You're not catching me off guard anymore and enjoying it.

He remained in his office for the rest of the morning. As the clock struck one p.m.—lunchtime, I gathered my bag, ready to head out. Paul's door swung open and he strode towards me, the confidence in his advance making my imagination run riot instantly. My heart stopped dead before leaping into a frenzied beat. Was this it? Was this the moment he would pin me against the wall and ravage me until the end of time?

"Chicken tikka?"

I stared back dumbfounded, my fantasy of him pushing me back against the wall and owning me bursting like a balloon under a pin.

"The sandwich shop. That is where you were going, right?"

I nodded, words finally forming into sentences in my mind but still not reaching my voice box.

"Well, I'm going there, so do you want me to get yours for you?"

"Um, ok, thanks." I started fishing around in my bag for my purse, grateful for any chance to distract myself from my thoughts. "Let me get the money for you."

"I think I can afford to buy you a sandwich, Kyra."

With that, he turned and left. As the door closed behind him, I collapsed in my chair, frowning as I tried to figure this out. He was, without doubt, hitting on me. He had to be. But then I hadn't seen him around other women so maybe this was just him.

Fifteen minutes later, when he came back with my sandwich, I still sat in the same place trying to work out what the hell was going on.

I smiled and gave him my thanks as I took my lunch from him. He disappeared back inside his office, leaving me wondering about his actions once again. I headed to the kitchen to make a cup of tea and help calm my thoughts.

Unfortunately, daydreams of me spread over his desk took control once again as I stirred the milk in...and kept on stirring.

"Have you stirred that enough?"

I shrieked in surprise, jumped, and splashed tea all over the worktop as I dropped the spoon with a clatter. I turned to face him, my cheeks flaming up in an instant under his radiating gaze.

It suddenly struck me I had no way out of here because he stood in the doorway—the only way in and out. I felt like an antelope cornered by a lion.

"Daydreaming again?"

I nodded.

He stepped towards me and lowered his voice. "You really need to indulge me with your daydreams, Kyra. I'm curious."

"Oh, they're nothing. Just wondering what will happen in the soaps and stuff on TV."

"Ahh." He took another step towards me, the gap between us now barely more than a few inches. "And there was me hoping they might have been about me."

My mouth dropped open. "What?"

A beaming smile spread over his face as he took the last of the space between us. I didn't know where to look or what to say.

His attention fell to my mug. "Can I try your tea? Seeing as you always make me coffee."

I nodded. "But you never ask for tea."

"Well, I do like a bit of variety now and again."

My heart rate tripled. He reached past me, brushing my arms as he did so. A breath caught in my throat as crippling tingles from his skin touching mine nearly brought me to my knees. Our eyes met and I became lost in his brilliant blue eyes, nothing but oceans of devilry staring back at me.

He lifted my mug to his perfect lips and sipped my tea, letting out a small groan. My eyes fell to his mouth, fixating on them as they touched the rim of the mug. "Good tea. Is everything you make this good?"

"What...what do you mean?" My mind now raced in time with my heartbeat. Where was this going? Was he going to kiss me? Or was he just enjoying seeing me squirm?

"Anything." He shrugged his shoulders, trailing his tongue over his bottom lip. "Drinks, food, other things..."

Before I could even register his words, the office door slammed shut, alerting us to someone's presence.

The building tension melted like an ice cube in hot water. I scurried my way around him to see who the visitor was. Thankfully, no unexpected visitor, just one of the managers looking for Mr. Collins. Explaining the situation whilst quietly thankful for their intervention, I flopped down in my chair as they left.

Where the hell had that been going? What would have happened if they hadn't walked in?

Paul appeared in his office doorway as the main office door closed shut behind the manager. "Can I talk to you please?"

I knew for sure I wasn't imagining things now. I stood up and edged my way through his door, very aware of him stood to my left, hovering to close the door behind me.

As I passed through the doorway, coming to a stop just in front of him, he pushed the door, letting it slam shut as our eyes locked onto one another. His intense stare turned every cell inside me to jelly. My breaths came short and shallow as the tension between us bubbled to boiling point.

He stepped towards me and I stepped back, my entire body now trembling in anticipation of all my fantasies colliding together with reality. He stared straight through me, boring a hole through any weak defences I might have had against him.

"Paul—"

He rushed towards me, pushing me back against the door and stealing all the breath from my lungs. He grabbed my waist and pressed his lips to mine, kissing me with such hunger it rendered me not only speechless but completely motionless. As I opened my mouth, twirling my tongue with his, he clutched at my waist, his fingers digging into my sides. I wound my hands around his neck, running my hands up and through his hair.

Passion and urgency took hold of us both, raging desire spurring us into lust-fuelled action. He slid his hands up and down my body, exploring me over my clothes. I yanked his shirt free, desperate to feel his smooth skin. As soon as my hand touched the velvet hardness of his chest, I couldn't help but let out a small moan of joy.

Needing air, I broke our brief embrace, managing to whisper, "What the hell...?"

Resting his forehead against mine, he whispered, "I'm sorry...did I read you wrong?"

I couldn't help the grin spreading across my swollen lips. "No."

"Good. Now shush and enjoy it," he replied, planting his lips to mine.

Chapter Three

SEVERAL MINUTES LATER, WE came up for air, both of us panting. I had become a hot, flustered mess after feeling his taut, defined muscles beneath my fingertips. Being able to finally touch him achieved nothing but to further my need for him. Naked images of him flooded my mind, sending my imagination into overdrive. My ovaries were melting like ice on a hot plate.

"You ok?" he asked.

I nodded, a grin spreading over my face from ear to ear. He pecked my lips and then rearranged his shirt. Once he'd finished, he stood, staring at me, his lips folding into a cheeky smile.

I pushed myself away from the wall and smoothed down my clothes. "What the hell was that?"

Mischief flitted through his eyes as he said, "I'm sorry. I couldn't help myself any longer."

Those words, after what had just happened, sent my head into a complete spin. It felt so surreal to hear those words coming from him, from my boss. I faltered, not really knowing what to say back to that.

"You didn't slap me, so I'm guessing you're pleased I couldn't help myself any longer," he said.

I bit my lip and smirked at him. "You have no idea."

He came towards me and lifted his hand, brushing a stray piece of hair from my face. "Can I take you out to dinner?"

I giggled. "Is that just a formality before the inevitable?"

In mock horror, he slapped a hand over his chest. "What exactly are you trying to insinuate? I can behave for however long is required."

"Of course you can," I replied, laughing.

He narrowed his gorgeous blue eyes at me, his delicious mouth still curved into a heart melting smile. "That sounds like a challenge to me, Miss Wilson."

"Maybe it is," I said, giving him a cheeky wink.

"Friday night then. After all, we don't want you tired for work the next day, do we?"

I flashed him my best smile. "No, not at all."

By the end of the week, the atmosphere between us evolved into nothing short of animalistic lust, a primitive need to satisfy each other's cravings.

Paul handed me work at any given opportunity, stroking my fingers as he passed it over. Each piece I handed back would result in a closed door, stolen kisses, and disturbed clothes. I had a feeling dessert on Friday night would not consist of food—unless the food was on one of us.

The burning desire smouldering deep inside me was something I'd never harboured for anyone else. Something about him bewitched me, lost me in a world of insatiable daydreams, and made me question the true depths of myself.

I had never really been a relationship type of girl. The novelty of new things wore off quickly with me and it never took long for me to become bored. That of course, never did bode well for me or the poor guy who thought he could be the one to change my ways. Once my lust for someone burned itself out, their annoying habits and increasing need to steal my free time only irritated me to the point that I ended things within a few months.

My longest relationship had lasted six months which promptly ended when the guy confessed his undying love for me. Other than family, I had never uttered the dreaded 'L' word to anyone. Commitment scared me and I liked having options and knowing where my exits were.

I'd had a few one night stands here and there to keep my 'needs' satisfied, but other than that, my dating history looked sporadic at best and not what you would classify as experienced.

Paul, however, captured my attention to an extent I never knew a man could. I wanted him for more than one night, but at the moment, the alternative option to that scared me. To bare my soul to someone, to bond myself to them and only them...it made me shudder.

Yet a part of me, deep down, craved that stability, desired the closeness of having a partner, of having someone to rely on, someone to look forward to talking to every day about every little thing. Up to this point in my life, I just chose to ignore those deep feelings and blundered on in the best way I knew how.

Friday, I finished work, full of excitement and curiosity. I felt like I was walking on cloud nine, that this life wasn't possibly mine and my hot as hell boss couldn't possibly be taking me out for dinner tonight.

With my head way up high in the clouds, I realised I'd never been this high. Memories of smoking weed back in my teenage years sprung to mind and I thought to myself if only I'd had him to get high on back then, I'd have saved myself a boat load of cash.

As I grabbed the last piece of work to take to him, I undid an extra button on my blouse, revealing the curve of my breasts to whoever would dare look below my face. I sauntered into his office and couldn't help but give him a mischievous smile as I bent a little lower than necessary, giving him the perfect view of my cleavage.

He raised an eyebrow and ran his tongue over his bottom lip. "Anybody would think you were trying to seduce me, Miss Wilson."

"I think you're just being a little paranoid."

He grinned. "Oh really?"

"Or is that your line to try and seduce me?

He chuckled. "If I wanted to seduce you," he said, lowering his voice to a husky whisper. "You'd have been bent over my desk already."

"That's an awfully bold statement to make. You're very sure of yourself."

"I happen to be very sure of your reaction to me," he said, roving his eyes up and down my body.

My core temperature felt like it had risen ten degrees in the mere minute or so I'd been in his presence. He knew exactly what effect he had on me, and I couldn't deny it. "And is that a problem?"

"Not normally, no. However, I do recall you set me a challenge and I intend to complete it."

I stood up straight and grinned at him, biting my lip. I settled a hand on my breast, fiddling with the ends of my hair, and said, "We'll see about that."

I chose a strapless, black bodycon dress for my hot date. Slipping on a pair of nude stockings and some slinky black heels, I made the final adjustments to my hair and makeup before his timely knock at the door.

My stomach churned with anticipation at seeing him outside of work and what this evening would bring. I sucked in a deep breath before opening the door. I had to bite my cheek to stop the instant *'Oh my God'* reaction in my head coming out of my mouth.

Dressed in a soft lemon-coloured shirt and a pair of jet-black trousers, his dirty blonde hair smoothed down with gel and the faint aroma of cologne drifting towards me, he literally was the definition of sex on legs.

"Wow," he said. "You scrub up well." He winked and held his hand out, flashing me a dazzling smile. He dropped his voice and whispered, "You look beautiful, Kyra."

I blushed as I took his hand. "Thank you. You don't look too bad yourself."

He played the gentleman part and opened the car door for me. Once inside his sleek black BMW, the tension between us dissolved when our eyes met.

"You look really good," I said. "Like *really.*"

"Thank you," he said, giving me a warm smile.

We both giggled nervously as he started the engine, then eased into small talk on the way to the restaurant. It didn't take long for me to feel like I was on a date with a hot guy, rather than on a date with my boss. Just hearing his voice settled my nerves. I knew he wouldn't do anything untoward, and I knew he would treat me with nothing but respect.

As we pulled up at the restaurant, the conversation ended with him asking about my best friend, Molly, who also worked at the same company. Having spent the last two weeks sunning herself in Hawaii, I hadn't indulged her in this news over text. I had to tell her face to face. She would go berserk over this—Molly loved gossip. Glancing at the clock quickly—seven thirty p.m., I knew that she would currently be on a plane on her way back. Already forming sentences in my mind of how to tease her, I couldn't wait to see her.

Tonight, we were going to a small, cosy Indian restaurant not far from my home. They served the best prawn masala I'd ever tasted, and I couldn't wait to taste it again. I loved the inside with its traditional Indian décor everywhere from the brightly coloured elephant ornaments to the old oil paintings of tigers and forests. Soft but lively Indian music played quietly in the background setting the atmosphere.

A waiter led us to our table for two in the far corner of the room. With only twelve tables in the restaurant, service was always exceptional, and fast. The dark wooden tables were covered with a soft white tablecloth and the matching chairs each had their own colourful patterned cushion to sit on.

In the middle of every table, two pink candles were lit, their orange flames dancing almost in time to the beat of the music, giving the restaurant a warm, romantic vibe with the dimmed lights.

I didn't even need to look through the menu—I knew what I wanted from the minute Paul said we were coming here.

"That suits me," he said. "Because I knew what I wanted before we came here too."

I laughed. "And what are you having?"

"Wait and see," he said, winking.

When the waiter came to take our order, I ordered my favourite—the prawn masala with vegetable rice and garlic naan bread. When Paul ordered a Vindaloo, I nearly choked on my drink.

"It's not as bad as people think," he said, tucking into one of the poppadoms already on the table. "It's just like a normal curry except with more of a kick."

I raised my eyebrow at him. "Is that because all of your taste buds have been burned away?"

He laughed. "No. I just like to know that I've eaten something. If it's bland and has no taste, then I don't really feel like I've eaten anything. It may as well have been paper."

I shook my head. "I don't like ordering food I might not like. It's a waste of money and ruins the chance of a good meal."

"I like your logic. But I love spicy food and see it as a challenge."

I grinned and ran my tongue over my lips. "Is it just food you like spicy?"

The waiter appeared then with our drinks, making me wonder if he would return to this conversation once we were left to our ourselves again. The waiter finally left and I waited for Paul to continue.

He shook his head and chuckled. "I am completing that challenge this evening, Miss Wilson."

I reached for my drink and wrapped my tongue around the straw with deliberate, slow precision. His eyes darkened, glued to the sight of me stroking and flicking the end of the straw with my tongue.

I batted my eyelashes and in my most innocent voice asked, "So, what happens at work now?"

He hesitated for a second before taking his eyes from my tongue and looking at me. "What do you mean?"

"Well, isn't this kind of a bit weird? You are my boss."

He grinned, leaning across the table as he whispered, "From Monday to Friday, eight thirty to four, yes, I am. Outside of those hours, I'll be whatever you want me to be."

I dropped the straw and traced my index finger over my bottom lip. "That's a dangerous statement to make."

He poked the inside of his cheek with his tongue. "How so?"

"I couldn't possibly answer that. After all, you do have a challenge to complete." I grinned and then said, "On a serious note, what happens come Monday morning? Isn't it going to be a bit weird? I've been paranoid enough all week that people have noticed something."

He grinned. "I'm a director, Kyra. No one is going to challenge me except the other directors or Mr. Collins himself. Stop worrying."

"But isn't it frowned upon for employees to date?"

"It is advised against, yes."

"And you're my boss, which makes it worse."

"Stop worrying. You're not going to get into any trouble. Just relax and enjoy it for what it is, ok?"

I nodded, taking my time to sip my drink through my straw. Knowing full well his gaze was again fixed on my lips, I entertained the moment for as long as I could.

Our food then arrived, dissolving the building atmosphere like an antacid in a glass of water. I took a mouthful of my masala and nearly died on the spot from how beautiful it tasted. The creamy sauce blanketed my tongue with just a hint of spice. I loved it. Paul took a mouthful of his volcano on a plate and never even flinched. As we began enjoying our delicious dishes, the dreaded interview process began that seemed to be a staple for first dates.

"So, tell me about your hobbies," he said.

"I like reading when I have the spare time. I used to horse ride but haven't done that for a long time. I'm also doing a psychology degree so that takes up a lot of my spare time."

"Why no more horse riding?"

I squirmed in my seat, not wanting to touch on this too much. "Bad accident. I will do it again one day but not yet."

Purposefully to distract myself, I turned my thoughts to the perfect food, revelling in its taste. My mind started to wander further then, heading down roads of his tight abs just across the table, just underneath that shirt...all I had to do was reach across and touch...

"What happened?" he asked.

I flicked back to reality upon hearing his question, hesitating for a second as I realised I would have to tell him the whole story. "I was out riding one Sunday morning. It was really early, and I didn't expect much traffic to be around. I had just come off a field and only had a hundred yards to ride on the road to access the bridleway on the other side of the road. Some idiot came racing up behind me and had to slow down because of a lorry approaching from the other direction. He thought it would be funny to beep his horn. Unfortunately for me, my horse spooked, bolted, and ran across the road in front of the lorry. The lorry driver couldn't do anything. He clipped my horse's back end with the front corner of his truck and sent us flying into a dyke. He killed my horse but apparently, I'm lucky to be alive."

I said it as casually as I could to keep a lid on my emotions. The horse involved, Scotch, I bred myself from my father's favourite mare before my dad died. Scotch and I achieved a lot in the eight years we had with each other. Five years had now passed, and I still ached for him every day.

"My God, I'm so sorry. That sounds awful. What happened to you? And the guy who caused it?"

"He tried driving away from the scene, but the lorry driver blocked the road. Apparently as he tried to reverse up, a tractor came around the corner and penned him in from that direction too. He was arrested and eventually sent down for five years. He was high on cocaine and nearly three times the drink drive limit. It was no justice for me though. He'd killed my best friend through some stupid prank of wanting to show off in front of his mates. I had a broken arm, a broken hip, two broken legs, a punctured lung, a ruptured spleen, shattered ankles, and a fractured skull. I was in the hospital for months and out of work for a year."

"That's awful. I'm so sorry to hear that. You're ok now though?"

I nodded, smiling as I delved into my food. Silence fell over us as we both cleared our plates. I tried to push thoughts of Scotch to the back of my mind, but it never worked, he was always there and always would be.

After the waiter took our empty plates, Paul picked the conversation back up. "So, the psychology degree. What's that about?"

I grinned, my hopes and dreams flooding through me. "I want to be a criminologist."

I was studying part-time through the Open University. The course would take six years before then specialising. After that, I would have to gain a doctorate at a university, which would be another three years.

"Impressive. Does that mean you'll be leaving us one day?"

I nodded, trying to curb my enthusiasm. "One day." Downing the rest of my drink, I decided it was his turn to answer questions. "Enough about me. What about you?"

"Me?"

"Yeah. What are your hobbies?"

"I'm a bit of a film geek. I am also quite partial to a book or two here and there. I go fishing every so often and I like to ski too. That's about it."

I pursed my lips as his eyes twinkled with the hint of a secret. I let it go, pushing the questions of secrets away. "I guess you're always busy at work?"

"Yeah, you could say that."

I blushed as I thought of the next thing I wanted to ask but I had to know. "Do you mind me asking how old you are?"

He grinned. "I wondered if you'd ask that. I'm thirty-five."

I cocked my head to one side and sat back in my chair. "I'm guessing, as you didn't ask for my address, or haven't yet asked how old I am, that you read my personnel file?"

He laughed. "I'm sorry. Guilty as charged."

"That's creepy."

"Either creepy or using initiative. Depends which way you look at it."

I burst out laughing at his ridiculous logic.

The waiter came back, asking if we would like dessert. We both declined before asking for the bill. As we left, he took my hand in his, my breath hitching in my throat as we ambled to his car. I couldn't help but think how wrong this felt with him being my boss, but at the same time it felt so...right.

He pulled up on my driveway a short while later, opening the car door for me before then walking me to my front door. My heart started racing as my mind filled with wonder about this awkward moment we were fast approaching. He reached for my hand, gently taking it in his before lifting it to his mouth and kissing the back of it. Tingles pulsed through every inch of me, sending every cell inside me high with excitement.

"Thank you for a lovely night," he said.

I smiled, and feeling my cheeks filling with heat, I glanced away for a second. "You're very welcome. Thank you for a lovely night too."

"Can I call you tomorrow?"

I smirked. "You can call. Doesn't mean I'll answer."

He let go of my hand and settled his hands on my waist, pulling me in closer to him. "I had no idea you could be so awkward."

"Well, you do now."

His voice became a whisper as he inched closer. "I like it."

He leaned in and hesitated for the briefest of moments before brushing his soft lips against mine. He curled his arms around my body as his tongue parted my lips. We melted together in a gentle, tender embrace that left me breathless as he caressed my tongue with his own. My hands pressed against his solid chest, steadying my weakening knees.

After a minute or two, we broke our hold on each other, our noses touching and our eyes locked into a deep, wondering gaze. He moved one of his hands to my cheek, slowly stroking it with his thumb, each gentle touch making my heart skip a beat.

He whispered, "I shall let Cinderella go to bed."

I nodded, too stunned for words to formulate a sentence.

He leaned in and pecked my lips, before turning and walking back to his car. As he opened his car door, he winked and said, "Told you I could behave."

Chapter Four

I WOKE THE NEXT morning to the incessant ringing of my phone. Fumbling my way through the air, I managed to press the answer button somehow and croaked a greeting to the caller.

"I'm engaged!"

Molly's shrieking voice snapped me out of my half-asleep state as I struggled to comprehend what she just said.

"Ky? You there?"

I sat up, running a hand over my eyes. "Yeah. Sorry. What?"

"I'm engaged. Like, *engaged*, Ky."

I smiled at her excitement while trying to absorb her news. "Wow. Congratulations."

To say I was a little shocked was an understatement. Molly was your typical free spirit—tall, slim, a drop-dead gorgeous blonde, and not interested in relationships.

She'd been dating this guy, Chris, for nearly six months, which was a record for her. I had been more than surprised when she'd agreed to go on holiday with him.

"When can you come over? We have so much to catch up on." The tone of her voice told me that wasn't a question, but a demand. What Molly wanted, Molly always got.

I sighed as I threw back the bed covers. "Give me an hour."

A squeal of joy pierced my eardrums before the line went dead.

An hour later, I arrived at Molly's house, more awake and ready for her barrels of joy. I hadn't even opened the car door before she came running out, waving her new bling in my face.

She thrust her left hand in my face, giving me little option but to hold it and stare at the huge diamond ring sitting on her ring finger. "Wow. That's huge," I said, taking in the ginormous rock even a celebrity would have been proud of.

She nodded, her long blonde hair bouncing around with her enthusiasm. "I know. It's five carats and the band is platinum, not silver."

I raised an eyebrow and dreaded to think how much poor Chris had spent on it. Most likely his life savings. "So...how did he do it?" I asked, curiosity getting the better of me.

A broad smile swept across her face as she relived her special moment. "It was so perfect. We were in this gorgeous restaurant right on the sea front. There was a guy there playing guitar and singing love songs. Candles all around, stars in the sky, he got down on one knee under the moonlight, and ta-dah!"

I smiled. "I'm so pleased for you."

She grabbed my arm, dragging me out of the car before enveloping me in a bone crushing hug. "You know what this means?"

I stepped back, stretching out my shoulders. I raised my eyebrows, daring to ask, "What?"

She clasped her hands together and jumped up and down on the spot. "Shopping. *Dress* shopping."

I suppressed a groan, and somehow managed to give her a brilliant smile that faked my excitement. It wasn't that I was unhappy for her, it just didn't seem right. Before her holiday, she'd been detailing the hot personal trainer in her gym to me and how she thought he was coming on to her. Now, it was like he never existed. Still, she deserved someone decent, and Chris was a good guy.

As I followed her inside, my phone rang—**Paul** flashed across the screen making me burst into a genuine smile of my own. I realised then that this news would kill her.

When Paul started at the company a few weeks ago, Molly used any trick in the book to be upstairs in my office, poised seductively on the end of my desk in her short, tight skirts. Whenever Paul emerged from his office, he completely blanked her, not even acknowledging her with a hello.

Unfortunately, that only fuelled her fire more. By the time she was on her last day before her holiday, her heels were five inches high, her blouse buttons dangerously close to not even being done up, and her skirts so tight she could do little more than waddle like a penguin in them.

Grinning like a Cheshire cat, I ran back outside, answering his call. "Well, hello there."

"Good morning. I'm delighted you decided to answer."

I giggled. "It was accidental. I meant to press reject."

A soft, honey laden laugh trickled down the line, sending shivers up and down my spine. "Well, I'm guessing that answers my question, then. May as well hang up now."

"Didn't anyone ever teach you that if you don't ask, you don't get?"

"As a matter of fact, Miss Wilson, I happen to live by that rule. Are you free tonight?"

I bit my lip, stifling my need to jump for joy. "Perhaps..."

"No use playing hard to get after your seduction attempts this week."

"Touché. I suppose since it's you, I'm free tonight."

He chuckled. "Want to catch a movie?"

My mind started whirring with ideas already. "Sounds perfect."

We hung up after confirming times, which then left me to deal with Molly. I walked back inside, ignoring her prying glances, and sat on the sofa with a cheeky grin.

"Who was that?" she asked

I grinned. "My hot date."

"What hot date? Who? When did this happen? Details please." She leaned forwards, her arms resting on her knees, and her jade green eyes glistening with delight.

I shrugged my shoulders, trying to appear nonchalant. "He took me out for dinner last night. Nothing happened."

She wiggled her eyebrows with impatience. "So, who is it? Anyone I know?"

I bit my lip to stem my growing smile. "Paul."

She frowned. "Paul?"

"Mr. Connors to you."

She gasped, her jaw dropped before she covered her open mouth with her hands. "No way. You're freaking kidding me?"

"Nope."

She jumped out of her seat and sat down next to me, all but sitting on my lap. "I want details," she said, glee at the thought of gossip completely taking over her.

I grinned and patted her leg. "There are none. Yet."

***

As punctual as ever, Paul picked me up at six p.m. as we agreed. When I opened the door, I couldn't help my eyes roving over his fine form. Dark denim jeans hugged all the right areas and made it very difficult not to look at a particular area. His bright white t-shirt clung to his broad shoulders, clearly defining the ripped muscles all over his upper body. I had to bite my lip just to prevent any drool escaping.

He smiled as he looked over my own casual look of light-coloured skin-tight jeans and a fitted yellow halter-neck top. "You really do look good in anything, don't you?"

I licked my lips and grinned at him. "You haven't seen my best outfit yet."

He quirked an eyebrow and said, "Oh? Well, we have time if you wish to change."

I giggled. "I don't think you would want to take me out in my birthday suit."

He chuckled. "Never say never," he said, giving me a cheeky wink.

The drive over to the cinema seemed to dissolve some of the mounting tension, making me question whether it was all driven from my side. Did I need to calm it down?

I dismissed the thought as quickly as it arrived. Life was for living, and this situation with Paul wouldn't ever develop into anything more than something sexual, so what was the point in playing the wait game and testing his boundaries?

We arrived at the cinema early, which meant we had pick of the seats. Smirking to myself, I headed straight to the back corner. Paul raised his eyebrows as a quirky smile folded over his pink lips. Little did he know that I'd spent all afternoon thinking of devilish ways to seduce him in the darkness.

The lights dimmed, coating us in shadows, and within seconds he dropped his hand over my forearm, sweeping his fingertips across my skin as he began tracing tiny, hair-raising patterns. I tried to ignore the goosebumps popping up all over my body but my racing heart thumping against my rib cage distracted me completely from the beginning of the movie.

I sucked in a deep breath and let it out slowly, allowing him to feel like he had the upper hand for a few minutes. Once I had calmed my body and cleared my mind, I relaxed my hand into his lap, resting it just above his knee. I started brushing my fingers across his leg, ever so carefully inching my way towards that area. I stared hard at the screen, intent on not making eye contact with him, all in a bid to appear as innocent as possible. After several minutes, I reached his inner thigh, and I heard him inhale sharply as I grazed my fingertips a little too close for comfort.

He shifted in his seat then leaned over and whispered in my ear, "I know what you're doing."

I dared to look at him, almost losing my breath at the fire sparking in his sapphire eyes. "I don't know what you're talking about."

He came closer, his nose in my hair and his lips skimming against my ear as he said, "You know damn well what I'm talking about."

I batted my eyelashes several times and shrugged my shoulders. "I've no idea," I whispered back, allowing my little finger to stroke against his bulge.

He gasped and pushed his face further into my hair. A second later, I felt his teeth nibbling on my ear lobe. Shivers ran down my spine and settled in an electrified bundle right between my legs.

"See?" I whispered, my breathing a little ragged. "I've no idea what you're talking about."

"You carry on and you won't even be able to talk," he said, his voice a husky whisper. He pulled back and looked at me, the intensity of the blaze burning through his eyes making my heart skip a beat. "Kyra..."

I forced a smile, not wanting him to see how affected I was by this too. "Yes?"

I continued my torturous assault on him but said nothing more as he turned his attention back to the screen. Every so often, he would let out a slow, deep breath before fidgeting in his seat.

The instant the film finished, he grabbed my hand and pulled me out of my seat, marching us out to the car in fervid silence.

I dared to steal a sideways glance at him as I bit my lip to curb my grin. A muscle in his cheek twitched, his shoulders were tense and squared, and his focus fixed straight ahead on the car. Everything about him screamed a darkened sense of being, his ash blonde hair now the only light to the charged atmosphere between us.

As we closed in the last few feet towards the car, he swung me around and pressed me up against the cool metal with his solid body. My breath caught in my throat from the sudden movement, and before I could stop my world from spinning, he cupped my face between both of his hands and planted his lips on mine, sending me into a whole new whirling reality. He parted my lips with his tongue, entwining my tongue with his, demanding I submit to him and let him take control. I didn't even fight. I could do little but melt into him as I allowed him to take control of every essence of me with his assertive kiss.

After a couple of minutes, he broke our heated moment. We stared at each other, both of us breathing with short, ragged breaths. His assault on my senses had left me speechless and weak at the knees.

As I stared at him, seeing the intensity of the passion simmering in his eyes seared right through my soul. In that moment, I knew I was done for. I would never be able to get enough of this man.

"That was the least I could restrain myself to in public," he said. "Think yourself lucky."

His words triggered something in my brain—a challenge. He had dominated me with that kiss, but I couldn't let him think I was so easy to knock off balance.

I held his fiery eye contact and moved back towards his lips. As I hovered over his mouth, making him think I was going to kiss him, I reached out and grabbed his crotch, making him jump from the sudden contact. "That was the least I could restrain myself to, so think yourself lucky."

His eyes clouded over with a mixture of mischief and lust. "Oh, Miss Wilson..."

I grinned and let go. I turned around and, as I opened the car door, purposefully pushed my ass into him. He muttered something under his breath and strode around to the driver's side, his jaw set in a hard line.

He sat in the seat, turned the engine on, and put his seatbelt on, not looking at me once. The only noise between us for the entire ride home was the roar of his engine as he drove as fast as possible back to mine.

Every single second of silence seemed to pressurise the atmosphere even more. My head and my heart were racing like a herd of wild horses, scattering in all directions as to which way this situation would go. Had I pushed him too far? Was he angry? Should I have waited for him to test the boundaries instead of me teasing him?

Finally pulling up on my driveway, I jumped out of the car before he'd even put the handbrake on and ran to my front door. As I fumbled with the key in the lock, my hands shaking slightly, the hairs on the back of my neck stood up. I could feel a radiating heat behind me, closing in on me like an ominous shadow.

I turned around and inhaled a sharp breath. His eyes were gleaming with nothing but a wild mix of primal need and lust. He closed the distance between us, accelerating my heart rate to speeds I didn't know were possible. As our noses all but touched, his lips lingering above mine, he reached behind me and twisted the key in the lock.

The second I heard the lock click, I held my breath. My mind went blank. I heard the door handle being pushed down before the door creaked open. He pulled his hand back and settled it on my waist as our eyes met.

My entire body started trembling in anticipation of what was to come. I opened my mouth to say something but didn't even get chance to draw a breath before he crushed his perfect lips to mine and pushed me back inside the house.

Chapter Five

I N HIS WILD FRENZY, he pushed me up against the hallway wall, his tongue clashing with mine as he ran his hands up underneath my top and over my skin, heat following every inch of skin he touched.

I heard the front door slam shut and couldn't help but feel a little apprehensive as to how things would play out now we were behind closed doors. This guy was insanely hot and very confident in handling a woman. He seemed to already know how to make me melt like butter on hot toast.

He pushed himself against me and I could feel the bulge in his jeans pressing against my stomach. My mind ran haywire, filling my head with images of us naked and how good it would feel to have him inside me, our bodies skin on skin, taking each other to pleasures unknown. Just those thoughts alone turned me on and the little bundle of electricity between my legs only tingled more and more for a release with each passing second.

He broke our kiss, his chest rising and falling with short, ragged breaths. "Do you have any idea how much you teased me in there?"

I couldn't back down. I couldn't let him have the upper hand and think he had complete control of me. "You think that was teasing?" I lifted a hand to his cheek and grazed my nail across his soft skin. "Sweetie, that was nothing."

Our eyes were locked in a heated gaze, both of us trying to figure out what would happen from here. I reached for his t-shirt and inched my way underneath it, carefully caressing my way across his taut abs. His skin, as soft as silk, made me want to trace my tongue all over it. Hell, at this rate, I would quite happily lick ice cream off him until I had no tongue left.

I kept my eyes on his as I continued touching him. Every second that passed seemed to deepen the intensity of the hunger burning in his eyes, making me want to push him to the limit and see him snap. I wanted to know what he would do if I pushed him too far.

As I traced my hand around to his back, relishing in the delight of his incredible body underneath my hands, I cupped his face with my free hand. He closed his eyes and shivered ever so slightly. I took my moment and trailed my nails from his shoulder blade down to his lower back, smiling as a small groan rumbled in his throat.

I moved my hand from his face and slid it into his hair, massaging the back of his head with my fingertips. With one hand on his lower back and the other on the back of his head, I pressed him against me, pulling his mouth down to mine. I brushed my lips over his before kissing my way down his neck, covering any bare skin with soft kisses.

He shuddered and wrapped his arms around me, digging his fingers into my sides. He nuzzled into my neck, his breaths skimming over my neck and giving me goosebumps.

I reached the crook of his neck and found myself enveloped in his scent—a deep, masculine fragrance tinged with orange and vanilla. The more I inhaled, the longer I wanted to stay. He was becoming a drug to me, and I knew I would be his hardest, most faithful addict.

My kisses turned into little licks and nibbles as his delicious skin and irresistible scent became too much to not enjoy. I kissed my way up to his ear and gently took his earlobe between my teeth. The instant I nipped the sensitive skin, a quiet moan escaped his throat and he tightened his arms around me.

I smiled, pulled back, and kissed him on the lips, lingering for just a few seconds before whispering, "But we don't want to get you too excited now, do we?"

He stared back at me, his eyes darkened over with a deep carnal hunger. "I think it's a bit late for that, don't you?"

I grinned. "I can give you a cold shower if you'd like."

He leaned into me and started pressing tantalising kisses to my neck whilst running his fingers up and down my sides. I closed my eyes and revelled in feeling his touch on my skin. He touched me so light yet firm, confident yet tender. I knew I was done for—our clothes hadn't even come off yet and I was already like putty in his hands.

He kissed my ear and whispered, "And I could give you something else if you'd like."

With my body raging like a volcano, my head and my heart finally in sync and screaming for the same cravings, I replied, "Give it to me then."

I wanted him, *needed* him, now. I knew the instant those words left my lips that I was in for a devilishly good time that I would definitely not forget for a long time to come.

Our eyes met, a second of uncertainty flickering between us before a slow grin folded across his gorgeous face. He hovered his mouth over mine, teasing me with the moment of when he would finally kiss me.

Leaving me hanging for his kiss, he turned his attention to my top, gently brushing his fingers against my skin as he peeled it from me and threw it over his shoulder. Adrenaline surged through my veins as I stood before him, topless, except for my black lacy bra. He grinned as he roved his eyes over my chest with a hungry gaze a lion would be proud of.

"This isn't fair," I said, flicking my eyes to his t-shirt.

"As the lady asks," he replied, whipping off his own top.

As his t-shirt fell down to the floor, my eyes roamed down the length of his bare chest to those incredible abs—all six of them. What I'd pictured in my head as I felt his body with my hands hardly compared to seeing it for myself.

Wow.

Never had I been stunned by a man's body before, but this guy left me speechless and breathless. I couldn't wait to get my hands on him and get my fill until I passed out from pleasure.

After several seconds of eyeing each other up, our eyes locked, both of us teeming with raw passion and animal needs. He pulled me into him and clawed at my bra as I grabbed at his belt, desperate to release whatever he had hidden in there.

My bra fell down my arms and I shook it off me in a split second before undoing the button and the zip on his jeans. As soon as I had room to slide my hand inside his boxers, I took my first feel of him, and I was not disappointed. He had a girth I could barely wrap my hand around and the perfect length. My excitement notched up ten levels just feeling him in my hand.

He nipped at my neck with his teeth and said through ragged breaths, "Seriously, here?"

I started moving my hand up and down his shaft and replied, "I don't care where. I just need you. Now."

A small groan left him before he grappled with my jeans and pushed them down my legs along with my black lacy knickers. As I pulled my feet out of them, he dropped his own jeans and boxers, standing naked in front of me and leaving me absolutely hypnotised by his body.

He glanced down my naked body and then said, "You're right. That is your best outfit."

I licked my lips and said, "Come and enjoy it then."

In the blink of an eye, he wrapped his muscled arms around me and lifted me up. My legs naturally curled around his waist, drawing him into me like a snake coiling around its prey. He pushed me back against the wall, his hardness pressed against my ass. Kissing his way down my cleavage, he teased breathless gasps from me as every part of me ached for him like the desert thirsts for the rain.

When he moved his velvet mouth to my breasts, his tongue flicking over my sensitive nipples, waves of uncontrollable desire flooded me instantly. Bundles of sharp tingles settled between my legs, driving me insane as the need for my release dominated my mind.

He moved a hand down my side and stroked the inside of my thigh, leaving me quivering in anticipation. Expectation had never been so thrilling or driven with such a primitive need. As he brushed a finger over my folds, I trembled as my mind and body became totally overwhelmed with desire.

Licking and nipping at my skin, he made his way back up to my mouth, kissing me with an urgent demand. He slipped his tongue between my lips at the same time he thrust himself inside me.

We broke our kiss and both groaned in relief, the promise of our wants and needs now so close to being met.

With his forehead pressed against mine, and our noses touching, he whispered, "You good?"

Too breathless to speak, I nodded.

He traced the outline of my lips with his tongue, then slid his tongue back inside my mouth, playing a slow dance between us as he started moving, his rhythm hard and gaining tempo with every stroke.

Breaking our kiss, he moved his way down to my neck, nipping the soft skin in the crook of my neck with his teeth. Potent throbs of pleasure shot straight between my legs, leaving me to float in a dizzying mix of ecstasy and pain.

I closed my eyes in sheer bliss as he continued to satiate both of us. I couldn't help but dig my nails into his back, each new scratch seeming to fuel him with more urgency as he reached me deeper and harder.

The coil deep inside me began to scrunch together, promising me my sweet relief. His relentless, vigorous movements hit the spot every time and I was nothing but a lamb to the slaughter, completely at his mercy within minutes.

As he moved away from my neck and down to my chest, he skimmed his tongue over my nipple, giving me my moment of liberation. Almost as if I'd had the breath knocked out of me, I let out a strangled cry as I spiralled down into my world of decadence.

Seconds later, I felt him pulsing inside me, his sudden stop and quivering legs telling me he'd found his own sweet release.

"Don't stop..." I said, gasping the words like a beggar fraught for food.

He lifted me away from the wall and hugged me against his body. I wrapped my arms around his neck and pressed a kiss to his cheek. He cupped my ass with his hands and started to lift me up and down on him with such strength I thought he would split me in half.

As he increased his rhythm, I could feel another orgasm building and I wanted to soar over that edge again. I grasped at his hair and lost myself in the ocean of divinity he had me drowning in.

He slowed down for a second and tilted my hips backwards ever so slightly. The instant he moved again, he hit my spot from such an intense angle I couldn't help but cry out his name. Within seconds, I felt like I would pass out as he gave me another mind-numbing release. Every cell inside me shook from the amazing assault on my senses.

Stumbling back against the wall, he let go of me and set me down on my feet. He steadied himself against the wall with a hand and took a few deep breaths. I leaned my head back against the wall, trying to catch my own breath and cool the throbbing tingles trickling through me.

"I certainly didn't expect that tonight," he said.

I grinned. "You're a bad liar."

"Scouts honour," he said, slapping a hand over his heart.

I laughed, and suddenly became very aware of his eyes wandering over my naked body. Despite what had just happened, I felt very bare and made my excuses to run upstairs for my dressing gown.

When I came back down, he had his jeans back on, making me feel just a little sad that he was leaving after such a fun night. I sat down on one of the steps in my fluffy lilac robe and watched him get dressed.

"I guess this is going to be awkward Monday morning," I said, feeling my cheeks redden with heat.

"Hmmm," he said, coming up the steps to kiss me. "I've never done it in an office before."

"You are kidding, right?"

He narrowed his eyes. "No. Why, have you?"

"No, I haven't. I meant you can't be serious about doing it in the office."

He chuckled. "All in good time."

My mouth dropped open in shock. "That is not happening in my workplace. I am not going to be sacked for having sex with my boss on his desk."

"And who is going to sack you? Your boss?"

I imagined old sour faced Andrews walking in on us in the heights of passion and giggled.

"What are you giggling at?"

I told him, which gave him a quirky smile.

"I think it would give that old codger a heart attack." He took a hold of my hand and said, "So, what now?"

I frowned. "What do you mean?"

"Do you want me to stay...or do you want some beauty sleep?"

I shrugged my shoulders. "It's up to you. I'm not a demanding type of woman. I presume as you got dressed that you're going."

He grinned. "Ok." He tugged me to my feet and slid his arms around my back before whispering in my ear, "I want to stay. I want a proper session with you."

A broad smile burst onto my face as shivers ran down my spine. "Hmmm. I won't argue with that."

Chapter Six

WE INDULGED IN SOME cheese on toast to refuel us whilst watching some questionable horror movie on the TV. After an hour or so, and the poor heroine of the movie ending up dead, we headed upstairs, an ever-present atmosphere growing between us with each step we took.

As soon as I shut the bedroom door, Paul grabbed my wrists and tugged me towards him before whirling me around and throwing me on the bed. I grinned. I loved it when a man let his dominant side shine through.

I stared back up at him, biting my bottom lip, and watched as he took his t-shirt off, allowing me the delight of seeing his delicious body once more.

"I think you've got a little bit of drool escaping," he said, tapping the corner of his mouth.

I laughed. "I don't care if I'm slobbering like a rabid dog. The view is totally worth it."

He chuckled and eased himself onto the bed, his legs either side of mine. He moved himself up, inching his way towards my mouth.

"And now you can touch," he said, bending in the crook of my neck and giving me a soft kiss.

I shivered from the sensitive touch and wrapped my arms around his back, stifling the moan in my throat as I felt his beautifully sculpted muscles underneath my fingertips. I wanted to trace every line with my tongue, twice.

He kissed all around my neck, almost giving me a necklace of delicate kisses, before he pressed his lips to mine and began to massage my tongue with his. The slow, lazy rhythm started to drive me crazy within seconds.

After a minute or so, I seized my moment and rolled us over so I sat on top, admiring the view beneath me. I pinned his arms out to the sides like a set of wings and grinned. Seeing the fantastic Paul Connors beneath me, at my mercy, was a sight I'd always remember and definitely cherish.

He flashed me a grin and then gave me a cheeky wink. "Oooh, dominant. I like it."

I flashed him my best smile before tracing my tongue around the edge of his lips. As he closed his eyes and tried to capture my tongue between his lips, I slid my right hand off the bed and reached for my play toy.

The second he realised what I'd done, his eyes flew open and he quirked his eyebrows up. "Really?"

I grinned like a Cheshire cat as I notched the leather wrist restraint a hole tighter. "Oh, come on. Where's your sense of adventure?"

He broke out into a slow, lazy grin, his sapphire eyes twinkling with mischief. "Oh, believe me, there's nothing wrong with my sense of adventure. I just didn't think this was you, that's all."

"Mr. Connors," I said, reaching across the other side of the bed to grab the other cuff and strap him down more. "You have no idea. You shouldn't judge a book by its cover, you know."

"Oh, I'm definitely not. But I am definitely looking forward to seeing how this story ends."

I laughed and kissed the end of his nose before crawling down the bed.

"What are you doing?" he asked.

I grinned back at him. "You didn't think I'd just have wrist restraints, did you?"

He chuckled and replied, "I'd be disappointed if you did."

I strapped in his ankles and then resumed my position on top of him, straddling his waist as I grinned at him from such an awesome vantage point.

"I can see it's not only horses you're confident with between your legs," he said, grinning.

I laughed. "Still want to see how this ends?"

"I can assure you, Miss Wilson, I most definitely do. I am liking this. A lot."

"You're starfished on my bed, completely restrained, and you're liking it?"

His eyes lit up with fire as he licked his lips. "I'm all for the woman doing all the work."

I raised an eyebrow. "That's awfully sexist of you. You might regret saying that. Do you wish to retract your comment?"

"And what happens if I don't?"

I shrugged my shoulders. "I couldn't possibly say."

"I think I'll deal with my punishment then. I reject my right to retract my comment."

I smirked. "Don't say I didn't warn you."

I removed my dressing gown, leaving me sat naked on top of him. I bent down and kissed my way up his body, right from his droolworthy V lines to his rock-hard pecs. As soon as I saw goosebumps appear on his body, I reached over to my bedside table and opened the top drawer.

He moved his head to see what I was doing. "Dare I ask?"

I rummaged around in the drawer until I found what I wanted—a black silk blindfold. I pulled it out and dangled it off the end of my index finger whilst giving him an innocent smile.

"Is that it?" he asked, his voice full of mocking. "I thought you could do better than that."

"Did I say I was finished?"

I lifted myself up on to my knees and inched my way up the bed until his head sat directly underneath my body. He lifted his head up and stuck his tongue out as he tried to bury his tongue between my legs.

Pressing my palm against his forehead, I pushed him back down to the bed and tutted at him. "Did I say you could do that?"

"At least play fair," he said, pouting. "You can't sit there and expect me to not want to lick you."

"And why not? You're a big boy. You can handle your own cravings, surely?" I slipped the blindfold over his head, leaving it on his forehead for second as I said, "Are you wishing you'd retracted your comment yet?"

He grinned. "I think I can handle a bit more."

I pulled the blindfold down over his eyes, then leaned down and whispered into his ear, "Let's test that, shall we?"

I nibbled at his earlobe, grinning as he shivered. I moved off him completely, sitting on the edge of the bed as I went back into my drawer, looking for the one thing I enjoyed using the most—a long, white feather.

Closing the drawer, I sat next to him, letting the anticipation and the silence build in his mind. He knew I was there, but he didn't know when or where the next touch would be. I watched and waited, and sure enough, only a few seconds passed before he parted his lips, his chest rising and falling with shallow breaths.

I trailed the tip of the feather across his stomach, a broad grin breaking out on my face as he jerked and then muttered a curse. The restraints creaked from the sudden, forceful tug on them. I lifted the feather from his stomach, waited a few seconds, and then traced it across his chest, dancing it ever so lightly over his nipples. He shuddered, yanking on the restraints again.

"You're going to pay for this," he said, his voice a hoarse whisper.

I couldn't help but smirk. I repeated the process over every inch of his body, waiting a few seconds before targeting a new area, enjoying the trembles coursing through his body. By the time I reached his inner thighs, small moans were escaping his lips and the wrist restraints were under constant pressure.

Throwing the feather to the floor, I sat between his legs and replaced the feather tip with my lips, nipping just a little at his skin. He groaned and shivered, spurring me on to kiss my way around his inner thighs, and the crook between his legs, touching everything except what he wanted me to touch.

As the restraints continued to squeak and his breathing became raspier, I cupped his balls in my hand, making him judder. He sucked in a sharp breath as he tugged against the restraints, only this time straining metal replaced creaking rope.

I massaged his balls between my fingertips, a slow gentle kneading that pushed small groans of pleasure from him. I moved my head down and replaced my fingers with my mouth, sucking the tight skin between my lips and tracing patterns with my tongue.

A hiss sounded through the air followed by a, "Fuck."

I grinned and let go, kissing my way up towards the main prize. I licked at the base of his shaft before tracing my tongue all the way up his length. When I took him in my mouth, I treated him to the knowledge I had no gag reflex.

"Jesus Christ, Kyra." I reached down to massage his balls whilst I continued to suck. The instant my hands curled around his sack, he bucked his hips and said, "What the fuck are you doing to me?"

I let go, flicking my tongue over his end as I did so, making him twitch. "I did warn you."

"You'd better hope I don't get out of these, young lady."

I laughed. "Young lady? Oooo, someone sounds a little angry. Let me help you with that pent up frustration."

I moved and straddled his chest, removing the blindfold. He blinked a few times, his eyes settling on me with an animalistic hunger. Holding his eye contact, I slipped my index finger inside my mouth, leaving my lips open as I wrapped my tongue around it.

He drew in a deep breath as his entire body tensed beneath me. I slid my finger from my mouth and trailed it down my body, skimming it over my breasts. As my nipples hardened, his eyes grew darker.

"This is your last chance to stop before I get out of these and fuck you into next week."

I giggled and wiggled my eyebrows at him. I sat up on my knees and let my hand fall between my legs. I started pleasuring myself, giving him the perfect view of everything.

He clenched his jaw as he stared at my finger, totally transfixed by what I was doing to myself. The growing tension in my core was building with every second. A familiar tingle ran through me, and I let out a small moan as my release came close.

"I fucking warned you," he said, his voice deep and hoarse.

I glanced down to see his handsome face creased with a dangerous mix of lust and desire. To my absolute horror, he started pulling at the restraints with all his might, his muscles flexing under the strain. His face turned red and he let out a groan just as the thin D rings holding the rope to the restraints pinged with a heart-stopping jingle. All four of them were broken and he was completely free.

A surge of adrenaline shot through me as he sat up, grinning like the cat who'd got the cream.

"Hi, there," he said, winking.

I smiled and whimpered, "Hi."

He wrapped his hands around my back and drew me closer to him, slipping his tongue inside my mouth as he rolled on top of me. Seconds later, he broke our kiss, and in one swift move, flipped me onto my front, chuckling as I shrieked in surprise.

Grabbing my hips, he dragged my ass up into the air as he wrapped my long hair around his wrist, yanking my head backwards. With his free hand gripping my shoulder, he pushed himself inside me and let out a groan of relief.

I almost choked on my sharp inhale of breath as he reached my inner depths, tiny explosions already beginning to spark. He started moving in and out of me, fast, hard, and unforgiving. I moaned with pleasure, wanting it harder and faster.

He pulled harder on my hair, driving me faster to my release. His ragged breathing and the sound of our bodies hitting each other filled the air, fuelling us both to our end. My entire body screamed with pleasure as he hit all the right spots.

The sheer carnal nature of the raw, hungry lust between us set me on a heavenly spiral, that familiar wave I so craved ready to drown me once again. He let go of my hair and moved both hands to my hips, somehow increasing the pace even more.

Seconds later, a potent throbbing tingle exploded between my legs and I finally let go, my head whirling as I floated away on a cloud of ecstasy. He thrust himself inside and stilled, letting out a loud groan of relief.

I could feel him pulsing inside me as he collapsed onto my back, panting for breath. After a minute or so, he moved, flopping onto the bed with a big grin.

"I did warn you," he said.

"I'm not complaining. I'll happily have that every day of the week. Maybe even twice a day."

He laughed and raised his arms in the air, shaking his wrists with the cuffs still attached. "Think you need some new ones. Extra strong perhaps."

I laughed and shook my head, rolling underneath the duvet.

He joined me, curling his arms around me. "I wasn't too rough, was I?"

"No. I can take a bit of rough."

He chuckled. "I'm not even going to respond to that." He squeezed me tighter as he kissed my head. "You mind if I join you for a good night's sleep?"

I smiled and shook my head. I tried my hardest not to dissect this too much as I fell asleep in the most perfect pair of arms I could ever wish for.

Chapter Seven

"**G**OOD MORNING, GORGEOUS."

A smooth voice woke me from my peaceful slumber. I rolled over and smiled "Morning yourself."

"You feeling ok?"

I nodded, shivering as he trailed his fingers down my stomach. "You?"

He leaned over and pecked my lips. "Better than ever."

I rolled back over in an attempt to climb out of bed, but I barely got one leg out of the covers before he wound his hands around my middle, kissing my back and pulling me against him. The warmth of his chest and the solidity he offered were becoming dangerously addictive even after one night.

As he started kissing his way across the back of my shoulders, I closed my eyes and relaxed. When he moved to my neck, gently nipping at my skin in between kisses, I couldn't help the small moan that escaped me. I could feel his erection pressed against my back and all I could think about was how amazing he'd felt inside me last night. The more I thought about our frenzied sex in the hallway, the more excited I became.

He slipped a hand down between my legs, letting out a quiet groan as he felt how turned on I was. "Are you always so ready?"

I blushed and simply replied, "You turn me on."

Lifting my ass slightly, he repositioned himself and slid inside me, nibbling at my shoulder. "I think that's the best news I've heard yet."

He moved with a slow, teasing rhythm, coaxing me to my blissful place with such a languid pace my desperation to reach it almost made me want to scream at him. He grazed one hand over my breasts whilst the other held my hair back from my neck, giving him all the access he desired.

I lifted my left arm and reached behind me, raking my hand through his hair, pulling him down closer to me. He bit at the crook of my neck, sending jolts of electricity straight between my legs. As he brushed his thumb over my nipple, I sucked in a sharp breath. I didn't know what to think about—his mouth, his hand, or his dick. All of the amazing sensations flooding me at once was nothing short of pure ecstasy.

After a couple of minutes, he picked up the pace and skimmed his hand down my stomach to my clit. He started playing, matching the rhythm of his fingers to that of his hips. As my sweet release coiled tighter in my core, I truly felt like I was floating on a cloud of divinity. Nothing could be better than this. Sex with Paul Connors was mind blowing. I grinned and bit my lip—I'd been right from the beginning—he was, in fact, a God. A sex God.

A delicious buzz coursed through me, slowly increasing in intensity as my relief came closer and closer with every touch, every move in and out of me. I wished I could lay like this with him for days—I would never get enough.

When he took my earlobe in between his teeth, I fell over my edge, crying out in joy as I revelled in my leisurely fall of ecstasy. Seconds later, he stilled and groaned, kissing the side of my head as his own enjoyment spilled into me.

He ran his fingers down my side and kissed my shoulder. "I don't think I'll ever get enough of you."

My heart skipped a beat as my insides warmed with happiness. "Same."

The shrill ringing of his phone obliterated our sexy Sunday morning into a million pieces, interrupting the moment completely. He groaned in frustration and rolled away from me, reaching over the edge of the bed for his jeans.

"Shit." He leapt out of bed, pulling his jeans on with one hand as he greeted the caller. "Hi, Dad..."

I frowned at his worried tone of voice and pulled the duvet up around my chin.

"Yes, Dad...no, Dad...yes, ok...I'm sorry, ok? I left my phone on silent in my pocket. No, I'm not...yes...yes, ok...bye."

He sighed and stuffed his phone back in his pocket as he ran his hands through his hair. He took a deep breath and then met my eye contact. His beautiful sapphire eyes were full of stress and concern, his handsome face streaked with panic. I'd never seen a look like this on him and I definitely didn't like it.

"Everything ok?" I asked.

He forced a smile, but the anxiety in his eyes didn't lessen at all. "Yeah, everything is fine." He pulled his t-shirt on, then picked his socks up from the floor. "Listen, I hate to kiss and run but I really need to go."

I faked my own smile, trying to hide my disappointment. "Ok. No doubt I'll have Molly ringing soon anyway."

He sat down on the bed and pulled his socks on. A minute or so later, he jumped up and walked around to my side of the bed, leaning over me to give me a deep kiss. "I'll call you later, ok?"

"Sure."

With that, he bounded down the stairs before roaring down the street in his car.

All day Sunday I watched my phone, eager for any call or text from him. I ventured round to Molly's to give her as few of the details as possible, staying for something to eat just to help take my mind off the ever-absent Paul.

I found it very unnerving how a guy could have such a profound effect on me, especially after such a short amount of time. Usually, I enjoyed my freedom more than being with a man, yet here I was, checking my phone every two minutes and moping around because one hadn't called.

When Monday morning came around, I woke up and grabbed my phone, hoping to see a text or missed call whilst I'd been asleep but there was nothing. My heart sank. My mind started wandering, filling with anxiety as I cursed myself for thinking that this could have been anything other than a one-night stand. All I'd done was properly fulfil the role of a slutty PA.

By the time I'd dressed myself, I'd played out at least twenty scenarios in my head of the directors calling me in for a disciplinary meeting, detailing my extracurricular activities for all to hear, then sacking me.

By the time I locked the house and jumped in the car to head to work, I had, in my imagination, lost my house, lost my car, moved into a house share just to have a roof over my head, and had a job on minimum wage canning beans in a factory.

As I drove to work, I forced myself to suck in deep breaths and count to ten. Being a drama queen would help nothing and no-one. There would be a reasonable explanation for his lack of communication.

I arrived at work, walking into the office with my breath held. As soon as I realised I was the first one in, my anxiety lessened a few degrees. I made myself of cup of tea and as soon as I took my first sip, realised what an idiot I'd been worrying myself sick for the last hour.

Almost halfway through my tea when Paul came in, he breezed into the room, headed straight for his office, and closed the door behind him without so much as a word or even a look at me.

Immediately, anger began boiling in my veins, filtering through every cell in my body. How dare he treat me like this. Who did he think he was? Just as I was debating barging into his office full of fury, he yanked his office door open, making me jump.

A stern look edged his handsome face, flooding my mind with worry. "Kyra, have you got a minute?"

My heart started pounding against my ribcage like a madman in a padded cell. I stood up and smoothed my pencil skirt down before taking a deep breath and heading towards him. I locked eye contact with him, trying to gauge his mood, but his eyes were glazed over, giving absolutely nothing away.

He moved to the side as I walked through the doorway. As I passed him and turned around to face him, he closed the door behind him. Before I could think anything at all, he closed the gap between us and cupped my face in his hands, gifting me with a tender kiss on the lips.

As he kissed me, I became enveloped in his heavenly scent of oranges and vanilla. When he wrapped his arms around me and pressed himself against me, I became completely and utterly lost all over again.

He broke our kiss after a few seconds and said, "Good morning, beautiful. You look rather radiant today."

I narrowed my eyes at him. "Morning..."

He eyed me with suspicion for a few seconds and then said, "Are you ok?"

I raised an eyebrow in response. I didn't feel words were really needed.

After a couple of seconds, he widened his eyes. "Ah...I'm sorry. I was a complete ass. I'm so sorry I didn't call you yesterday. I bet you thought the worst of me by this morning, didn't you?"

I folded my arms across my chest. "Rightly so, I think."

He trailed his hands down my arms, uncrossing them, before settling his hands in the curves of my waist. "I'm sorry...am I forgiven?"

"What exactly have you done to earn my forgiveness?"

A glint of mischief filtered through his eyes before he grinned. He wound his arms around my back and stroked his hands up and down my back. He nuzzled into my neck and inhaled a deep breath. "You feel so good, you smell so good..." He tickled my skin with his tongue, giving me a surprise shudder. "You taste so good. Is there anything not good about you?"

Despite the fact my resolve was melting like an ice cube over a steam grate, I couldn't help my sarcasm. "Yes. My temper when I don't get a call."

He chuckled and opened his mouth to say something when the outer office door banged shut. I jumped, my heart racing to a million miles an hour as I realised we weren't alone anymore.

"Where's Kyra?" I heard Andrews ask.

Whoever he spoke to said nothing.

"Hmmm," Andrews said. "Is Paul in?"

Footsteps closed in towards Paul's office, sending me into panic mode. I smoothed out my clothes and stepped back from Paul. I pressed my hands to my flustered cheeks, hoping by some miracle it may take some colour out of my cheeks.

Paul stayed cool, not reacting in any way at all. He took the element of surprise away and opened the door before Andrews did.

"Ahh, Paul," he said, peering in the office with his beady eyes and seeing me. "Kyra, I wondered where you were, dear. Could I have five minutes when Paul is finished with you, please?"

"Of course," I replied, struggling not to smirk as I thought to myself it could be hours before Paul would be finished with me.

"I'll be done in a few minutes, John," Paul said, closing the door on Mr Andrews. He turned back to me and reached for my hands, pulling me into his chest. "Now, shall we finish up here?"

I could do nothing but grin like a little girl as I divulged in the deliciousness of Paul Connors once more.

Just as the clock struck lunchtime, my phone rang from an outside line. I frowned, wondering who it could be.

"Hello. Kyra speaking."

A deep male voice laughed down the line. "Well, hello, young lady."

I squealed in delight. "Ashley? Is that really you?"

"The one and only, my lovely. What time is your lunch?"

"Now. Why?"

"I'm outside."

I grabbed my things and charged out of the door like a bull in a china shop. Taking the stairs two at a time, nearly breaking my ankle several times, I bulldozed my way out of the building and straight into Ashley's open arms for a giant hug.

As I screamed with joy, he picked me up and swung me round before kissing my cheek.

"What are you doing here?" I asked, getting my breath back. "You said you wouldn't be back until the week-end."

He set me down on my feet with a big grin. "I wanted to surprise you."

I grinned and took his hand, leading him to the café on the other side of the street. "Come on. We have lots to talk about."

I loved my older brother more than life itself. After our dad died a few years ago and Mum remarried and moved to America, it left just me and Ashley against the world. We had grown very close over the past few years, even more so since he came out and he realised that I wouldn't disown him just because of his sexual preferences.

Mum still found it hard to come to terms with, but I had a feeling that was more to do with her leech of a new husband than anything else. Just thinking about him gave me the creeps.

Ashley, with his dark good looks, natural charm, and sharp dress sense, always had a line of female attention to bat away. Not outwardly extroverted, and giving off a very macho, alpha male energy, no-one would ever think he was into men.

We sat in the café, ordered our food, and caught up on all recent things. Ashley had just spent the last year travelling in Australia. We'd had sparse contact due to his outback locations and lack of phone signal, plus being busy enjoying himself.

"Enough about me," he said, sipping at his coke. "Tell me about you. What's been going on with you?"

Bubbling with excitement over Paul, I couldn't wait to tell him my news. Right on cue, as I said his name, Paul emerged from work, making his way down to the sandwich shop at the end of the street.

I pointed him out with a grin on my face like a Cheshire cat. "That's Paul."

Ashley raised an eyebrow. "That's your boss?"

I nodded.

"That you had mad, passionate sex with in your hallway? And in your bed?"

"Yep," I replied, grinning like an idiot.

He let out a low whistle. "Wowsers. You might even have some competition from your brother."

I laughed. "Very funny."

He gave me a cheeky wink. "He's a bit of all right, Ky. You've done good there."

I shrugged my shoulders, trying to downplay it. I couldn't afford to get carried away on hopes and dreams. "You know what I'm like, Ash. It's only a fling."

He lowered his voice and looked at me, a touch of seriousness floating through his dark eyes. "Ky, I know your usual look when it comes to men and that isn't one of them. Have you finally met a guy you want a proper relationship with?"

I pursed my lips. "I don't know, we'll see."

"Aww look at my lil sis, all fussed up over a guy—finally." He reached out and patted my cheek, chuckling.

I batted his hand away. "Shut up."

We ate our food, thankfully off topic of Paul, and when it came time for me to go back to work, I felt sad that I had to leave my brother again. He always lifted my mood and made me feel good. When he told me he would be coming round for tea tonight, I couldn't agree fast enough.

Ashley walked me back to work, pecked my cheek, and disappeared. Feeling happy and like my soul had finally been satiated with a dose of my brother, I headed back inside. I even allowed myself to think that with my brother back in my life, and the unexpected appearance of Paul in my life too, maybe things were finally falling into place for me.

Making my way straight to the kitchen for a cup of tea, I flicked the kettle on and lost myself in musings of replaying my conversation with Ashley.

"So, who's the hunk then?"

The sound of Paul's voice made me jump. I turned around to see him leaning against the doorframe, his arms crossed over his chest.

A playful smirk twitched at my lips. "You saw him then?"

He nodded. "It was kinda hard to miss him giving you a loving kiss before he left you at the front door."

I bit my lip to curb the laugh creeping up my throat. "Scared you might have some competition?"

He licked his lips before he smiled. "I think you should be worried of the competition."

My playful mood dropped like a stone through water. My heart did a triple backflip, stealing my breath from me for a split second. Did he mean he had another woman in his life? "What's that supposed to mean?"

"He's gay, Kyra. It stands out a mile off."

A wave of relief washed over me before I wondered for a second why I felt such disappointment at another woman potentially being in his life. Did I need to re-evaluate exactly how I felt for this guy?

Deciding that now was not the time to go down that road, I gave up my game and admitted the truth. "He's my brother. And yes, he is gay. How did you know? He does so well to hide it."

He shrugged his shoulders. "I've met my fair share over the years."

I raised my eyebrows, probing for an explanation, but he didn't give one.

"What are you doing tonight?" he asked.

"Having food with my brother."

"Oh, ok. I was going to ask if I could see you, that's all. I don't have much spare time this weekend."

The thought of not seeing him this weekend sank my heart to my feet for the second time in one day. "Well, I don't know what time we'll be done but you could come over afterwards if you wanted?"

He smiled, dropping his arms to his sides. "No, it's ok. I'll leave you to it. I'll book you in for tomorrow night instead?"

I smiled and agreed, already looking forward to an evening of me and him tangled between the sheets.

The rest of the day ticked by painfully slowly, each passing minute seeming to want to torture me further by prolonging me from seeing my brother even more. Finally, after what seemed like an eternity, the clock ticked onto four p.m. and I had my freedom until tomorrow morning.

I scooped up my things and with all the other directors gone, dared to venture into Paul's office to say bye. He sat at his desk, scribbling away with his blue and gold fountain pen on a stack of papers nearly three inches high.

"I'm heading home. I should think Ashley will be gone by nine in case you change your mind or want to give me a call."

Not even looking up from his work, he said, "You don't need to say bye to me, Kyra. It's not like we're in a relationship. Go have fun with your brother and I'll see you tomorrow."

His words stung like I'd been hit with a thousand bee stings. "How can you say that after how you greeted me this morning?"

He looked up from his desk, his sapphire eyes full of thought. He set his pen down on his stack of papers and pursed his lips for a few seconds. "Ok, I'll be straight with you. I saw your reaction in the kitchen when I mentioned you might have competition. I know the conclusion you came to. I don't want you thinking that this anything other than what it is."

A barb of disappointment laced adrenaline shot through my heart. "And what is that exactly?"

"Fun. We're just having fun. Nothing more, nothing less. But just for the record, there are no other women in my life to the degree that you are."

I frowned, trying to decipher his words. Was there a hidden meaning in there? Had I managed to thaw a part of him to let someone, *me*, in? I pushed the thoughts away for now and decided he was right—we weren't in a relationship, but since when did saying bye for the night and being polite mean that we were?

All the way home I couldn't help but overthink the strange conversation. By the time I pulled up on my driveway, I decided I had to stop overanalysing every little word he said and just take the situation for what it was.

Right on cue to distract me further, Ashley pulled up, his face beaming with happiness and carrying Chinese takeaway and a bottle of wine.

"You read my mind," I said, getting out of my car. "Trouble is, I don't think one bottle of wine will be enough."

He grinned and lifted his t-shirt up to reveal another bottle of wine tucked in the waist band of his jeans. "That's why I have the spare."

I opened my door and let Ashley go in first. "Oh," I said, following him inside. "I forgot to tell you earlier. Guess who's engaged?"

He turned around and looked at my left hand, making me laugh. After a couple of seconds he quirked an eyebrow up and said, "Don't tell me it's who I think it is."

I giggled. "Yep. Molly got engaged."

"To the computer geek?"

I nodded and started getting the plates out of the cupboard.

"Pffft," he said, his face creasing into a dark scowl. "That girl is something else. She can't keep her legs shut for more than two minutes. She's the definitive meaning of Tesco—open twenty-four seven. She'll never get married, especially not to him."

I sighed, not really liking his opinion. "Ash, that's a bit harsh. She just enjoys herself. She's a good friend."

He dumped his chow mein out of the foil container onto his plate and looked me square in the eyes. "That girl is trouble, Ky. You mark my words."

Chapter Eight

As soon as I woke the next morning, I had a stupid grin on my face. Ash had surprised me last night by announcing we were taking a trip to London this weekend so we could spend some time together.

Sitting at my desk daydreaming of the weekend, my joy quickly evaporated when I remembered today was the directors' monthly meeting. That meant not only would all of them be in the office, but I would have to take minutes whilst fighting the urge to fall asleep.

With the clock ticking closer to nine a.m., I found myself puzzled as there was still no sign of Paul. Trying to push thoughts of him to the back of my mind, I set my things up in the meeting room before making all their drinks.

Walking back to the meeting room several minutes later with all their cups of tea on a serving tray, I nearly dropped the entire tray when I wandered in to see Paul grinning at me—from the seat next to mine.

My heart accelerated instantly, filling my body with fuzzy tingles. Doing my utmost to keep myself from making eye contact with Paul, I set all the cups of tea around the table at their seats before taking my seat, mentally willing my flustered body to calm the hell down.

The company owner, Mr. Collins, strolled in just as I sat down. In his mid-fifties with washed out blue eyes, a stern face, but a good body, he had a few lady friends that I knew of. Despite his age, I could see the appeal. He reminded me of a less good-looking George Clooney.

Clapping his hands together as he shut the door, he soon rounded our attention. "Good morning. I hope everyone is settled and ready?" A concurrent murmur from around the table sounded along with nods of heads. "Good. Then let's begin."

I took a deep breath as I poised my pen, trying to force myself not to think about Paul beside me. Before I could think anything further, a hand slid across my knee, as an all too familiar voice whispered in my ear, "Yes, let's."

I jumped from the sudden unexpected contact, inhaling so sharply I ended up coughing.

Mr. Collins glared at me, one eyebrow raised. After a few seconds, his impatience won through. "Are you done, Kyra? We have a lot to get through today."

I nodded, taking a sip of my water as I swore at Paul under my breath.

Paul kept his hand on my knee, making me grateful and regretful at the same time for wearing a skirt today. After several minutes, he began brushing his fingertips along my thigh with a feather light touch. The gentleness of it sent my heart soaring to new heights. I bit the inside of my cheek to stop myself from letting out small gasps of pleasure. I glanced up at him from the corner of my eye, giving him my best I'm going to kill you look.

He didn't even look back at me, his focus solely fixed on Mr Collins. He continued his slow tease of my skin, his pink lips twitching at something of a smirk as goosebumps rose on my leg. Seconds later, a violent shudder shot down my spine catching the attention of Mr. Harris, who sat on the other side of me.

He turned to me, his beady eyes scanning my face. "Are you cold, dear?"

Feeling anything but cold right now, I had to lie. "A little."

"Would you like me to turn the air con off?"

I faked a smile. If anything, I needed it colder and blowing straight on me. "Just turned up a degree or two will be fine."

He nodded and smiled as he pressed the temperature button on the remote control.

Mr. Collins's demanding voice cut through the air. "Kyra, are you paying attention?"

"Yes, sir. Mr. Harris was just—"

"I don't want your excuses. Did you get what I just said? About broadening our horizons in Europe? Namely Germany and Switzerland to start with?"

I nodded, not daring to meet his burning gaze as I carried on with my notes. Paul gave my knee a gentle squeeze. For the briefest of seconds I felt relieved that he would now cease his little game.

However, I soon found myself lost in a weird mixture of elation and disappointment as he crept further up the inside of my thigh, his voice never faltering once as he addressed Mr. Collins about his plans for a German division.

When he finished talking, he inched even higher up, stroking his fingers over the outside of my silk underwear. My breath hitched in my throat, and I bit down on my tongue. Heat flooded my body, settling between my legs with a dull throb.

He moved his fingers slightly and settled them on my clit, applying a little more pressure. The dull throb turned to a barb of hot tingles, making me close my eyes for a brief second and suck in a deep breath. I let my breath out slowly and stole a glance at Paul whose delicious, kissable mouth had tweaked up into the curve of a victory smile.

He danced his fingers across my underwear, searching out the edge. My heart started pounding as the reality of getting caught started to dawn on me. Trying to write the minutes and keep up with Mr. Collins had now become an extremely hard task. I could only register every other word in my head, let alone draw enough focus and strength to write it.

As Mr. Collins carried on, I stifled a whimper as Paul slipped his fingers underneath my underwear. When he moved his fingers, gliding down over my sensitive folds, I couldn't help but gasp, a mixture of shock and delight.

Embarrassment consumed me and I faked another cough before reaching for my glass of water. I tried my hardest to ignore the enquiring looks from a couple of the directors. Somehow, I resisted the urge to squirm in my seat and cross my legs. He had me hooked on his touch like a crackhead addicted to their next hit. The electric surges he drove around my body, jolting my muscles with sensations I never knew possible, were impossible to ignore.

He spent the next several minutes tracing his fingers along my entrance, filling me with excitement and apprehension as to if, or when, he would finally slide inside. When he finally delved a finger inside me, I kept my head down and scribbled furiously in my notebook, pushing my hair forwards to block out at least part of my tomato coloured face.

Trying to keep my breathing at a steady pace became a fruitless task as the rhythm he played inside me, hitting my spot every time, had my insides coiling, ready for that sweet release I really needed right now. If he carried on, I knew I would end up begging him to take me right there, regardless of who was watching.

Thankfully, for everyone involved, Mr. Collins finally announced break time. "Right. Time for a fifteen-minute break before we get back at it."

I looked at the clock, surprised to see it was after ten a.m. already. No wonder my thoughts were bordering on public sex. Being played with for over an hour would drive anyone to the edge of insanity.

Rushing to the ladies' room for a brief reprieve, I leaned back against the smooth, cool tiles, grateful for any sort of cold on my body. I took a few deep breaths, trying to calm my aching body but my mind would not let me forget what had just happened.

Just as I debated relieving myself merely to appease my body, the door swung open, Paul striding in with a devilish grin on his handsome face. He closed the door and flicked the lock.

My heart somersaulted, knowing full well what was coming next. He grabbed my face, meeting our lips in a rough kiss, his tongue searching out mine with hungry desire. In nothing but a moment of sheer passion, we yanked at each other's clothes in a desperate bid for bare skin.

With his trousers around his ankles and my skirt hitched up to my waist, he grappled with my thong as I found my way inside his boxers.

He slid his fingers inside me once more and pulled back from our kiss to whisper, "Always so ready."

"Shut up and fuck me," I whispered back, before planting his mouth back on mine.

He moved his fingers and thrust himself inside me, both of us groaning in relief. Our lips parted, our noses still touching, and our eyes locked in a radiating stare. I lifted my legs and wrapped them around his waist, needing to feel him deeper inside me.

"Harder," I whispered.

He drove himself further inside me, a whisper of a hiss escaping through his gritted teeth. My entire body ached, pulsing twinges shocking every cell within me. I needed my sweet release, and I wanted him to give me it—now.

He started moving hard and fast, each stroke pushing breathless gasps from my body. I needed to scream to let some of my tension out, but I knew I couldn't. I dug my nails into his arms in an effort to get rid of some of my need to cry out, but all that did was fuel him into an utter frenzy.

Within a matter of seconds, my tight coil sprung free. He covered my mouth with his, letting me moan into him. As my orgasm washed over me, my muscles quivered from the manic assault.

He leaned his head on my shoulder and bit my skin as he stilled, emptying his own frustration with a shaky sigh of relief.

As he fought to get his breath back, he kissed the end of my nose and gave me a wicked smile. "Lesson number one," he said. "I can tease too."

Chapter Nine

A FTER BEING THE LAST one to re-join the meeting, earning myself a disgruntled stare from Mr. Collins, I managed to work through the rest of the morning without a hiccup.

Lunchtime arrived so off I trundled to the kitchen for another round of drinks whilst they all indulged in the catered food and discussing the joys of golf.

As I reached for the milk from the fridge, a pair of hands snaked around my waist before delicious lips gifted kisses over my skin.

I turned round, grinning. "I think you've done enough for the time being."

Sapphire eyes twinkled back at me, full of mischief. "Really? I could have continued."

"Oh, really?"

Taking the milk from my hands, he grabbed my wrists, spun me around, and pinned me up against the wall. Before I could even think anything further, he pressed his lips to mine, sliding his tongue inside my mouth and teasing my tongue with his. As he ran his hands up and down my body, I could do nothing but melt into a liquid pool. If anyone had walked in at that point, I really couldn't have cared less.

After a few seconds, leaving me utterly breathless, he said, "I like you in a skirt."

I smiled at him. "I guess there's no need to see me tonight now, is there?"

He pulled back and frowned. "Are you insinuating I only want you for sex, Miss Wilson?"

I giggled, reached for his pale blue shirt and pulled him back closer to me. "I'm not insinuating anything, Mr. Connors. I am merely pointing out the fact that we are not in a relationship so that leaves this only being about sex."

He narrowed his eyes slightly, curiosity swimming through them for a few seconds. "Let's get on with the drinks before they all start moaning."

He helped me with the drinks before we ventured back into the meeting. Finally, a little after three p .m., the meeting came to an end. As all the directors piled out, I stayed behind, checking through my notes. Mr. Collins always demanded the minutes within forty-eight hours, which meant I had over ten pages to sort through before Thursday morning.

I sighed as I ran a hand through my hair, wondering how the hell I would get this done alongside my normal workload.

Paul sauntered back into the room and took a seat next to me. He leaned over and kissed me, his lips lingering with a touch of tenderness. "I'm really sorry but I'm going to have to cancel tonight."

"I know."

"What do you mean you know?"

"Well, you've satisfied yourself for today. You've no need to see me tonight now."

He chuckled and shook his head as he took my hand, brushing his thumb across the back of it. "That's not it at all. It's family stuff. I'm sorry."

I shrugged my shoulders. "It's fine, no worries."

He smiled as he stood up. "I need to go. I'll see you tomorrow."

Pecking me on the cheek, he strode out of the room without so much as a second glance.

The next morning, I decided I would wear trousers, purely because Paul said he liked me in a skirt. I couldn't have him thinking I dressed myself according to his likes.

When he came out of his office to meet me, he chuckled. As I flashed him a triumphant smirk, Mr. Harris strode into the room, barking at me to get in his office now.

I threw a surprised look Paul's way, only for him to shrug his shoulders with a frown. Not wanting to irritate Mr. Harris any more than he already was, I dropped everything and ran after him.

Several minutes later, I emerged with a list as long as my arm of things he wanted done as a priority. He knew I had the meeting minutes to complete but he didn't care. It was my problem to figure out.

With a sigh, I sat down, wondering where to start. I decided a decent cup of tea would be the best place to start as well as being the answer to my problems. Stomping into the kitchen, grumbling away to myself, I had no idea I was being watched until a familiar, silky voice slid through the air.

"Enjoy your alone time with Harris?"

I turned around and narrowed my eyes at him, cursing as I spilled some milk on the worktop. "Why? Jealous?"

He barked a loud laugh. "Of Harris? Definitely not."

I smirked. "Oh, so you would be jealous if it wasn't him then?"

He grinned. "I'm saying nothing that could potentially incriminate me."

Laughing, I said, "Oh come on, you're a big boy. You know how to share."

"Oh, I definitely do." He reached out and took my hand. "So, what did he want, anyway?"

I sighed. "If you must know, all he's done is peed me off. He's given me a list a mile long of things he wants doing this week. He knows I have the meeting minutes to do but he doesn't care." I shrugged my shoulders. "Looks like I won't be getting a lunch break or be going home on time."

He pulled me into his arms, amusement dancing through his eyes as he placed a kiss on the tip of my nose. "Hmmm. What I take from that is that we will be alone in the office after hours. That could be interesting."

I rolled my eyes and laughed. "What would be even more interesting is me explaining to Harris that I haven't done his work because his fellow director was too intent on bending me over his desk after hours."

Wiggling his eyebrows up and down, he quirked the corner of his mouth up and said, "Now there's a thought...bending you over Harris' desk..."

I burst out laughing. "That is a very tempting thought ..."

He pecked me on the lips and said, "I'll leave you with that," as he winked and disappeared.

The rest of the day blurred by. I didn't even stop for lunch. Paul, bless his heart, went out at lunch and bought me a sandwich. I finally finished Mr. Harris' list of tasks just before five p.m., but I had to make a start on the meeting minutes at least before I went home.

Making myself another cup of tea with an extra sugar, I plonked myself back in my chair just as Molly came in, asking if I was ready to go home.

I shook my head. "Too much to do."

"Oh. I wanted us to have tea together." She pulled a full-on sulky pout. "I've got some news."

I raised an eyebrow, full well knowing she would tell me anyway.

"We've set the date." She clapped her hands together and squealed. "November first—make sure you book it off. And I want us to go dress shopping so book July seventh off too."

I really didn't need this distraction right now, but I knew if I didn't fill out the holiday request form in front of her eyes, she wouldn't ever leave. I sighed and nodded my agreement to her as I scribbled on the request form.

Perched on the end of my desk, she whispered, "So what's been going on with you and Hot Stuff?"

Right on cue, Paul strode out of his office, flashing me a winning smile. When he noticed Molly, his smile vanished in an instant, his sapphire eyes clouding over with a prickly darkness.

Molly straightened her back, pushing her shoulders back and her boobs out whilst twiddling her blonde hair round her finger. In her sweetest, sultriest voice she said, "Hi, Mr. Connors."

Paul said nothing, glanced at the door, and sauntered out of the office in silence.

Her behaviour annoyed me. She knew how I felt about Paul yet she still insisted on flirting with him. The fact he never reacted was irrelevant. She was crossing a line. However, having an argument with her right now would not help me get my work finished.

Instead, I just simply said, "Molly, you're getting married in a few weeks."

"Nothing wrong with window shopping."

"There is when you know how I feel about him."

The instant the words left my mouth I wanted to rake them back in. Her jade green eyes filled with surprise as her cheeks flushed pink. "You're right. I'm sorry. I was being totally inappropriate."

No, Molly. You were just being you, is what I wanted to say but I kept the thoughts to myself.

"I kinda need to crack on with these notes," I said. "I'll see you tomorrow."

"Ok, yeah, see you tomorrow."

She glanced at me as she stood up, an awkward tension hanging in the air between us. I didn't bite back at her very often but on the odd occasion I did, she never knew how to react.

Thankfully, nothing more was said and she left me in peace with my mountain of work. I continued to plough through it, surprisingly not distracted by thoughts of Paul or anything else.

When my stomach began to grumble, I dared to look at the clock to see it was nearly seven. Sighing in defeat as I realised I'd also have to come in early, I muttered a curse and started gathering my stuff together whilst the computer shut down.

Just as I stood to leave, Paul strolled through the door with a mischievous grin plastered on his handsome face. "Working late?"

I glared at him. "I'm not going to even dignify that with an answer."

He walked to me and held his hand out. "Come on."

I frowned. "What? I'm not in the mood for games, Paul. I need to get these notes done before the morning."

"I know. Stop worrying about it. He's not going to sack you for handing him his minutes in late, and if he does, then he'll have questions to answer. Come on, you need food."

"Paul..."

"Shut up and get your cute little ass out that door."

Chapter Ten

M ANHANDLING ME INTO HIS car, he completely ignored my futile attempts to tell him I needed to go home and rest because I had to be up early to get my work done.

He settled in the driver's seat and smiled. "Just shush. I know you need food so just relax and indulge yourself."

I sighed and did my best to calm my mind from stressing too much. Whilst more than glad I was being taken away from work, I couldn't help but panic about facing Mr. Collins with an unmet deadline.

As we headed down the road and turned onto a narrow country lane, I couldn't help but wonder where the hell we were going. "Where are we going?"

"There's a little pub I often come to when I'm not busy. They serve good food and it's private."

I smiled and watched the scenery of fields and old farmhouses out of the window, imagining myself riding Scotch across all the farmland, the wind in my face and the sound of his hooves filling my ears.

After twenty minutes, we pulled into a gravel park around the back of a light-green coloured pub. A black wooden frame hung off the side of the building— '*The Dog and The Bone.*'

I stepped out of the car, a little dubious as to where the hell he had brought me. We were in the middle of nowhere at a place that looked like it had certainly seen better days. Pushing my pessimism whilst mentally chastising myself for judging a book by its cover, I followed Paul's lead and headed towards the side door.

As Paul opened the door, it creaked loudly, making me look twice at its black iron hinges. I couldn't help but smile as I realised that this place was full of nothing but old charm. I stepped inside, a wall of heat from a roaring open fire on my left hitting me instantly. Old oil paintings hung over its brick red breast with various scenes from horses hunting to a shaggy looking poodle.

Red and gold wallpaper covered the walls, contrasting the aged floral carpet we stood on. On the right sat a dark wooden bar, a stout, grey-haired man standing behind it with a broad grin on his face.

"Paul, how lovely to see you. We missed you last week."

Paul smiled as he headed over. "Hi, Phil. How are you doing? I was busy last week, sorry."

"No worries. Usual?"

Paul nodded. "And a Tia Maria and Coke for my friend here, please."

I raised an eyebrow. "Do I not even get a choice in what I want to drink?"

He grinned and led us over to a table. "Stop being awkward."

We browsed through the menu in silence as Phil brought our drinks to us. I was so hungry I could have eaten everything on the menu and then some. A few minutes later, we had placed our orders with Phil, leaving us all but salivating at the thought of food coming any minute.

Needing to distract myself from my hunger, I decided to quiz Paul. "Do you come here every week?"

He hesitated for a split second before replying, "Yes. If I can."

"What do you mean if you can?"

He pressed his lips together for a brief second. "I have a family business to take care of after I finish at Collins's."

I raised my eyebrows, a mixture of surprise and intrigue flooding me. I hadn't expected that. "Oh. What kind of business?"

He scratched the back of his head, licking his lips before he answered. "Um, it's a little difficult to explain."

"I'm all ears."

He attempted a smile, but his eyes held nothing but a blank stare. "It belongs to my parents but as they insist on handing the business down to me at some point, they kind of insist I'm as much a part of it as they are."

"That's understandable. They've obviously spent a long time building it up for you."

He nodded.

"So, what is it exactly?"

He shuffled in his seat and replied, "They're in the leisure and entertainment industry."

Thinking of cabarets on cruise ships, my eyes lit up. "That sounds fun. Like holidays and stuff?"

"Yes, that kind of thing."

"Oh, I see. So, you come here for a night off or something?"

He nodded. "Wednesdays are the only nights when I'm not really needed so I tend to make the most of my free time and come here for decent food and peace and quiet."

I nodded, understanding his situation. Taking a sip of my drink, I began to think of my ideal holiday. It used to be a choice between the Maldives and going to a horse ranch to learn to rope cows. My ideal spot had been Texas whilst dad had always wanted to visit Colorado. I would go one day, in honour of him.

Thinking about Texas unfortunately brought forth thoughts about my mother and her new husband. I hadn't spoke to my mother in two years, since the day she remarried. The younger cowboy she had decided to attach herself to for life was not what he appeared to be, but unfortunately for me, my mum refused to see it.

Unwelcome memories of the leech haunted my sleep all too frequently and I prayed every day that she would one day believe me over him but as of yet, that hadn't happened.

Not wanting to think any more about Mum and her husband, I decided to pry further into Paul's business, but luckily for him, our food turned up.

I stared at the two huge oval plates, my eyes bulging out of their sockets as I took in the heaped pile of food, the odd pea dropping off the edge of the plate and onto the floor.

As Phil set the plate down in front of me, my mouth dropped open. "I'm never going to eat all of this."

Paul grinned. "Yes, you will. It tastes too good to leave it."

I hadn't ordered anything fancy, just a lasagna, but from the first mouthful I could tell it was all home cooked and it was just delicious. I felt really at home in front of the fire, eating proper homemade food. All I needed was a blanket, a comfy sofa, and the TV and I would be set for the night.

Paul smiled as I hoovered my food up. "Good?"

I nodded. "Almost as good as you."

After a quiet ending to our evening last night, nothing more than a simple kiss before we parted ways, I arrived at work a little before seven in the morning feeling rather rested and relaxed, despite the mammoth task that awaited me.

Being the only one in the building, the eerie silence sent chills down my spine. My solitary footsteps echoed up the empty staircase, making me check behind me every few seconds as paranoia began to creep in.

I hurried into the office and dumped my bag on my desk with a defeated sigh as I glanced at the stack of paperwork on top of my keyboard.

I did a double take as I spotted a bright yellow post-it note stuck to the top of the first page with a heart stopping message written on it.

Thought I'd give you a helping hand. XXX

I picked the papers up and scanned through them. My mouth fell open in shock. They were the minutes from the directors' meeting—complete. My scrawled notes were stacked in my filing tray.

Had Paul really done this? I was gobsmacked to say the least, and also now slightly annoyed I'd gotten up early for no reason.

I sighed and decided seeing as I was already here, I may as well stay and either leave early today, or bag the time up to claim back another day. Making myself a cup of tea, I decided just for my own peace of mind, I would check through the minutes for errors. I settled back at my desk and started scanning through the pages, however, as I suspected, I couldn't find fault. I actually couldn't have done a better job myself. How on earth he'd read my terrible notes I had no idea.

Just after eight, in strode my Greek god, a broad grin on his handsome face. "Hello, you," he said.

"Morning," I replied. "You could have told me you were doing this. I wouldn't have bothered coming in at seven otherwise."

He crossed his arms over his chest and raised his eyebrows. He mimicked a high-pitched voice as he said, "Oh, thank you, Paul, for helping me. That was so nice of you. I really appreciate it. What can I possibly do to thank you?"

I rolled my eyes. "For fucks sake..."

He put his tongue in his cheek. "Well, seeing as you're offering to thank me..."

I snorted. "I don't think so. Thank you, though. I am grateful."

He dropped his arms to his side and came to the edge of my desk. "You're very welcome. I didn't want you stressing, and I couldn't be doing with politics from Collins if you were late with them."

I frowned, undecided whether to be insulted he thought I couldn't meet my deadlines or wondering what politics he could have with Collins over some unfinished minutes. I shook my head and dismissed both thoughts.

"I need July seventh off. Dress shopping with Molly."

"She's actually going through with it, then?"

I nodded.

"That guy needs a medal."

"Hey, she's my best friend, you know."

"Sweetie, I think a lot of people would call her that. Namely men."

"Paul!"

He tilted his head back and laughed. When he looked back at me, he waved his hand through the air dismissively. "Yes, okay. Fine. Put it on your holiday sheet. If you get my drift," he said, winking.

I frowned. Was he saying what I thought he was? "Um...am I being dumb or are you insinuating—"

"Yes. Now shush about it and make me one of your lovely teas. Please."

I relaxed back in my chair, a grin enveloping my face as I realised he was giving me a day off without using up my holiday quota. Sleeping with a director seemed to be full of perks.

Chapter Eleven

F OUR P.M. ON FRIDAY couldn't come around fast enough. All day I'd had ants in my pants as the buzzing anticipation for the weekend consumed me. As soon as the clock hit four, I packed up my desk and all but ran for the door.

But God damn me if that hot sex God, Paul, didn't stop me first. "Where are you going in such a rush?" he asked, his eyebrows arched upwards.

"Why? Worried you might have some competition?" I replied, smirking. I tapped my finger on his chest and then said, "But we're not in a relationship so there is no competition, right?"

He grinned. "Right." He shrugged his shoulders and then said, "I've just never seen you in such a rush to go anywhere."

"I'm going to London with Ash."

He reached out and settled his hands on my waist, pulling me in towards him. "All weekend?"

I nodded. "You said you were busy so I made plans."

A flicker of surprise flashed through his eyes. "Oh. Well, have a good time. Do you mind if I call when I can?"

"No, of course not."

He smiled and pressed a kiss to my forehead. "You make sure you stay safe. If you get in the wrong place at the wrong time—"

"I'll be fine. We'll be hitting gay bars anyway."

He grinned and cocked his head to one side. "Which will have lesbians in as well."

I smirked and bit my bottom lip. I dropped a hand and brushed it across his groin. "Well, maybe that's something I'm not immune to."

"What?"

I gave him a cheeky grin. "Well, I have always been slightly curious..."

He started laughing. "Interesting."

"Isn't it just?"

He pressed his lips to mine, parting my lips with his tongue as he massaged me into a bubble of hot surges and tingles. After a minute or so, he stopped it with a smile. "Go and have fun. I'll speak to you later."

Ash picked me up from work, my luggage already in his car. His bundle of energy had nothing on mine as he almost bounced out of his seat the entire three-hour trip down to London.

We pulled up outside of a Premier Inn in the depths of Covent Garden. Ash bounded up the stairs after we checked in, unlocking my door and throwing my bags on the huge bed.

He turned round, grabbing my shoulders as his dark eyes danced with joy. "I want you showered and changed in an hour."

He charged past me to his room next door as I stood there rolling my eyes at his kid-like energy. Once left in peace, I showered and proceeded to rummage through my bags for a dress to wear. I pulled out my favourite red lace number and a pair of black high heels to go with it. Pinning my hair to the side, I curled a few random pieces before attacking myself with hairspray.

Just as I finished my makeup, Ash banged on the door, demanding to be let in. I sighed and let him in, wondering if I'd even had the full hour to get ready yet.

He let out a low whistle and nodded his approval of my outfit. "Check you out."

I wrinkled my nose up at his aftershave. "Are you wearing Joop again?" He knew I hated that aftershave.

"So, come on then. What's going on with you and Mr. Hot Stuff?"

Deciding to let his ignorance of my question go, I smirked and shrugged my shoulders. "It's just sex."

"Sis, don't lie to me. I know you."

"Are we ready?" I asked, grabbing my bag.

He nodded.

I ushered him out the door, barely remembering my room key card. "Ash, it's barely been a week. We've had more sex than conversations. That's all it is."

He held his hands up in a surrender sign, grinning. "So, if he suddenly appeared and declared his undying love for you, what would you say?"

I laughed. "You should be asking what I would do."

He chuckled. "Ok, ok. But in all seriousness, taking him out of the equation, don't you ever want to settle down? I am waiting to be fun Uncle Ash."

I sighed as we made our way down the corridor. "Ash, I'm only thirty, not fifty. I'm not going to tie myself down to someone just for the sake of it. It has to be right."

It suddenly dawned on me that even if I had a child now, I would be fifty before they left home. That was a scary thought. Why hadn't I settled down before now? A cold realisation hit me that, actually, I really did need to take this seriously if I wanted that normal life I craved yet was too afraid to commit to.

"I get that, sis, I really do, but when are you going to stop being so afraid? Fear is in all of us but you're letting it rule you."

I thought about his words for a moment. He was right, but I wasn't going to tell him that. My stubborn streak emerged, batting away his good sense. "If I get desperate for kids, I'll go to a sperm bank."

Ash burst out laughing, shaking his head. "You're impossible."

I ignored him, changing the subject. "Right, where are we going?"

He grinned, grabbing my hand and squeezing my bones into a sickening crunch. "We're going to a beautiful little club called The Tiger's Eye. There's someone I want you to meet."

I instantly knew he'd met someone. I couldn't wait to meet him—this was a first for Ash, introducing me to one of his partners. The club was only a ten-minute walk from the hotel. As I revelled in the fact I was out on a night out, which I'd not had for ages, my phone vibrated.

Paul: Hope you're enjoying yourself. Let me know whether she's a blonde or a redhead. I'm already sorted for a brunette. ;-) xx

Me: I'll let you know once I'm finished with her. ;-) xx

Paul: Take some pics or a video for me. ;-) xx

Me: Sorry, I'll be too busy. I'm sure your imagination can come up with something better. ;-) xx

The club had three levels to it. I raised my eyebrows at Ash as he described each level as more risqué than the one before. He instructed me under no circumstances to go to the third floor. A shot of dread ran through me as I pushed unwelcome thoughts and climbing curiosity from my mind.

We left the ground floor with its black marble floor and quiet music, climbing a set of white marble stairs that curled round in a loose spiral. We came to a wide landing, a plush red carpet spread out over the floor leading us to a set of double doors. Bright lights and thumping music streamed out to us as we approached our destination.

Opening the doors, we were greeted with an incredible sized dance hall. The same black marble spanned the floor in here with a huge bar the length of the room to the left and a line of red velvet booths to the right, each lit with a hanging chandelier. The DJ pumped out feel good tunes to the crowd of bodies all upon each other, hands and feet mingling into one giant mass.

Everywhere I looked there were girls on girls, guys on guys, and guys on girls. It seemed like anything went in here—if it had a pulse and you fancied it, then away you go. That alone made me a little nervous and Paul's warning of staying safe kept repeating itself in my mind.

We ordered our drinks before I turned round, scanning across the room. "So where is he?"

He grinned like a school kid and pointed to the DJ booth.

I raised my eyebrows. "Really?"

He nodded, throwing me a wink. "And he bangs as well as his tunes."

I choked on my drink, spluttering as he laughed next to me.

He patted me on the shoulder. "I'll be back in a minute."

I watched his broad back disappear into the crowd, trying to hide my awkwardness at standing in a strange place on my own. Not only was it an unfamiliar place but somewhere full of predators searching out their next prey.

"Hey."

I turned round at the sound of the silky-smooth voice to be greeted with a fantastic-looking redheaded woman. A couple of inches taller than me with a perfect hourglass figure, I couldn't describe her as anything other than simply stunning. Her green eyes glittered with intrigue as she stood next to me, scanning over my face. Dressed in a simple black halterneck dress, it contrasted her soft, pale skin to perfection.

I smiled, finding myself unable to take my eyes off her. Something about her just captivated me.

She held a hand out, her nails long and perfectly manicured. "Tessa."

I took her hand, ignoring my racing heart. "Kyra."

"I've not seen you here before."

I wondered how often she came in here to warrant a question like that. "I'm just here for the weekend with my brother."

"Where is he?"

I pointed to the DJ booth.

"Your brother is Ben's new beau? Wow. I've heard he's quite something. Ashley, isn't it?"

I nodded as I began to wonder how on earth he'd met this guy in the first place.

"So, what are you doing here? Other than your brother? You can't possibly be single."

I smiled. "It's complicated."

She nodded. "So, where is he? Or she?"

"He is doing family stuff this weekend."

"So how is it complicated?"

I was slightly taken aback at her forward approach but maybe speaking to another female, and getting an outside point of view, would do me some good.

"He's my boss. We've had more sex than conversations. It won't go anywhere."

"Ah." She curled her fingers around my arm, causing me to jump in surprise. "Never mix business and pleasure. It always ends in tears. Is he hot?"

I grinned. "Like you wouldn't believe."

"Well, the way I see it, you're just enjoying him for sex." She trailed her nails up and down my arm, leaving a trail of goosebumps in her wake. "Which means..."

My heart skipped a beat. I couldn't deny I found her alluring to say the least. I suddenly found myself understanding how men became fixated on a woman. Hell, I was a woman and even I found myself attracted to her.

As much as I had always been curious about being with a girl, I knew for a fact if I did it, I would regret it afterwards. I knew I would feel dirty and wish it hadn't happened. However, I couldn't ignore the fact that the curiosity was there.

I stuttered, distracted by her gentle touch as she crept closer to me. I couldn't stop looking at her; she bewitched me in a way I'd never known before.

She smiled before biting her plump red lips. My heart rate spiked as she moved into me, our chests touching as she wandered her fingers up my arm. I felt trapped, helpless. She was like a vampire luring in its next meal—seducing it into a good time before ripping its heart out and devouring it.

So lost in my thoughts, I didn't even realise when her mouth casually brushed over mine. When I finally registered the fact a woman had her lips on me, I wriggled out from under her grip, babbling my apologies.

"Tess, leave her alone for goodness sake," a deep voice boomed from next to me. I turned around to see a burly, sandy-haired, hot as hell guy stood with Ash, their arms around each other.

Tessa grinned before releasing me from her clutches, hugging the guy and then Ash.

Ash stepped forwards, his beaming smile telling of his happiness. "Ky, this is Ben."

Ben took my hand, gracing the back of it with a tender kiss. We swapped pleasantries before they both disappeared back into the darkness.

Tessa resumed her place at my side, violating my personal space and then some. "He's nearly finished his set. He'll be back soon."

I nodded, shuffling back and creating some space between us with a nervous smile.

She laughed. "I'm sorry. I get a bit carried away when I see someone I like."

I smiled. "Sure. No hard feelings."

My bag vibrated with another text.

Paul: So, where have you gone, sexy legs? Xx

Me: Some seedy club called The Tiger's Eye. There are definitely tigers in here. xx

Tessa bought me a drink as an apology, gesturing for us to take a seat in one of the red booths on the other side of the room. I accepted, pleased to have a seat and someone to chat to whilst Ash was enjoying himself with his new bloke.

Paul: I bet they're all cubs compared to you. ;-) xx

Me: I actually doubt that. xx

Paul: Well, why don't you catch one and let me know? ;-) xx

I giggled before ignoring his text, stuffing my phone back in my bag.

Tessa and I indulged in some small talk before she gestured towards the dance floor. I hesitated, which only served her to run over to the bar, reappearing with six shot glasses. I balked at the Sambuca shots, raising my eyebrows at her.

"Come on," she said.

She downed hers in quick succession, pushing mine towards me as I followed her lead. Before I knew what was happening, she'd grabbed my hand, leading me towards a spot near the DJ booth, which housed two metal poles on a stage.

I raised my eyebrows. "You are joking, right?"

She laughed. "No. Get up and work that shit."

As I debated my options, Ash appeared from nowhere with another two shots and a cheeky grin. I sighed before downing them. No one knew me in here anyway, may as well let myself go and enjoy myself.

I grabbed the pole, working my way around it, swinging my legs and hips all over the place. Before I knew it, Tessa joined me, running her hands down the length of my body as we moved in rhythm to the music. I closed my eyes as she pulled my hips back into her. She wandered her hands over my chest as I continued to gyrate against her.

A massive cheer from a group of guys caused me to open my eyes. I grinned, the alcohol taking a hold as I really let my hair down. I ran my fingers through my long locks before turning round to face Tessa and grabbing her own delicious curves. Our eyes met in a sparkle of desire as we inched our lips closer together.

The whoops and roars from the crowd below us only served to fuel my actions further as I pressed our lips together, our tongues meeting in a slow dance which burned me to my core.

We parted after several seconds, continuing our seductive dance much to the enjoyment of the men below us. I glanced around the room, trying to avoid eye contact with anyone. The lights from the DJ booth highlighted the doorway for a brief second, causing my heart to drop like a lead weight to my feet.

There he stood, staring at me—Paul.

Chapter Twelve

M Y HEART RESTARTED WITH a resounding thud,
racing to a million miles an hour when our eyes
met. I scrambled off the stage, words jumbling together in
my mind as I thought of something to say to him. As I approached his burning gaze, any comprehensible sentences
melted away, leaving me stood in front of my Greek God
with nothing to say.

He crossed his arms over his chest, the corner of his
mouth tweaking up into something I couldn't quite name.
"Hi."

My cheeks erupted, scorching my already heated skin.
"Hi."

"Having fun?"

I blushed, dropping my eye contact and staring at the
floor. "I..."

"I saw the whole thing, Kyra. I've been stood here quite a while."

I dared my eyes to meet his once more, his smouldering look shooting dread through my body. "I'm sorry...I just kind of..."

He lifted a hand, a gentle touch tilting my chin up to him. "You have nothing to be sorry for, Kyra. It's not like we're in a relationship or anything, is it?"

My heart splattered at my feet for a second time, disappointment and rejection mingling with it into a mangled mess. I shook my head, faking a smile. "No, I guess not."

He dropped his hand, his beautiful blue eyes scanning over my face. "I do like you, Kyra. I like you a lot. I'm just not a relationship type of guy. It doesn't fit well with my life and the type of person I am."

Somewhere deep inside, anger started boiling, trying to force its way to the surface. I snorted at him as I crossed my arms over my chest, taking a step back. "Thanks for the heads up, like, a week ago."

He smiled. "But if I did ever change that about myself, then you would be the first to know."

I threw my hands up in the air. "Lucky me." I sighed before I burst out laughing. "Well, at least I know where I stand. In the meantime, I'm going to live for the moment."

He raised his eyebrows. "Which means what, exactly?"

I grinned, blew him a kiss, and made a beeline for Tessa, who was still working her stuff on the pole. I jumped back up on stage, settling my hands on her waist as I pulled us together.

She raised her eyebrows as I inched our lips closer. "Someone had a change of heart?"

"You only live once, right?"

She grinned before gluing our mouths together, her tongue massaging my own with an aching desire. Whoops and jeers resounded from our group of watchers on the dance floor, both of us smiling as we broke our kiss.

As Ben finished his set, the music changed tempo slightly as the new DJ took over. We climbed down from the stage, strange hands patting us on the back and groping our bums as we walked through the throng of people.

"Wooo! Go, sis!" Ash said, bounding towards me with a grin on his face.

"Shut up."

He grinned before handing me another two shots of Sambuca with a wink. "I'm disappearing for the night—if you get my drift."

I laughed. "Sure. Paul is here, anyway."

He looked around, his eyes settling on my sex God's fine form. "I shall make sure I say hi. See you in the morning."

I bid him good night before heading to the bar for yet more unneeded alcohol. Tessa ordered our drinks as I watched Paul and Ash share a short exchange. Downing my drink in one go, I smiled as Paul sauntered over, his blonde hair twinkling under the disco lights.

"Where's your brother going?"

I smirked. "For an early night."

He laughed as he shook his head. "Just me and you, then, I guess?"

I shook my head. "Nope."

He frowned.

"I'm going for an early night too."

He clenched his jaw and narrowed his eyes as the fun in them hardened over with something I might dare label as jealousy. "With who?"

I grinned, wrapping my hand around Tessa's waist. She responded by curling her own arm around my waist.

He looked from me to Tessa, then back to me. "Are you serious?"

"Totally."

He smiled and folded his arms over his chest. "So, you're just going to leave me high and dry?"

I ran my tongue over my bottom lip and let the alcoholic fuzz in my brain do the talking. "Not like we're in a relationship or anything, is it? I didn't ask you to spend three hours in a car to come and see me."

"Touché."

I started walking past him, my grin ever growing. I turned back, gesturing towards the door with my head. "You coming or not?"

He grinned in response and followed us out.

As we stepped outside into the fresh air, the alcohol I'd consumed seemed to hit me all at once, sending me into a new spin as we made our way back to the hotel. When we entered my room, Paul disappeared into the bathroom, leaving Tessa and me alone.

"You sure about this?" she asked.

I nodded, smiling as I tried to steady my whirling mind.

She leaned into me, pressing her soft lips to mine and slipping her tongue inside my mouth. Our hands mirrored each other's movements, both of us fondling over our feminine curves. Shivers covered me from head to toe. A small moan escaped me when she brushed a hand over my chest, new waves of lust rushing through me.

I broke our kiss for a second. "Take it off. My dress."

She smiled before working her way down my neck with her soft lips, catching all my sensitive spots with an expert touch. She unzipped me, pushing my dress to the floor in one swift move. She took a moment to look at me in my black lacy underwear, biting her lip as she did so. In less than a second, her own dress found its way to the floor as she revealed her own bright red silk lingerie.

She settled her hands on my hips, then ran her fingers over my body and around my back, releasing my bra in one swift move. I shivered as goosebumps covered me from head to toe, anticipation and excitement heightening everything.

I copied her movements, my heart pounding as I took her bra from her gorgeous body. Our bodies pressed together, soft skin to soft skin, I could do nothing to fight the moment even if I wanted to. Her velvet curves and her sparkling emerald eyes were too much to resist.

As our mouths pressed back together, our tongues intertwining in a slow, teasing dance, we explored each others bodies with our hands, the gentle roaming leaving both of us covered in goosebumps.

She broke our kiss, leaving me wanting more of her delicious kisses. She kissed her way down to my neck, nibbling at the skin. I gasped, mentally willing her to move down to my breasts. What felt like hours passed, but was only seconds, before her tongue caressed my nipple with gentle licks, working spine tingling patterns over its soft surface.

Violent shudders coursed through me, each one settling between my legs with a throbbing ache, making me want to pull her hand down south and give me my release, now.

"Fucking hell."

I jolted back to reality and opened my eyes to see Paul stood by the bed, watching us. His sapphire eyes glittered like gems under sunlight. In the heat of the moment, and totally consumed by pleasure, I'd completely forgotten about him.

I smiled at him and closed my eyes, allowing Tessa to push me on the bed. She crawled on top of me, continuing her sensual assault on my breasts, driving me insane, as she worked her way down my body. She glided her fingers down my legs, sweeping my thong off in one smooth movement.

Paul groaned, and I looked over to see him undressing himself. Tessa distracted me from him as she kissed the inside of my thighs. I squirmed with an overwhelming anticipation of what would happen next.

She licked me, from bottom to top, making me jolt from the sudden but divine touch. When she placed her mouth on me, teasing slow circles over my tender spot, I could feel my core tightening within seconds. I couldn't help but buck my hips up to her, wanting her to consume more of me.

I'd had some good oral sex with men, but this, this was something else. I struggled to calm my breathing as I silently begged for her to give me more. She slid a finger inside me, instantly going straight to my G spot. I could do nothing but close my eyes and let heaven come to me.

A familiar hand covered my left breast, teasing my hardened nipple with a thumb. I opened my eyes to see Paul hovering over me, his breathing heavy and ragged. He pressed his mouth to mine, taking control of me as he continued to play with my nipple.

I closed my eyes and let out a moan, needing some sort of relief as this incredible wave kept building in my core, still not ready to jump free. Tessa increased the pressure on my G spot, bringing me to the point of not even being capable of kissing Paul.

Seconds later, the two of them had me floating in an ocean of decadence as my body let go, too overwhelmed by the sensual assault from both of them. As everything tingled and fizzled from my toes to my head, neither of them let up. Tessa kept going with her tongue, the lazy but firm circles on my clit ensuring me of another release that was so close.

Paul broke our kiss and moved down to my breast, taking it in his mouth and flicking the tip of my nipple. The quick, fierce jolts of pleasure settled straight between my legs and in Tessa's mouth.

She started moving her finger in and out of me, making me think only of Paul and the way he would thrust himself inside me. Just thinking about Paul fucking me pushed me over into another sweet release.

I let out a cry of relief, my eyes locking with Paul's. He knew what I wanted, somehow, and growled at Tessa to move. As my world continued to spin, my body trembling from my orgasms, Paul plunged himself inside me, taking me to a whole new level.

Tessa climbed up the bed and settled herself next to me. My muscles weak and overloaded with pleasure, I still managed to find the energy to reach for her and slide my fingers between her legs to repay her the heaven she'd given me.

Within seconds, Paul slid out of me and pulled me up to my feet. He spun me around and wrapped his arms around my waist, sliding his hands up to caress my breasts. He nuzzled into my hair and nipped at my earlobe, making me shiver.

In a gruff whisper, he said, "You're mine."

My drunken haze couldn't focus too much on the meaning of his words but when he ordered Tessa to move to the top of bed and sort herself out, I tried desperately to cling on to some sort of reasoning behind his words, but I could do nothing but let him take control.

He pushed me back down onto the bed, face down, and thrust inside me. Keeping his hands on my breasts, he played with my nipples to the point I cried for him to fuck me harder to give me my release.

Wrapping my hair around his wrist, he moved his free hand to my clit and started rubbing it as he pounded into me harder and harder. It didn't take long for me to find my third climax, and I could do nothing but collapse, my body completely wrung out and exhausted from such an overload of pleasure.

Tessa gasped and I forced my eyes open to see her at the top of the bed, her mouth in a perfect O as she found her own joyful release. Paul let go of my hair and stilled inside me, letting out a shaky groan.

He leaned over me, kissing my back, before moving away from me. Saying not a word, he walked into the bathroom and shut the door.

Sobering up at a rate of knots, I looked at Tessa who quirked an eyebrow up and said, "That was...interesting."

My head spinning, I could think of nothing but what had just happened. What the hell did I just do? With my boss?

Chapter Thirteen

I woke up Saturday morning with a pounding headache. In the fuzzy parts of my brain, I could hear something jingling. I blinked a few times, trying to adjust my sore eyes to the dimly lit hotel room.

As I sat up, I gasped in horror when I saw a woman in my bed. Her silky red hair splayed out on the pillow like something from a seductive photograph. Then it hit me. Like a herd of stampeding bulls, all my jumbled memories fell through my mind, fragmenting their own picture show of last night's events.

The bathroom door opened, revealing a stark-naked Paul looking mighty fine in all his glory.

He grinned at me. "Morning."

I groaned and clasped a hand to my head. I met his amused gaze, squinting as his words from last night filtered through my mind. Right from where we stood of not being in a relationship to him tearing my touch from Tessa and telling me that I'm his.

What did it all mean? Why was he not a relationship guy? Why did he come down here if he wasn't interested in something more committed?

I pushed the thoughts away, not needing to dissect them with a hangover. I pulled the duvet back and stumbled towards the bathroom. "I need a bath."

I turned the bath taps on before realising I had no shower gel to clean myself with. Wrapping a towel around me, I walked back out to see Tessa getting herself dressed. Paul sat in the chair in the corner of the room, looking at something on his phone.

She flashed me a dazzling smile. "Hey. I had a good time, thank you." She zipped her dress back up and then said, "For what it's worth, I think you two should definitely reconsider your 'fun' arrangement."

I frowned. "What do you mean?"

She gave me a lazy smile. "Well, let's just say that's the first ménage a trois I've had where the guy makes his singular interest rather clear."

Heat flushed through me as I realised that, really, the poor woman had ended up enjoying herself more than either of us. But what exactly did that mean?

I glanced at Paul who didn't react at all. Faking a smile, I nodded at Tessa, not quite clear-headed enough to make sense of her words just yet. She ran for the door, making her excuses for having work in less than an hour.

As the door slammed shut behind her, an uncomfortable silence fell in the room. Paul didn't even look up at me, so I said nothing and walked back in the bathroom. I shut the door behind me before slipping under the bliss of the bubbles. My peace lasted for barely two minutes.

"Kyra..."

I groaned hearing Ash banging on the room door.

Several seconds later, I heard him say, "Hey, Hot Stuff."

"She's in the bath," Paul replied.

Ash's voice boomed through the bathroom door. "Ky, get out here."

"No, I'm having a relaxing bath."

"Ky," he said, his voice deep and commanding. "Get out here, now."

I sighed and muttered swear words under my breath as I got up and wrapped a towel around me. Poking my head around the door, I said, "What do you want?"

Ash smirked back at me, his eyes lighting up at impending gossip. "Did I just see Tessa leaving your room?"

"Is that all you got me out of the bath for?" I rolled my eyes. "Go away, Ash. I'll speak to you later."

"Holy shit. You did, didn't you?"

I didn't dignify him with a response except for shutting the door in his face.

"Time to go," Paul said. "She'll talk to you later."

"All right, gorgeous, chill out," Ash replied. "Tessa is quite a fun girl, isn't she?"

"I wouldn't know."

"Oh, come on, man, we're all grown-ups."

"And some things still remain private."

"Fine." Ash's voice changed slightly, his tone lowering as he turned serious. "Let me put it another way. Did you stick your dick in another woman in front of my sister?"

"*Ashley!*" I yanked the bathroom door open, absolutely fuming at my brother. I glanced at Paul, who stared at Ash with nothing but a blank look on his face. "That's enough," I said, "Out. Now."

"What?" His dark eyes told me he was more than serious at this moment in time and I had no idea why. "I'm just trying to have a normal conversation about sex and Mr. Uptight here is refusing to."

"Ash, I'm your sister. This is weird enough. Get out."

Ash ignored me, turning his attention back to Paul. "Alright, let's cut to the chase. What are you doing with my sister exactly?"

I interrupted before Paul could even open his mouth. "We're having sex. That's it. End of."

"Yeah, you've told me your side already, but from what I've heard from Tess, it's not quite that simple."

Paul shrugged his shoulders. "We're having fun. It's nothing serious. I'm not a relationship kind of guy."

I glared at Ash, hating him for making me hear those words again. I fought back the tears that threatened to cover my eyes and swallowed the lump in my throat. "Satisfied?"

"Not completely, no, but it'll do for now." Ash raised his eyebrows and chuckled. "How awkward is this going to be on Monday morning?" He turned and left, the door closing shut behind him.

The tension left between me and Paul became so intense I felt as if I could reach out and snap it.

"Kyra..."

He said my name in such a soft tone it coated me in shivers. I ignored him and started closing the door. I couldn't do this now. Not again.

"Kyra, we need to talk."

I sighed and said, "About what?"

"You know what."

I smirked. "If I knew what, then I wouldn't be asking, would I?"

He folded his arms over his muscled chest. "What was that? Last night? I mean, I'm not complaining, but it's like someone flipped a switch and boom, off you went and jumped into bed with a woman. Where did that come from?"

I shrugged my shoulders. "I told you I'd always been curious."

He narrowed his eyes and took a few steps towards the bathroom.

"Fine," I said. "You said we're just having fun because you don't do relationships, so I figured I had nothing to lose. Why not?"

"I see." He rubbed his chin between his thumb and forefinger, his face harbouring a thoughtful look. "So, despite the fact I may change my mind at some point, you decided to put the final nail in the coffin by involving another person in our sexual relations?"

My heart raced to new heights as dread and regret tumbled through my body. Had he just said I'd stopped any chance of us getting together? I looked down at the floor, wishing I could curl up into a ball and rewind time.

My stubborn side chose its moment to show itself and I met his eye contact with a defiant tilt to my chin. "Yes. I'm not waiting for anyone." I closed the door to finalise the conversation before reopening it again. "Besides, most guys would love what happened in here last night, and you're complaining? Pffft."

He raised his eyebrows and twitched his lips into something of a smile. "I understand you don't want to wait but expecting me to declare my commitment to you after a week is a little high expectation, don't you think?"

"I have high expectations and patience isn't my strong point."

"Clearly."

I scowled at him. "Why the hell did you come down here anyway?"

He ran a hand through his hair and looked away. "I wanted to see you."

"And you couldn't have waited until Monday?"

He sat back on the bed, his elbows on his knees as he cradled his head in his hands. "I thought it would be a nice surprise."

"Surprises are usually a relationship type of thing, Paul. You can't take me out for dinner, ask to see me in the evenings, follow me three hours down the road, and then act shocked when I think this is going somewhere."

He remained silent for a few seconds before his eyes met mine, somewhat empty. "When you put it like that, I'm sorry. I guess I have given you false hope. I shouldn't have come here."

My heart sank and my urge to cry became too overwhelming. "Wow. You really are a piece of work. Just go, please."

I slammed the door in his face before he could respond. I clicked the lock as loudly as I could to make a point. Sliding back inside my now lukewarm bath, I switched the hot tap on, cursing under my breath at all the interruptions I had at just wanting a damn soak in some hot water.

A gentle knock tapped at the door. "Kyra..."

"I'm not listening."

"I'm not going home until you talk to me."

I snorted. "Enjoy your stay, then."

"Stop being awkward, Kyra."

"I will. When you stop being a confusing asshole."

"I like you, you know this. I've told you plenty of times."

"Yep," I said. "I know. I get it. It's the whole 'it's not you, it's me' thing."

A loud sigh came from the other side. "Friends with benefits, Kyra. That's the best I can offer you."

I smirked as I sank under the bubbles. "Fine. Whatever."

Chapter Fourteen

AN HOUR LATER WE sat in a posh café a few minutes' walk from the hotel. Ash insisted on taking us there for lunch so I could meet Ben properly. He actually seemed quite sweet. I liked him. Broad built but well-toned with sandy-coloured hair and dark eyes, his face always wore a pleasant smile, and his manners were second to none.

Ash detailed me on how they met in Australia. "Hell of a coincidence, don't you think, Ky? We live in the same country but never meet yet travel to the other side of the world and bam, we meet. It's like it was meant to be."

I forced a smile on my face. "Yeah. Totally meant to be."

He caught the sarcasm in my voice and glared at me. "Why can't you be happy for me? Just because Hot Stuff here is as much of a commitment phobe as you, don't take it out on me."

Ouch. That stung. I bit my tongue, playing the one in the wrong. "Sorry. I'm just a bit tired."

He smirked. "Yeah, I bet."

He laughed with Ben over a memory from their trip whilst I turned my attention to the menu, which I'd already read five times over. Ash was picking up the bill as a treat for all of us. When the waitress came over, I took great delight in ordering the most expensive food on the menu. I blew Ash a kiss and sat back in my chair, smiling at his scowling face.

Ash clasped his hands together, leaning on the table. "Anyway, I'm glad Hot Stuff here decided to show up."

I lifted an eyebrow. "Why?"

He flitted his eyes across to Ben before he sent a beaming smile my way. "Ben and I are going to live together and we're going to spend a few days house hunting down here."

My jaw dropped open. "What?"

"We've been together over six months. It just feels right."

"So let me get this right." I rested my elbows on the table, glaring at him for all I was worth. "You come back after being away for a year, which may I add, you barely spoke to me for the duration of. Not mentioning you didn't even tell me the proper date you were coming back. You then whisk me down to London for a weekend for us to spend some time together but all you really wanted was to spend the weekend with your new boyfriend and then spend a few days house hunting? Tell me, if Paul hadn't showed up, how was I getting home?"

He looked at me as he ran his tongue over his lips. "I'm sorry, Ky. I didn't realise it sounded quite that bad. I was just excited about you meeting Ben and sharing our news with you. I didn't quite think of how you may feel..."

"No." I stood up, scraping my chair back against the polished floor with a spine-chilling screech. "That's your lot's problem, isn't it? You men are just incapable of thinking about anything except your fucking dicks."

I stormed out, my temper getting the better of me to say the least. I found a wooden bench a few hundred yards away and sat down, taking deep breaths to calm myself. Thinking over my little outburst as I cooled my temper, guilt began to wash over me as I realised Ben probably thought I was a first-class bitch by now. More than anything, I was shocked at Ash and his hidden agenda. Why hadn't he just been straight with me from the start? I could have at least then had a contingency plan in place to get myself home if needed.

As I contemplated going back with my apologies, Paul appeared, a blank expression on his face. I rolled my eyes, sighing as I looked the other way.

The bench moved slightly as he sat down next to me. "I presume that was a little dig at me there?"

"Don't flatter yourself."

"Kyra, I know what I said isn't what you wanted to hear but I'm not going to fill you full of false promises. That wouldn't be fair on either of us."

I nodded, biting my lip to stem my flow of tears. I blinked for all I was worth before turning to face him. "Yeah, it's fine."

He smiled, taking hold of my hand. "Are you going to come and eat your food? Ash is currently moaning he's paying a fortune for food you're not going to eat."

I laughed and nodded. After apologising to Ash and Ben, it was decided I would be catching a lift back home with Paul.

Unfortunately for me, this meant not only leaving sooner than expected but sitting in a confined space with my hot Greek sex God for three hours. Fortunately for me, my lack of sleep from last night claimed the best of me and within minutes of hitting the road, my heavy eyelids won the battle and I fell asleep.

At some point later, I woke up, immediately glancing around me to see where we were. The answer was nowhere near home and I'd only been asleep for half an hour.

Great.

The thought of the atmosphere between us drove me to want to ignore it in any way possible; sleep was my answer to that.

Just as I closed my eyes again, Paul said, "Welcome back." I turned my head to see him grinning at me, his handsome face melting my heart all over again. "Do you mind if I make a quick stop at my house before I drop you off?"

I smiled. Hope began to reignite deep down that this was his little way of letting me take a peek inside his life. "No, of course not."

"We tend to have a few people over on Saturday nights. Mum usually sends me out with a shopping list."

I frowned. "Every Saturday?"

He turned his attention back to the road. "Most."

Silence fell between us, and the main roads melted into quiet back roads as he drove us deeper into the blissful countryside. As the roads became narrower and more dirt than tarmac, a pair of huge black iron gates appeared before us at the end of a rather long driveway.

Held in place by two sturdy red brick pillars complete with ornamental lions on top, they took my breath away with the intricate metal work entwining all over them.

Paul pulled up in front of them, opening the window to type in a key code on the silver number pad stationed a few feet away from the entrance. The gates glided open, allowing us to pass through. My jaw dropped open at the landscaped gardens surrounding us. The perfect gravel driveway edged to perfection with fancy curb stones kept us away from the neat green grass.

Hundreds of trees hung overhead, obscuring us from the view of anyone around. Drawing closer to the edge of the tree lining, a fantastic sprawling mansion emerged into our view.

Complete with a carriageway drive, stone water feature in the middle, and steep steps up to the front door, it was everything you would expect to see in a Jane Austen novel.

I turned to Paul, my mouth wide open. "You live here?"

He chuckled and nodded. "It's my parents' house but I have the west wing to myself."

I raised my eyebrows as I shook my head. Thinking of my own small abode, I felt somewhat embarrassed that he'd seen where I lived in comparison to this.

He opened his door and hopped out. "I'll be back in a minute."

I nodded, my eyes already trailing over the vast expanse of the amazing building. Paul jogged his way up the cream-coloured steps, entering through a set of dark wooden double doors, which housed a fabulous lion's head brass knocker.

After what seemed like an age, I checked the time to see he'd been gone nearly twenty minutes. Entranced by the house, I found myself climbing up the steps and tiptoeing through one of the ajar front doors.

I gasped, finding myself inside an exquisite entrance room. The ceiling was so high it made me dizzy. A beautiful gold chandelier hung from the middle of the room and a dark wooden staircase sprawled up the centre, parting left and right at the top with its soft, red carpet. The white marble floor sparkled under the bright lights, highlighting the level of cleanliness this home kept.

A dark wooden door to the left of the staircase caught my attention, its brass door handle twinkling at me.

"Paul?"

My voice echoed around the empty space and I couldn't help but smile. What an incredible house to live in. I stepped towards the door, careful of making any noise in this quiet setting. Pulling it open, I gasped as my eyes settled on a middle-aged man with a woman on each arm. He was leaning back against the marble kitchen surface whilst each woman nuzzled their way round his neck.

My cheeks erupted with heat and I didn't know where to put myself. "Oh my. I'm so sorry."

His grey eyes danced with amusement as he flashed me a dazzling smile. "Have you come to join the party, gorgeous?"

Chapter Fifteen

MY MOUTH WAS OPEN, but my lips and tongue would not cooperate into forming words. For every step he took towards me, I took several back, clattering back against the door, which had closed behind me.

"Aw, come on, honey. We don't bite. Unless you want us to." He gave me a cheeky wink as he released one of the women, stretching his hand out to me.

I shook my head, my hands fumbling for the door handle in a blind panic. I didn't dare remove my eyes from where he was.

"Who did you come with?"

I found the door handle and pushed, falling through the open doorway. "Paul."

He stopped in his tracks, his facial features changing in an instant. He actually wasn't that bad looking for his age. "You're Kyra?"

My breath caught in my throat, and I nodded.

"I can see why he's not been himself lately. Please forgive me. I'm his father, Roger."

I gave him a weak smile as I continued to back my way to the front door.

He chuckled and followed me. "Not the best introduction."

"I...should probably get back to the car."

"Don't be silly. Come in here and have a drink. Paul is talking to his mum upstairs. He'll be down in a minute."

My jaw dropped as I took in his words. "His mum?"

"Yes. My wife. You know, it usually takes two to make a baby."

My eyes flashed to the kitchen door, which was slowly closing on the two women who were watching us intently.

He looked behind him and then back at me. "Ah. I'm guessing Paul hasn't told you about our family business?"

"He said you do holidays and stuff."

A wry smile played across his lips. "Is that what he called it?"

Leisure and entertainment I remembered were his exact words. I pieced those words together along with the fact his dad was getting it on with two women in the kitchen whilst his mum sat upstairs.

Holy moly. I began to panic. They're swingers. My eyes flickered back to Roger once the penny dropped with a mind spinning realisation.

"You just figured it out, huh?"

I nodded as I held my hands up. "I think I need to go."

"Don't be daft. Come on."

"No. Really. I need to go."

I ran back across the shiny floor, cursing my choice of wearing stupid flip-flops. Still, I'd thought it was only a car ride home. Slamming the heavy doors shut behind me, I debated taking his car since he'd left the keys in it, but I didn't know the key code to open the gates, nor did I fancy being arrested for theft. Not tonight anyway.

I attempted to run across the gravel only for the stones to keep lodging themselves between my toes and under my feet. I stopped, ripping the useless shoes off before stepping onto the grass. Power walking my way under the darkening tree line, I tried to ignore the sound of Paul shouting to me in the distance.

"Kyra!"

I broke into a run as I tried to hide the hot tears that sprung from nowhere.

"Kyra!"

A dawning horror struck me as I realised I was in the middle of nowhere with no way of getting home. I could call Molly to come and get me, but I couldn't be doing with the interrogation. Not wanting to let this on to Paul, I marched on, determined to make my way out of those gates and keep them as a barrier between me and him.

The sound of padding on the grass behind me told me he'd caught up with me. Before I knew what was happening, he grabbed my arm, swinging me round to meet him.

"Kyra—"

I yanked my arm free, tears spilling down my cheeks. "Don't touch me."

"Kyra, please. I can explain—"

"Explain what? Your dad feeling up two women in the kitchen whilst your mum is upstairs?"

He ran a hand through his hair and sighed. "It's complicated."

"Complicated? Is that what you call it? Because to me it looks like they're swingers."

He looked down at the floor, staying silent.

"Holidays and stuff? Leisure and entertainment? Wow, you must have really had a good giggle when I bought that one. This is your family business? That you're supposed to be taking over?"

He nodded, avoiding eye contact with me.

"Have you been sleeping with other women whilst we've been sleeping together?"

His eyes flashed to mine, widening. "No."

"How am I supposed to believe that?"

"I haven't. I promise. It wouldn't normally have stopped me but—"

"I beg your pardon?"

He closed his mouth, then ran his hands over his face.

"You dirty bastard. You better not have given me AIDS or anything!" I turned from him, continuing my persistent walk to the gates.

"I haven't. We're all tested every three months. Everyone is monitored very closely."

I stopped in my tracks, disbelief hitting me like a freight train. I turned around, rage oozing from every part of my body. "Oh, well, that's okay, then. We'll have one massive orgy because the doctor says we're all clean. Wayhay."

A pained expression flashed across his face as he stepped towards me. "Ky..."

Not knowing what to do with my boiling temper and sheer frustration, I threw one of my flip-flops at him as I screamed at him to leave me alone.

He jumped to the side, dodging it by millimetres. "Where are you going?"

"Home. Alone."

"Let me take you."

"You are kidding me, right? You are fucking kidding me?"

"You're miles from nowhere. Come on, don't be daft. You don't even know where you are."

I snorted. "I know exactly where I am. At some fucked up house of horn or whatever you call it. I bet you've got some purple room of passion or whatever in there, haven't you?"

He smirked at my sarcasm and shook his head.

"You know what, you were right earlier. You shouldn't have come down to London. In fact, you shouldn't have ever come anywhere near me. Is that what this was?" I motioned between me and him. "You wanted me in your sick little club?"

He hesitated for a second, which was all the reply I needed.

My lips curled into a snarl as I boiled over. "Well, here's your answer." I threw my other shoe at him, smacking him square in the face.

He barely blinked and just stood staring back at me, completely blank.

Fishing my phone from my pocket, I brought up Google Maps, which dealt me some unwanted news. I was fifteen miles from home—ten of which were these country roads. I sighed and continued my relentless march. I was not giving in. Turning my back on him, I continued on towards the gates.

"Kyra, let me take you home, please."

"No."

"You've got no other way home. Just let me make sure you get home safe."

"If I have a choice between sharing a six-foot space with you or walking for the next eight hours, I think I'm making it obvious which one I prefer."

He sighed. "Kyra, please, come on, be sensible."

I whipped around, and before I could even think, I reached out and slapped him across the face. "Leave me alone. From now on you are nothing more to me than my boss. Do I make myself clear?"

He nodded, the dimming twilight bathing half of his gorgeous face with a magical glow.

"Outside of work hours, I want nothing to do with you in any way, shape, or form. Do you understand me?"

"Yes."

"Good. Right now is outside of work hours so piss off back to your orgy or whatever and leave me alone."

I blundered back into the trees, debating calling my ex, Simon, for a lift. I knew he would gladly help but he would also expect me to repay him in kind. I sighed as I walked faster, trying to take the evening chill from my skin. Part of me wanted to give in and accept Paul's lift but my stubborn side would not allow it. I dared to look back and felt partly relieved to see he'd gone.

As I tried to busy my mind from the encroaching darkness and the gnarled branches trying to reach out to me, I heard the crunch of tyres on gravel behind me.

I sighed when I realised he wasn't giving in with taking me home. I ignored him as I heard his engine rumbling away behind me.

"Kyra, get in."

I carried on walking. The gates less than thirty feet away.

"Get in the damn car before I pick you up and put you in."

I reached the gates, debating my options. I would not show weakness and ask him for the code. Instead, I decided scrambling up and over the pillars was my best option.

"You can't get out unless I let you out."

"Are you threatening me?"

"No, I'm pointing out the obvious to stop you being so damn stubborn. Get in the car, Kyra."

I shot him a glare that would have curdled milk, clearly telling him where to stick his idea of me getting in his car. Turning my attention back to the red pillars, I worked out a decent run up would give me enough power to jump up before climbing up and over.

So busy thinking about my calculations of speed and distance, I didn't even register his footsteps behind me. The next thing I knew, a pair of strong arms wrapped around my stomach in a vice-like grip before they picked me up and sat me in his car.

Chapter Sixteen

H IS CAR FILLED WITH a pressurising discomfort whilst he drove me home. I stared out of the window, my body turned away from him. I was seething with anger, my nails digging into the soft flesh of my palm as I struggled to contain my emotions.

The instant he reached my driveway, I threw my seatbelt off and jumped out before he'd even stopped the car. I unlocked my door in record time and slammed it shut before running upstairs and jumping into my bed. He banged on the front door for fifteen minutes before he gave in and drove off. He called my phone repeatedly to the point I had to turn it off.

Sleep would be the only relief here. Not even bothering to take my clothes off, I huddled up under my duvet and forced myself to sleep.

By the time I woke on Sunday, I already knew the day would be a total write off. I woke with a splitting headache, which evolved into a killer of a migraine. I buried myself in my bed, still not even bothering to turn my phone on.

By the time Monday morning came around, I felt no better. The thought of facing a day at work and seeing Paul only ensured I called in sick. I spoke to Molly, batting off her offers of coming to see me at lunch.

I fell back asleep after swallowing a mountain of pills. Sometime later, an incessant banging on my front door disturbed my peaceful slumber. I sighed and heaved myself out of bed, cursing Molly for not listening to me when I told her to leave me be.

I opened the front door and froze when I saw Paul stood there. I scowled at him before shutting the door in his face. Unfortunately, he stuck his foot in the door, pushing his way inside.

"Are you okay?" he asked.

I clutched at my head and backed away from him. "Leave me alone, Paul."

He closed the door behind him, walking towards me with a hand outstretched to me. "I was worried about you." He placed a hand against my cheek, cupping my face with such a delicate tenderness, I couldn't help but enjoy it. "I care about you."

I gazed into those soulful sapphire eyes of his, losing myself for a moment. That was all it took—one touch from him and I couldn't stop myself from succumbing to him like a mouse to a lion.

"Get off." I pushed his hand away, my head only hurting more as tears threatened to flood me again. "Don't touch me."

He backed away a couple of steps, concern flashing through his eyes and creasing his forehead. "I thought you were avoiding me."

"Please," I said, snorting. "Don't flatter yourself that my world revolves around you."

I wandered into the kitchen, searching out more tablets. A pounding thud resounded through my head and I clasped at it with a painful groan. My knees buckled as an arrow of pain hit my temple.

He caught me in his arms, curling them around my waist and supporting my weight. "Are you okay?"

I pushed him away from me, clutching at the worktop for support. "Do I look okay to you?"

He pressed his lips together. "Do you need anything? Is there anything I can do?"

"Yes. You can go away."

"Ky, come on. Why be like that?"

"I thought I made my feelings about where we stood perfectly clear." I squared my shoulders and summoned all my strength to glare at him with all the ferocity I could muster. "Why is it I have to accept it when you tell me no, but you don't want to accept it when I tell you no?"

"I never told you no."

"Yes, yes you did. Over and over again you made it very clear where you stand on relationships. I get it—I've never wanted to commit to anyone seriously, but you..."

my voice cracked, and tears flooded my eyes "...you were *different*. I wanted to commit to something. With you."

His beautiful eyes swam with water as despair filled them. "Ky, I can't. You know I can't."

I nodded. "I know, but that doesn't mean I want to keep hearing the rejection. It hurts me, Paul. Why can't you understand that?"

He fell silent for a minute then said, "I'd never thought of it like that, I'm sorry."

I turned to the cupboard and grabbed a glass. "Please just go. My day is bad enough as it is."

"I want to help you—"

"Then disappear."

Silence fell between us for a moment. "You didn't reply to any of my texts."

"Well, considering I spent all day yesterday like this, I wasn't really in the mood for anything, let alone dealing with you. Plus, my phone has been switched off since Saturday night. I wouldn't expect that to change any time soon either."

"I'm sorry, Kyra. I never wanted any of this to happen. I just...I wanted to make sure you were ok."

I walked over to the sink and filled my glass with water. "Since when does company policy require a director to come to an employee's house when she calls in sick anyway?"

He dropped his eye contact, looking at the floor as he nodded. "Ok. I get the point. I'll go."

I didn't even bother to dignify him with a response. He let himself out as I popped some more pills and crawled back to bed. I didn't move from my bed at all for the rest of the day.

When I called in sick again on Tuesday, I prayed to God he wouldn't make an appearance for a second day. My prayers were answered—in part. I'd made the mistake of turning my phone on early Tuesday morning and instead found my phone bombarded with texts which wasn't much better than having him appear on my doorstep.

Ash called me late in the afternoon. "Jesus, Mary, and Joseph. She's alive!" he yelled. "Where the hell have you been for the past four days?"

"If I told you, you wouldn't believe me."

He chuckled. "Try me."

I took a deep breath and told him everything that happened between when I left him and right to the current moment.

"Oh. My. God," he said, almost screaming with excitement. "Get your ass out of bed. I'm coming round and I'm bringing food."

I sighed and hung up, figuring I ought to at least shower rather than curse him with my greasy hair and B.O.

Two hours later, he burst through my front door, the delicious smell of fish and chips following him in. My low mood lifted to a degree. Considering I'd not eaten properly since Saturday morning, my stomach thought my throat had been cut and growled at me every time I dared to open my eyes.

He grinned, lifting up the bag. "Hungry?"

"I could eat a scabby cat." We headed into the dining room, and as he served the food up, I frowned. "What are you doing back anyway?"

"We decided to live up here in my house." He took a bite of his fish. "Anyway, less of that. That's boring. Paul. Wow, do I have some news for you."

I frowned. "What do you mean?"

A beaming smile folded over his lips as he picked up a handful of chips and rammed them in his mouth. "Well, when you told me about what happened, it suddenly clicked. When I first met him, I knew I'd seen him somewhere before, but I couldn't remember where. Then when you said about his parents and the business, it dawned on me."

He jumped from his chair, retrieving my laptop from the other side of the room. He stuffed more chips in his mouth as he waited for it to boot up. A few seconds later, he tapped away quickly before spinning the screen round.

"Is that his dad?" Ash asked.

I looked at the screen, almost choking on my mouthful of fish when I saw Roger's rugged face staring back at me from the homepage of a website. A stunning blonde accompanied him in the picture. I guessed she was Paul's mum.

"What the hell is this?"

"His parents own the biggest swingers' club in the country. They own a string of night clubs up and down the country for straights, gays, bis—anything goes. They are the bees knees when it comes to fulfilling your greatest desires. Then they have an exclusive level club, which is where all the really wild stuff happens. It's called The Triple C. You have to be accepted into this circle—you can't just join. There are certain...parameters you must meet."

My head felt like it wanted to explode. "What? Are you actually being serious?"

He nodded. "Read it."

I browsed through the website, reading the long list of locations for their nightclubs which included The Tiger's Eye. Nearly every major city had one of their clubs. I was stunned into silence as I dared to click on the link for The Triple C. It refused me access, inviting me to set up an account to view further information.

I spun the laptop back round. "It won't let me in. What is it?"

He grinned. "It's basically a club for couples who want to indulge their fantasies with other couples. They do allow singles in but not many. You have to be something exceptional. Being good looking is a must for getting in there. Apparently, they keep files on everyone—they ask your deepest darkest fantasies, what you do and don't like, and match you to similar minded people. Basically, they're sex match makers."

"That's...weird."

"But genius if you think about it. How many marriages fall apart because one of them isn't getting their fantasies fulfilled so they go off and pay some hooker or escort to do it with them? This is a way for couples to accept each other's fantasies and let them be acted out safely, properly, and with no lies, sneaking around, or anything else. They've apparently saved a lot of relationships."

I shook my head and curled my top lip back in disgust. "From letting wives see other women sleep with their husbands? I just don't get it, Ash. It's wrong on so many levels."

He shrugged his shoulders. "It works both ways. A lot of men get off watching their wife with someone else. It's just human nature. We're all different."

"What does Triple C stand for?"

He grinned. "Crave, Choose, Come."

"Ewww."

He laughed at my reaction as he continued eating his food.

I picked at a chip, my appetite somewhat repressed after seeing this. "So what is your point of telling me all this?"

"To try to make you see it's not some seedy gig like you're thinking. It's just adults who are free with themselves and comfortable with letting their partners be with other people. There is a massive difference between having sex with someone and being with someone in a relationship. For these people, it's just a simple division, as easy as that."

"How do you know so much about all of this anyway?"

"A gay friend of mine got into The Triple C with his partner."

I suddenly remembered how Paul had noticed straight away that Ash was gay. That was how he knew—he was around all sorts, all of the time.

"This is just too much. What am I supposed to do with this information?"

"Make an informed decision."

"About what exactly?"

"I don't know. Paul...whether you fancy trying it out or not."

"You are kidding me, right? Please tell me you are kidding?" I was beyond mortified my brother was even suggesting this to me.

"No, not at all. What have you got to lose? You'll be in an exclusive club with direct links to the owners, not to mention sleeping with one of them. Not only that, but you'll be also surrounded by other hot people who just want to have fun. You are freaked out about settling down, Paul doesn't do relationships, so what's the issue?"

I narrowed my eyes at him. "Did he put you up to this?"

"Who? Paul? No. I'm just looking at it from a different point of view, Kyra. What's wrong in having some fun whilst you wait for Mr. Right to come along?"

I glared at him and stared down at the table. I didn't know what to say because in all honesty, I couldn't really argue against his point. I was single. If I was married or with a partner and being presented with all of this, then my reaction would be totally justified. But why was I freaking out about indulging myself with some gorgeous people with no strings attached?

"It just feels wrong. I'd just feel like a complete slag."

He laughed. "I wouldn't worry, Ky. You and I both know of a certain someone who has had more pricks than a second-hand dartboard and she still walks around with her head held high. There's no way you'll work your way past her number."

"Ash, stop it."

He folded up his empty fish and chip papers and stood up. "Right, anyway. Time for me to go. My programme starts in ten minutes, and you need to go back to bed. You look like death warmed up."

I rolled my eyes, and packed my food away for later on, or maybe even tomorrow. I sure as hell couldn't face food right now. We said our goodbyes and as I headed back to bed, I found myself pondering over his words. Maybe I could make sense of all this with a clear head after a decent sleep.

Chapter Seventeen

I WENT INTO WORK the next morning, still very much in the same mind set as I had been since Saturday evening. I wanted nothing to do with it despite Ash's little talk. The second I stepped through the door, Mr. Andrews commandeered me, steering me into his office before giving me a twenty-minute talk on his entire client database, which he wanted redone.

He was halfway through his monotone drone when I heard the office door click shut and Mr. Harris walking across the floor.

"Is Kyra still off?" he asked.

A second voice answered that stilled my heart in an instant—Paul. "I don't know."

"Can you call her, please, Paul? She should be ringing in sick every day she's off and speaking to one of us, not her friend downstairs."

"If she calls before we're in, there isn't a lot she can do except leave a message, is there?"

Harris went silent for a moment before he snapped at Paul. "Just call her."

"You are not my boss, Harris. Get one of the admin girls to call her."

I heard Paul's office door slam shut and moments later, Harris' followed suit. Struggling to contain a smirk, I finished listening to Mr. Andrews before heading back out to my desk.

I made my ritual cup of tea, then sat at my desk, quietly humming away to myself as I worked through Mr. Andrews client files.

"Kyra?"

I lifted my gaze to see Paul standing in front of my desk. My breath caught in my throat when I looked at his beautiful sapphire eyes. I wanted to melt at his feet. Using every last ounce of strength in me, I focused my attention back down to my work, not even dignifying him with an answer.

"Can we talk, please?"

My heart started racing at the thought of being alone with him again. I could feel my body responding to his presence already. I refused to look up at him but gave him an answer. "What about?"

"You know what."

"If it's not work related, then no, we can't talk."

"Is that it? You're not even going to hear me out?"

"Hear you out about what?" I took a deep breath, and looked up at him, only to be met with his pained expression. "You have your life and I have mine. That's it. Simple."

He sighed and ran his tongue over his lips. My mind began betraying me, showing me memories of what that tongue could do to me. I pushed the thoughts away, my heart continuing to race.

He took a step closer, his eyes imploring for my sympathy. "Just five minutes?"

I sighed and crossed my arms over my chest. "Fine."

I stood up and followed him into his office, marching to the other side of the room before turning to face him. He started coming towards me, arms outstretched.

"Don't." I held my hand up to stop him. "You can talk from there."

"Ok."

A long silence fell between us whilst I waited for him to speak. I glared at him, secretly enjoying watching him squirm. "Well, you have approximately four minutes left."

"Look, I know what it looks like, but I didn't start something with you in order to get you involved in all of that."

"At the moment, Paul, that is the least of my worries. I'm more concerned with the fact you've been sleeping with other people whilst sleeping with me."

"I haven't."

I snorted at him. "Please. I didn't fall from the Christmas tree yesterday."

"I'm telling you the truth. I have no need to lie."

"Yes, you do if you think you're going to involve me in all of that...stuff."

"I know it's weird to most people but it's how I was brought up. I don't know any different. You can't miss what you never had."

"So, you've never had a normal relationship?"

He faltered for a second before answering me. "One. When I was younger. It was a long time ago now, though."

"What happened?"

He cleared his throat. "She went off with someone else."

"Oh." Something inside of me softened but I ignored it. "How old were you?"

"I was sixteen. We both were."

"Oh. So, what is this, then? Your way of dealing with the fact you got cheated on?"

He shrugged his shoulders. "It's all I know. I just kind of fell into it after her and that's all I've known since. I've spent nearly twenty years like this. The year I had with her doesn't really compare. The way I see it, there are no jealousy issues, no complex dealings of relationships, no expectations, no arguments. It's just all easy and I can pick and choose as I please to an extent."

I raised my eyebrows. "It's 'all just easy' and 'picking and choosing as you please'? Are you being serious right now? You talk about it like women are pieces of meat."

"No, I didn't mean it like that. Sorry, that came out wrong. What I meant was that my life is easy. I am just me. I don't have to worry about anyone else or anything else that goes with it. When it comes to sex, I have what I know."

I shook my head, chuckling. "Wow. And I thought I was screwed up."

"I'm not screwed up, Kyra. It's just how my life is. Just because it's different to yours it doesn't make me wrong."

"It makes you wrong to me."

"Why?"

"It's dirty, it's wrong. What happened to the sanctity of marriage?"

"You'll be surprised how many relationships this has saved. We provide a place for people to have their fantasies but still have their partners too. It's a win-win."

"How exactly? I know for a fact if I was married, I wouldn't want my husband acting out his fantasies with some other woman, I'd want him to act them out with me."

"But not everyone is like that. Some women only like sex once a week, once a month, not at all. Or they only want it in certain positions. Or they won't play and experiment. Would you deny your husband the experience of trying something out just because you didn't like the thought of it?"

"If that involved being intimate with another woman, then yes."

"Coming from the woman who won't commit? Yet you speak about it like you're experienced in the area."

My jaw clenched as I hardened my stare on him. "You pompous bastard. How dare you. If I remember correctly, I've made it perfectly clear where I stand on commitment with you. You're the one who won't commit."

I stomped towards the door, my anger boiling once more. As I passed him, he grabbed my arm.

"Ky..."

Before I knew what I was doing, I reached out, slapping him across the face with a hell of a crack. He loosened his grip and I shook his hand from me, reaching for the door handle.

"Ky, I'm sorry, I shouldn't have said that. I'm just trying to make you see it's not like you think it is."

"Why is that so important to you?"

"Because I liked the time we spent together."

My heart flipped upside down at his confession. I closed my eyes and took a deep breath. A deep ache began to grow in my chest as I thought of his touch, his kiss, his skin against mine. That one simple sentence made me question my own beliefs, the whole point of me being mad at him. Then I remembered the words he whispered in my ear when we were in the hotel room with Tessa.

"You're mine."

I opened my eyes to see him stood within arm's reach, his eyes sweeping me up in their captivating gaze once again. "I..."

"We had fun, right? We enjoyed our time together. Why should my parents' business stop us enjoying each other?"

My arguments melted into oblivion, and I became lost in a hazy ocean between his twinkling eyes and his silk laden voice. "I...I'll think about it."

He shrugged his shoulders. "Ok." He grinned before giving me a cheeky wink. "I'll give you a week."

I narrowed my eyes at his reference to our conversation on Saturday. Snorting at him, I strode out of the door, muttering various curses under my breath as I headed for the bathroom. Locking the door behind me, my mind wandered back to what happened in here a mere few days ago.

A deep yearning grumbled in my gut as I struggled between my head and my heart. I knew I didn't need his complications in my life but my God, I did want him.

Chapter Eighteen

P AUL DISAPPEARED DOWN TO Devon with Mr. Collins for most of the week. It was a blessing in disguise because it left me to clear my head without his presence sending my hormones into overdrive. I couldn't deny I craved his touch, his mouth on mine, his hands roaming over my body. Just the mere thought of him had me in hot flushes.

Ash spent most of the week convincing me to pick up where we left off. My heart and head were in a constant tug of war, which was frustrating enough without him trying to nudge me in one direction.

I decided over lunch with Molly to ask for her opinion. "Do you remember what it was like before you met Chris?"

"Yeah, course I do."

"Did you feel bad about your history when you met him?"

She giggled. "You mean all the guys I've been with?"

I nodded, smirking.

"No. I had to have a life before him. It's not like he's a virgin either."

"Do you ever miss it? Your life before him?"

She shook her head. "I don't need to miss anything. That was just amusement, fun, whilst I waited for the right guy."

I smiled, nodding. Her words made sense.

"Why do you ask?"

I shrugged my shoulders. "I don't know. I just know that this thing with Paul isn't going to go anywhere, and I don't know whether to cut it off now or carry on until I meet the right guy."

She squealed in excitement. "Are you thinking about settling down?"

"Eventually, yes. But I don't want to get all caught up with Paul only to be knocked back when I have to end it for someone else."

"Maybe he'll change his mind. You never know."

"Not likely. Trust me."

"Well." She reached across the table, gripping my forearm in excitement. "Chris has a younger brother who is single. He is lurvly. You will love him."

I rolled my eyes. "Molly, seriously."

"Trust me, you will love him. He's gorgeous, charming, funny, a true gent, and he's loaded. You get the whole package you get with Paul except he wants commitment so he's better."

I laughed. "And probably got a micro penis."

She spluttered on her drink as I said it. "If Chris is anything to go by, then definitely not."

"TMI, Molly. TMI."

Grinning, she continued on. "Well, he's back from America in the next couple of weeks so maybe you can happen to come by the house when he's back."

I smiled "We'll see."

By the time Friday arrived, I had reached no decision whatsoever. I had no definitive answer to give to Paul when he returned this morning. Both Ash and Molly seemed to have the opinion that having fun whilst waiting for Mr. Right was fine. Molly didn't know the full story behind it all, though, and I was worried about being sucked into the whole thing. Ash seemed to think it was some sort of adventure and I would be a fool to pass up the opportunity.

I decided I would just go with the flow. Whatever scenario arose with Paul, I would just deal with it at the time. I didn't want to prepare for one thing and something else happen instead. He walked in just after nine o'clock, flashing me a dazzling smile before he went to his office.

My heart started thudding the second I saw him. I began to wonder whether this was something I had to get out of my system so I could consider meeting Mr. Right. If I cut it off now, I would always be having these reactions to him. I couldn't be with someone else if I kept feeling things like this for him. It would be wrong and wouldn't sit right with me.

I was so lost in my thoughts I didn't even register him staring at me from his open doorway until he spoke.

"You coming?"

I looked up in surprise at hearing his voice and those words. What they meant in my head with my current train of thought meant the complete opposite to what he intended.

"Sorry?"

His eyes held a mischievous glow. "We need to talk. You've not spoken to me all week. I think we need to settle this, don't we?"

I blushed and nodded. I took a deep breath and stood up, smoothing out my clothes before making my way towards the delicious specimen of a man before me.

He didn't move from the doorway, only turning slightly so I could brush past him on my way inside. It was impossible not to do so and I knew he'd done it on purpose.

I turned around to face him as he closed the door and snapped the blinds shut. "So, how many women did you find in Devon?"

He grinned. "Anyone would think you were jealous, Kyra."

I snorted. "Jealous of what exactly? We're not in a relationship remember."

He closed the gap between us with a couple of steps. "Let's face it, you can't resist me. You don't want to admit it, but you want to give in, don't you?"

I scanned over his handsome face. My heart was already picking up speed, my chest tightening. "You're very cocky."

He winked. "You would know…"

I narrowed my eyes as I began to think of what he was hiding underneath those perfectly fitted clothes. This was his intention all along, and I hated to be giving in to him—mentally, not physically.

As I raged an internal battle with myself, he brought his hand to my arm. His eyes met mine as he traced it across my skin, leaving a trail of shivers in its wake.

I closed my eyes, trying to ignore the surges of tingles his singular touch sent through me. Before I knew what was happening, his soft lips were on my neck. He left a trail of gentle kisses across my skin before his hands picked at my blouse, easing each button undone. His mouth continued to induce me into a sensual filled world as he made his way further down my chest.

He wound his hands around my back, and gently pushed me backwards. I met the cool surface of the wall just when the last of my buttons popped undone. My breaths came in short, shallow rasps as he peeled my bra from my body. I opened my eyes to meet his own dancing with lust and desire.

As he inched kisses across my exposed breasts and tickled my nipples with his tongue, I realised just how much I'd missed him. Fierce shudders shot straight between my legs, and I had to bite my lip to contain my moans of joy.

His attention wandered to my pencil skirt, unzipping it in less than a second. As it fell to the floor, I mentally begged him to delve inside my underwear. I needed to feel him, skin to skin. His fingers stroking my sensitive spots would be all I needed to melt into a pool at his feet.

He began to work his way south with his luscious lips as he inched my lacy thong down my legs. I began trembling in expectation of where his delightful mouth was now heading. I ran my hands through his silky hair, clutching at him as a groan escaped me. Easing my underwear over my feet, he parted my legs with his hands. As he placed delicate kisses at the top of my thighs, he left me nothing short of a quivering mess as anticipation bettered me.

When he closed his mouth around my tingling sweet spot, my knees buckled. Drawing mind numbing patterns over me with his tongue, it didn't take long for me to submit to him. I was done, and I could do nothing but come undone for him.

When my legs gave way, he caught me with his strong arms as I struggled for my breath. He held me up and kissed my throbbing clit.

I opened my eyes in a haze of stars, my head still spinning. I think he'd just clarified which direction this was going to go.

Chapter Nineteen

I SPENT THE REST of the day on an unbelievable high. In pure Paul style, just as home time came around, he squashed any good feelings I enjoyed by revealing he was working tonight. The disdainful scowl that spread across my face said everything.

"You know I won't be sleeping with anyone else, Kyra. Just relax."

My internal war raged once again, making me wonder whether I could actually do this or not. "It just feels wrong, Paul. You're going to be in a house full of gorgeous women who are all up for anything that goes. It's just...weird."

He fell quiet for a minute. "Kyra, I don't want to make an issue out of this. You are reacting to this like we're in a relationship. It shouldn't matter what I do when we're not together—that's the beauty of not being with someone like that. This is a perfect example of what I was talking about when I said I don't do relationships."

His words cut deep as he confirmed yet again, he wasn't interested in anything more than this "friends with benefits" situation. I knew we weren't together, but I still couldn't help a tiny bit of hope rising that my Friday night would be filled with sex with my fuck buddy.

He came to me and took my hands in his. "I'm sorry to say that to you again, I know it hurts you. I'm just making a point, that's all."

I tore my hands away from him and grabbed my stuff before heading for the door. "Ok. Fine. But don't expect me to jump when you click your fingers."

I didn't hear from him for the rest of the night, which resulted in more hate-fuelled thoughts running through me. The more I thought about him and what he could be potentially doing whilst I sat home alone, the worse it became.

Saturday, I went for lunch with Ash, and I couldn't help but moan about the recent happenings.

"You need to grasp the whole idea of this fuck buddy thing," Ash said. "If you can't deal with it, then I think you need to reconsider."

"But fuck buddies are usually at it at the weekends, are they not? That's what most people do on a weekend." I sighed and then said, "Except me, of course, because mine is too busy wanking over other people getting fucked."

Ash laughed. "So join in, then. If you can't beat 'em, join 'em."

"Seriously? Don't go there again."

He pushed his half eaten salad around his plate, his amused expression disappearing as a serious shadow over took his features. "Have you heard from Mum?"

I narrowed my eyes and clenched my jaw. "No."

He pressed his lips together and reached across the table and placed his hand over mine. "I know she'd love to hear from you..."

I snorted. "Well, she has my contact details. It works both ways."

Ash sighed and rolled his eyes. He took his hand back and then put his fork down on the table which only foretold me of the lecture to come. "Come on, Ky. It's been a long time. The whole Tim thing is old news. Time to let it go and move on. Surely your relationship with Mum is more important than your hatred for him."

I shivered at the sound of Tim's name and glared at my brother. "The guy came onto me, Ash. I had to punch him to get him off me because the word 'no' means nothing to him. I don't hate him, I despise him. The man is an abomination of nature. He shouldn't be living." I stopped for a breath and then said, "Do you really think I'm the only one he's done that to? The sheer audacity to assault his stepdaughter on his god damn wedding day..." I shivered. "No, Ash. The fact my mother believes that parasite over me cuts deeper than anything else. She needs to come to me."

"Ky, come on. I told you this at the time and I will repeat it again now—Tim wouldn't do that. It was just a case of too much to drink and you perceiving the hug he gave you in the wrong way."

I narrowed my eyes at him and all but spat my next words out. "Since when does giving someone a hug involve sticking your hand up their dress or groping their boobs? The man cornered me, he trapped me, Ash, to the point my only way out was to punch him in the face." I shook my head and sat back in my chair, folding my arms over my chest. "I don't call two vodka and cokes too much alcohol. A six-year-old could drink that and not feel it."

Ash held his hands up in a surrender sign and said, "You have never liked him from day one. I think you saw an opportunity to vent your anger and dislike for him and punched him."

"I told him no and he wrapped his hand around my throat and started to choke me, Ash. Should I have let him strangle me to death so you could finally see him for what he is?"

"You're being a drama queen," he said, shrugging his shoulders. "It's as simple as that. Tim is very honest, genuine, and caring. The community over there adore him. He goes to church every Sunday. He's really not a sexual assault kind of guy."

I cocked my head to one side and said, "You know who else went to church every Sunday?"

Ash frowned. "Who?"

"Jeffrey Dahmer. Gary Ridgway. Dennis Rader. Hell, Rader was a cub scout leader and got elected to president of the church council. You can't judge a book by its cover, Ash."

He chuckled. "I see you're still watching your serial killer documentaries."

"It's part of my coursework, actually. Understanding the psychology of prolific murderers and what makes them do what they do. They felt that God and the church would help them deal with their darkness, but it didn't. All it became was a crutch."

"I don't think you can compare Tim to those guys. They're on completely different levels."

"But are they? You know where serial killers start? Torturing animals. You know where rapists start? Molesting women."

"I think you're taking this to the extreme, Ky. Yes, those situations with all of those murder guys happened, but that doesn't mean that every married, church going man is a rapist or a murderer."

I nodded. "I agree. But he is."

He sighed and ran a hand through his hair. "We're just going round in circles. I don't see that side to him, and considering it's your word against his, I have to go with the evidence in front of me—I know Tim and I've spent a lot of time with him."

My stomach filled with a nauseous ball of unwanted memories and rejection from my own brother. My heart dropped to my feet as I fought back tears. "You grew up with me and spent more time with me, Ash."

"I don't want to upset you, but I just don't see that side to him."

"Well, you be grateful for that blindness because what happened to me is something I will never forget. You didn't see the look in his eyes, Ash. He was so intent on getting what he wanted. He really scared me."

For the briefest of seconds, a flicker of hesitancy flashed through his eyes. Then he reached over and grabbed both of my hands. "I'm sorry that whatever happened affected you so much. I don't like thinking of you suffering from upsetting memories, but I do think it was a misunderstanding and too much alcohol on both sides."

"Whatever, Ash," I said, pushing my food away from me, my appetite gone.

He left the subject alone after that, departing not long after to trek down to London for Ben's set tonight in the club. By four o'clock, I was back home, alone.

With Mum weighing heavily on my mind, I decided the cleverest idea would be to reminisce through old photo albums. Of course, the idea turned out to be absolutely ridiculous and I ended up sobbing my heart out wishing everything had turned out different.

If only Dad hadn't died, if only Scotch hadn't died, if only Mum hadn't married a toy boy and moved abroad, if only we still had a good relationship. If only, if only, if only; those two words were the story of my life.

Tim, Mum's toy boy, was the epitome of a cowboy. I could understand why Mum fell for him. At an age gap of nearly twenty years though, I never understood why Tim, given his fine looks, healthy bank balance, and love of horses, couldn't find someone his own age.

Don't get me wrong, Mum, for her fifty-two years, looked damn fine. She took great pride in her appearance and cared for her body well. Unfortunately, after losing Dad unexpectedly, I had the opinion, to this day, that Tim was a rebound. Nothing more, nothing less. A hot, younger guy paying interest in an older, emotionally vulnerable woman? Who wouldn't fall for that?

But the two years that passed since the wedding day had done nothing but sour my memories of our relationship. When I told her, in front of Tim, what he'd done, the smug look on his face as she rebuked my claims would always haunt me.

Now though, in reality, too long had passed for either my mum or me to give in and pick up the phone. It hurt that she hadn't believed me, and it hurt that she picked him over me.

Lost in my thoughts and clutching onto a sofa cushion as I dried my eyes, I welcomed the distraction of my phone pinging with a text.

Paul: Are you busy tonight? XXX

I snorted and ignored him. Instead, I wandered into the kitchen and opened a bottle of wine. Always a good choice when feeling emotionally unstable. An hour and a bottle of wine later, I received another text.

Paul: I would love to see you. ;-) xxx

I hadn't forgotten my warning to him yesterday about expecting me to jump when he clicked his fingers. So again, I ignored him.

Definitely not in the mood for cooking, I ordered Chinese. Several minutes later, a knock sounded on the front door. I frowned thinking how the food couldn't even be cooked yet, let alone here.

I opened the door, rolling my eyes when I saw Paul staring back at me.

"Hi," he said, flashing me a winning smile.

"What do you want?"

"I came to see you."

I laughed. "No, you didn't. You came here thinking you could get lucky after you ditched me last night. I thought I made myself quite clear when I said I wouldn't be jumping when you clicked your fingers."

He chuckled and sighed. "Ok. I can see this is a bad time."

I raised an eyebrow as a response.

"So...I'll...see you on Monday."

"Yep."

I slammed the door shut, feeling rather proud of myself. I'd barely sat down before my phone beeped with another text.

Paul: You know I could make you feel better. ;-) xxx

I smirked at his words and persistence, but I refused to give in. I had to make a point. He couldn't control me like a dog.

Me: Doesn't mean you will. See you Monday.

Chapter Twenty

I HEARD NOTHING MORE from Paul. When I arrived at work Monday morning, I had a note on my desk detailing me he was out for the day. I smirked, wondering if this was due to my rejection of him.

Pushing thoughts of him to the side, I began to wonder about tomorrow which was dress shopping with Molly. The woman loved clothes. An actual fiend in clothes shops, she had been known to pick fights with people trying to take the last item in her size. At least tomorrow, there would only be the two of us in the shop.

Work breezed by, without so much as a word from Paul. Nothing from him overnight either, I tried not to let it bother me. I knew he was testing my resolve and I had to stand firm.

My hopes of a lay in on my day off were promptly shattered when Molly started banging on my front door like a woman possessed an hour earlier than planned. I groaned and let her in, even putting up with her chatting through the bathroom door about dress styles and trains and tiaras as I took a longer than usual shower.

When I moved from the bathroom to the bedroom to get dressed, she followed me, still talking away about dresses and fabrics. My nonchalant replies of "Yes," "Oh, really," and "That sounds nice," didn't switch on anything in her brain that I might not be that interested in wedding dresses this deeply.

The shop we were going to was approximately a thirty-minute drive from my house. We planned to leave forty minutes before her ten a.m. appointment time, just in case we hit traffic.

By 09:21, just as I grabbed my keys and my bag, she was snapping at me that we were late. Rolling my eyes and keeping my thoughts to myself, I locked the house before heading to her death trap of a car and praying to whatever Gods existed that I would survive her terrible driving.

Speeding, close distances, checking her make-up in the mirror, reaching into her bag for chewing gum—Molly held the title of a typical female driver. Her car, as a car, was perfectly safe. She made it a death trap.

Thankfully, we made it there in one piece and I couldn't get out of the car fast enough. No wonder Chris insisted on driving her everywhere. We parked in a two-hour free stay car park and walked into town. Being early morning, the streets were fairly quiet except for those hurrying about trying to get to work on time.

The shop wasn't on the main high street, it sat down a cobbled little side street next to an old Victorian building that had been turned into the latest branch of Lloyds. It wasn't a massive shop, but everybody local knew it for its beautiful dresses and exceptional pricing.

The olive green name board above the huge glass windows sported the name 'Belle Bridal' in a calligraphy style cream coloured scrawl.

As we opened the door, an old fashioned bell jingled above our heads, alerting the shop keeper to our presence. I heard the clicking of high heeled shoes on wooden floors just seconds before an older lady in a green tartan suit appeared from around a corner.

"Good morning," she said, clapping her hands together.

Her high pitched, fake pleasantry voice sent shivers down my spine. With her grey hair, five-foot height, petite frame, and glasses on a chain around her neck, she reminded me of my Nan.

"Hi," Molly said, rushing up to her and holding her hand out.

The lady smiled and held her hands up, taking a step back. "Nothing personal, dear, but I'm afraid I'm a bit of a germ phobe. Nice to meet you though. My name is Edith."

I pressed my lips together in an effort to not burst out laughing. Molly dropped her hand and stepped back, confusion and surprise filtering through her green eyes.

"Molly," Molly replied, her voice giving away the slightest hint of a shake.

"What a lovely name," Edith said. "Now, first of all, when are you getting married, my dear?"

"In three months. Just over. First November to be exact."

Edith quirked up a grey eyebrow. "Oh, my, that is quick." She darted her eyes to Molly's stomach and then smiled. "What sort of dress are you looking for?"

Molly, completely blasé to Edith's subtle hint, started off with her spiel of fabrics and cuts and what she thought would suit her body type best. Rolling my eyes at hearing all this again, I took my chance and wandered off to the rails, glancing through the dozens and dozens of exquisite dresses on offer. I couldn't help but wonder if I would ever get the chance to wear one for myself one day.

Lost in my own musings, I completely zoned out from the chatter in the background, or to be more specific, Molly's voice.

The next thing I knew was when Molly laid a hand on my shoulder and said, "Ky, why don't you find something you like?"

I did a double take. "What?"

She shrugged her shoulders. "I can't be the only one having fun. Come on, what harm could it do?"

I frowned. "I'm supposed to give you opinions on your dresses. Not only that but I think I'm missing the key ingredient that would require me to try on a wedding dress."

She laughed. "Oh, come on. Stop being a spoilsport. We're supposed to be having a girly day. This is for both of us."

I sighed, and as always, gave in. I carried on looking through the dresses, almost imagining that I might actually one day be doing this for myself. I stumbled across an off-white-coloured lace dress, off the shoulder, trailing down to the floor and two layers that crossed each other making the lace pattern seem extra intricate. I loved the simple style—classy yet elegant.

"That's gorgeous," Molly said, peering over my shoulder. "Go try it on." She glanced over at Edith and said, "You don't mind, do you, Edith? Seeing as my friend is the same size as me, she's like my own little dress model."

Edith waved a hand through the air dismissively. "Of course, not, dear. You go right ahead."

The disdain in Edith's watery blue eyes was very hard to miss and I couldn't help but wonder if it was the thought of two people's germs on her dresses that made her squirm. Either way, she was clearly paid enough to not say anything and deny the blushing bride her request.

Molly pulled out a sweetheart neckline cream coloured fishtail dress and followed me to the changing rooms, Edith scurrying along behind her to strap her in.

"If you need help, dear," Edith said, raising her voice. "Just let me know."

"I think I'm ok, thank you."

I hung the dress on the rail inside the changing room and stared at it for a good minute or more. Was this really a good idea? Would I just be filling myself with false fantasies of something that would likely never happen?

"Fuck it," I whispered to myself. "There's no universal law on trying on a wedding dress. It's just a dress."

I took off my jeans and t-shirt and slid the dress off its hanger, studying it carefully for hidden zips but could find none. Figuring it just must be a pull-on type dress, I slid it on over my head and inched down my body until all the creases were out.

I looked down at myself, seeing how the fabric hugged my body, and bit my lip as a broad grin started to spread across my face. Sucking in a deep breath, I turned to face the full-length mirror and see what I looked like.

I couldn't help but gasp, my jaw falling wide open when I stared at my reflection. The lace clung to me like a second skin, highlighting every part of me. The off-shoulder design drew attention to my bare neck and chest, making me look really slim and elegant. I pulled my hair out of its ponytail and let it fall down to my chest. The slight natural wave to my dark hair contrasted perfectly against the lightness of the dress. I scooped my hair up into a rough bun, letting some curls fall back around my face. The term 'seductive elegance' sprang to mind, and I couldn't help but smile. The more I stared at myself, the more I couldn't believe how a dress could change my entire appearance.

"Are you done yet?" Molly said, her screeching voice shattering my trance.

I let go of my hair and went to the curtain, pulling it back.

"Oh wow," Molly said, her hand flying to her mouth. "Ky, you look absolutely amazing. You have to buy that dress."

I shook my head. "Don't be silly."

"Why not? At least you'll be all set ready."

I laughed and looked down at myself again, touching the fabric. I loved it. "No, Molly. I am not buying a dress before I've even got a boyfriend, let alone a proposal. Besides, by the time I get down the aisle, weddings will be out of fashion."

She giggled and then motioned her hands over her own dress. "What do you think?"

The slinky dress clung to her tight body like a glove. The sweetheart neckline accentuated her big boobs, and the corseted top with the fishtail at the bottom gave her an almost perfect hourglass figure.

"You look incredible. It really suits you."

She nodded, grinning. "I can't believe I've found it already. It's the first dress."

I smiled and touched my own dress. "If it's the one, it's the one."

My mind decided that point in time would be the perfect time to conjure up images of Paul stood in a grooms suit, waiting at an altar for me. I closed my eyes for a brief second and forced them away.

Molly clasped her hands together and squealed. "You're right. I'm going to buy it."

I headed back into the changing room and as slowly as possible, took the dress off. Every part of me screamed to buy it before someone else did. My heart and soul wanted it so bad, but I had no need for it now, probably ever with the way things seemed to be going. My head overruled my heart and soul, and I decided I couldn't justify buying it. Where would my fun filled day of dress shopping be if I bought my dress now before I'd even been proposed to?

An hour, and two thousand pounds later, Molly drove us back to hers with orders for us to enjoy a takeaway this evening. Chris would be home around teatime with his brother, who he was collecting from the airport, so until that time, we could sort through colour schemes and flower options for the wedding.

We pulled into her driveway to see Chris's car sat there. She frowned, threw her seatbelt off and disappeared into the house before I could even blink. The car continued rolling forwards and I couldn't help but murmur a curse at her lack of care of even applying a handbrake. I yanked the handbrake up and then followed her inside. I'd barely taken my shoes off before she grabbed my hand and dragged me inside the living room.

"Ky, this is Scott. Scott, this is my best friend, Kyra."

I rounded the open door to see a tall, broad, dark-haired man. Beautiful chocolate eyes glistened with joy, an amused expression creasing his handsome face. Bronzed skin and an incredibly toned body, the white t-shirt he wore only seemed to further highlight his gorgeous good looks.

I blushed and glanced away. He was so hot it would be hard not to stare at him, and I had better control of myself than that. Or at least I thought so.

"Nice to meet you," I said, finding myself looking at him again.

He flashed me a dazzling smile. "And you."

Molly shoved me towards the sofa and then said, "Me and Chris need to discuss some wedding things, so you two just..." she motioned her hands back and forth between us "...we won't be long."

She gave me a cheeky grin before running off with Chris. I knew exactly what she was doing.

I dropped my eye contact from Scott and shuffled back on the sofa, picking up one of the cushions and cuddling it to my body as some sort of weird comfort.

He cleared his throat. "So, have you had a good day so far?"

"So far so good."

"Did she find her dress?"

I nodded and laughed. "First one. Thank God."

"That's good. I gather she has rather a lot of energy."

"You have no idea." I wrung my hands together as I tried to calm my nerves. "So, um, where have you flown from?"

"America. My father owns an oil company out there."

"Oh. Molly never mentioned Chris's father owned something as huge as that."

"We have the same mother, different fathers."

I nodded, understanding a little better how two brothers could look so different. Chris was a good-looking guy in his own right, but his thin frame, blond spiky hair, and nerdy glasses combined with his IT technician job did little to serve him up as a macho man. Compared to Scott here, they were like chalk and cheese.

"Where in America are you from?"

"Texas."

My heart skipped a beat as I realised we would have some common ground to talk about. "My mum lives out there. Her and her husband own a horse ranch."

"Really? Whereabouts?"

"Near Springtown."

"I know where that is. I'm from Wichita Falls. My dad owns a couple of rigs around the Scotland area."

I frowned. "Scotland?"

He tipped his head back and laughed. "Not Scotland, UK. Scotland on route two-eighty-one."

I giggled and buried my face in my hands. When I dared to look back up at him, the intensity oozing from his eyes made my heart pound against my ribcage like a drummer in a heavy metal band. I had little doubt that his whole attention was on me.

"Have you ever been to Scotland?" he asked, leaning forwards and resting his arms on his knees.

"Neither of them," I said, laughing. "Have you ever been to our Scotland?"

He shook his head. "I would like to, though. I've heard it's very beautiful. Maybe it's something we can tick off our bucket list together."

My breath caught in my throat. His direct approach caught me completely off guard. Yet his confidence was somehow charming and filled me with ideas that this guy knew what he wanted and would stop at nothing to get it.

"I'm sorry," he said, softening his tone of voice. "I can be too forward at times. Please don't hesitate to tell me to back off if I scare you."

"It's fine," I said. "I'm just not used to men being so decisive and thinking further ahead than a few hours."

"Well," he replied, giving me a mischievous wink. "Maybe I can help change your mind about men."

If I had been a block of ice on a hot grate, I would be nothing but steam by now. A giant cloud of steam. Scott had an aura about him that just hypnotised me instantly. Something about him drew me to him like a bee to honey. Was it the fact that he was different?

"That may be a challenge," I replied. "But we'll see. Nothing is impossible."

He lowered his voice and whispered, "I love a challenge."

My cheeks burst into heat as my heart galloped wildly inside my chest. I thought Paul was my 'one' because he affected me differently to my exes, but this guy was affecting me just as badly, if not more so, than what Paul ever had. Maybe he was actually different.

Maybe my attraction to Paul was nothing more than lust, sexual chemistry. This guy had already suggested about us doing something together and we'd only just met. Was that odd or was it romantic that he was already thinking this way? Had I had the same affect on him that he had on me?

Either way, I liked this. I liked the fact he saw me, liked me, and wanted to get to know me better—even if a trip to Scotland was a bit of a stretch for now, the intent was there. That was when I realised that intent is all I needed from Paul, but his intent had been clear from the beginning—sex, nothing more.

Molly and Chris shortly reappeared, and the four of us soon relaxed into chitchat and put on a couple of movies. Later in the evening, we ordered pizza, Molly very cleverly ordering a pizza for her and Chris to share, and then asking me and Scott what flavour we would like to share.

When the food arrived, Scott came and sat next to me so we were literally sharing the pizza from the box together. Molly, being Molly, decided to put on a horror movie, which she knew full well would make me whimper like a little girl. Blood and guts for entertainment was not my thing.

As I'm sure she predicted though, Scott stayed next to me for the entire length of the movie as I hugged the sofa cushion and watched parts through my fingers. When the two-hour long torture fest ended, I jumped up before she could put another film on and asked her to take me home. Being nearly eight p.m., I was more than tired after being up so early on my day off.

"Ok," she said, sighing and rolling her eyes. "I'll take you home."

"It's ok," Scott said, standing up. "I can drive her."

My heart stopped dead and my body flushed with hundred-degree heat.

Molly grinned, dug around in her bag, and threw him her car keys. "The sat nav is self-explanatory. Don't rush," she said, winking at him and taking Chris by the hand upstairs. "Speak to you tomorrow, Ky," she said to me, calling back over her shoulder.

Scott motioned towards the door and said, "Ladies first."

I hurried past him, my mind running crazy about being alone with him, in the dark, in a car, then at my house. I slipped my shoes on and turned around to see Scott holding the front door open for me. Then, as we reached the car, he opened the car door for me as well.

"Thank you," I said, glad he couldn't see my blushing cheeks because of the darkness.

For the first time ever, I felt safe and comfortable in Molly's car, even with a man I'd just met. His manly presence and his excellent manners only further comforted me that I had nothing to fear, and everything to look forward to—potentially.

We chatted about film likes and dislikes during the short drive to my house, interjected with me giving him directions. When we pulled up on the driveway, an awkward moment fell between us as neither of us really knew what to say or do.

"It was really nice meeting you, Kyra. I would definitely like to see you again."

My heart swelled with warmth and happiness. "I would really like to see you again, too. I've had a really good night with you."

He gave me a brilliant smile before saying, "Let me get the door for you," and hopping out of the car to come around my side and open the door for me.

"Thank you," I said, stepping out of the car.

"Don't mention it," he said, walking me to my door. "Could we perhaps swap numbers?"

I bit my lip to try and curb the massive grin escaping onto my face. "Definitely," I said, giving him my phone.

He tapped his number in and then called himself. Handing my phone back to me, he said, "Can I text you tomorrow?"

I nodded. "I would really like that."

He leaned forwards and pecked a kiss to my cheek, his subtle aftershave surrounding me in tones of sandalwood and vanilla. "Goodnight," he said.

"Goodnight," I replied, unlocking my door.

I hurried inside the house, desperate to shut the door and catch my breath. My knees were shaking and my heart doing backflips. A little voice in my head told me that this was how dating was supposed to be. This guy was ticking all the right boxes from day one. In that instant, I knew that my time with Paul was nothing but limited.

But to be honest, the thought of having someone as hot as Paul but without the commitment issues really appealed to me. For the first time in weeks, I crawled into bed thinking about someone other than Paul.

Chapter Twenty-One

F ROM THE MINUTE I opened my eyes the next morning, my thoughts were dominated solely by Scott. All the way to work, I kept reliving the moment at my door, where he leaned in and kissed my cheek. I even convinced myself I could still smell his aftershave.

At my desk, sporting a huge grin, I didn't even think once about Paul until he appeared in front of me. With his own beaming smile and pleasant good morning greetings, my heart melted at the sight of him once again, all thoughts of Scott vanishing into nothing.

"What are you grinning about?" he asked, narrowing his eyes with suspicion.

I shrugged my shoulders. "Nothing. I'm just happy."

"Are you talking to me today?"

"It would appear so."

He chuckled and disappeared into his office. I stood up to make the usual morning cups of tea, but before I could even take a step away from my desk, Molly burst through the office door, squealing in excitement. "He really likes you, Ky. Like, *really*. He wants to ask you out."

"Shush," I said, motioning my head towards Paul's office.

She threw a look of scorn towards the open door. "So what? At least Scott isn't afraid of relationships."

I resisted the urge to facepalm myself as a groan full of dread seeped through me. "Molly..."

"So, do you like him?"

A cough emanated from the open doorway. My heart skipped a beat. I knew before I even looked that Paul was stood there. Holding my breath, I dared to turn my head and look at him.

Leaning against the doorframe, arms crossed, and a hint of a smile tweaking up the edges of his lips, he said, "Don't stop on my account."

Molly glared at him. "Don't worry, we won't." She turned back to me. "So, do you?"

Heat burned through every fibre of my body as two sets of eyes awaited my answer. Neither answer I would give would satisfy them both. I glimpsed at Paul for a brief moment, remembering his words on where our relationship stood. I wanted him in ways he said he couldn't contemplate. Scott didn't seem afraid of taking things forwards and if he was settled in the idea of commitment, and intent on making me see him as different to other men, then he could be the very person to erase my fear of commitment.

"Yes, I do. He's really lovely."

Molly clasped her hands together and jumped up and down on the spot, her sheer excitement like a little girl in a candy store. In a whirlwind of shrieks, she turned and ran back downstairs.

An awkward silence fell between Paul and me for a few seconds before he spoke. "May I ask who is wanting to ask you out?"

I raised an eyebrow and folded my arms over my chest. "Why so interested?"

He shrugged his shoulders. "I'm not. Just a general wondering, considering her little personal dig at me."

"I don't think this is a conversation we need to have, Paul." I started making my way towards the kitchen. "I'm going to go and make the drinks."

"Okay, let me put this another way." He paused for a second, waiting for my attention. I turned back around to see his face edged with a serious tone. "You tell me what I want to know, or I'll discipline Molly for her disrespect towards a director."

I raised my eyebrows. "Wow. Really? You're going to pull rank now?"

"No. I'm merely offering to exchange...favours."

"Exchange favours?"

He smiled and stepped forwards, dropping his arms to his side. "Well, she's got a squeaky-clean record. Wouldn't want it tarnished with any formal warnings, would we? You do your friend a favour, and you do me a favour by answering my question."

I narrowed my eyes at him and spat my words out with venom. "Her fiancé's brother."

Surprise trickled through his eyes. "Oh."

"Have you finished?"

"And you said you liked him too?"

I sighed. "Well, you just heard that for yourself, did you not?"

He ran a hand through his hair. "I just—"

"What, Paul? We're not in a relationship, remember? This is one of the reasons you said as to why you don't do them. If someone wants to take me out and potentially take things further, then I'm not going to say no. Not when I have little else to keep me from doing so."

I winced as the last sentence flowed past my lips. I wanted to take the words back as soon as they came out, but I couldn't. He nodded, a mixture of resignation and hurt settling in his eyes before he retreated into his office in silence. My words had obviously hit a nerve, but I'd said nothing untrue. Maybe now he would understand how he'd made me feel every time he repeated the words that hurt me so badly.

I sighed and ran into the kitchen, biting back tears of frustration. Deep down, I knew he meant more to me than what I let on. I wanted nothing more than for him to stake his claim on me, but I knew it wouldn't happen. I had to make this cut between us at some point, despite my heart tearing into pieces at the thought of losing him.

"Kyra?"

I turned around to see him stood behind me, barely a foot of space between us. I blinked away my tears, but

I knew he'd seen them. He reached up with a hand and skimmed the back of it across my cheek. My heart soared with a dangerous, delicate mixture of hope and joy. Every cell in my body trembled with apprehension as I wondered what would happen next.

"I'm sorry," he said.

I nodded. "Ok."

"I understand now how much I hurt you before...whenever I said about where we stood."

I sucked in a deep breath and decided to give him the whole truth. "I just...you're the first man who has made me want more, Paul, made me realise that really, I need that. I crave the stability and comfort of having someone by my side, I want to know I have a rock, and I need to know that they're not going to run. I think that's what my fear is—abandonment. I wanted that one special person to be you. But all you do is tell me you can't give me any of that."

"I know." He dropped his hand from my cheek and took my hand in his. "I'm sorry, Kyra. I really am."

I sighed. "So where does this leave us?"

He grinned, pulling me into his warm body. "Well, until you're officially someone's girlfriend, it leaves us wherever we want to be..."

He crushed his lips to mine, sweeping me up in his comforting embrace. His tongue played with mine, each movement shooting throbs straight between my legs. I searched for the edge of his shirt, crawling my hands underneath in a desperate need to feel him bare.

He pulled away and whispered, "Can I take you out for dinner tonight?"

I smiled and nodded.

I spent the rest of the day on the edge of my seat, going back and forth between my head and my heart, wondering if I was being bad by liking one man, and then going to dinner with another. Ultimately, I told myself that nothing concrete had happened with me and Scott as of yet. If the roles were reversed, would he be shunning a fuck buddy for someone he barely knew? Judging from my experience of men, no.

As I left work, Paul confirming he would collect me at seven p.m., I couldn't help but wonder if all of this had been down to his jealousy. Perhaps there was still hope he might change his mind after all.

Chapter Twenty-Two

I WOKE THE NEXT morning, feeling happy and satisfied. I looked to my right to see Paul laid next to me and I couldn't help but grin.

He opened his eyes and smiled at me. "Good morning."

"Morning," I replied, still grinning.

"Shall we make it an extra good morning?"

He traced his fingers across my belly, sending shivers right through me. Just as I reached over and touched him, the shrill sound of his alarm cut through our anticipated bliss.

Rolling over with a defeated groan, he said, "I need to go home and change my clothes. Can't have people thinking I'm a dirty stop out."

I giggled and snuggled back underneath the duvet. I didn't need to be up for another hour at least. Watching him throw his clothes on, I admired his unclothed body for as long as possible. He gave me a quick peck on the lips before running down the stairs and out of the door.

Lost in my imagination of what we could be doing right now, I settled down for another hour of sleep before needing to face the day and get up. When my alarm sounded at 7:15, I groaned and tore myself from the bed, regretting my decision to stay in bed. I only felt even more tired than if I'd gotten up when Paul did.

Picking through my summer dresses for today's wardrobe choice, my phone pinged with a text message. Expecting it to be a cheeky message from Paul, I found myself slightly shocked to see it was from Scott.

Scott: Good morning, Kyra. I hope you're well. Are you busy on your lunch break today? Would you like to grab a cup of coffee maybe? Xx

I bit my lip as I stared at the text. How bad would it be if I went for lunch with him today considering that Paul had just climbed out of my bed? I felt bad. Deep down an uncomfortable feeling of being dirty started to climb through my veins, leaving me upset but also determined not to carry on making myself feel like this. This situation couldn't continue and only I could stop it.

Dinner last night had been fun, but Paul had made no mention of our arrangement or it potentially changing which only further clarified to me that this thing between us would only ever be sex.

Sitting back down on my bed, I forced away the tears that were trying to spring forwards and told myself to get a grip. There was no use in crying over spilled milk. The situation with Paul was what it was, and last night had happened. Never again.

I sucked in a deep breath and decided to call Ash. Maybe he could settle my mind.

"Don't tell me you need a save from a walk of shame?" Ash said, answering on the first ring.

I laughed. "No, not quite."

"Go on, I'm all ears."

I detailed him on last night, and then the situation with Scott, and how he seemed so different already. "And he's texted this morning asking if I would like to meet him for a coffee at lunch."

Ash let out a low whistle. "If I'm honest, Ky, it sounds to me like he's a guy who knows what he wants, and he goes after it. He's definitely not scared of coming forwards and that's exactly what you need. Of course, I'd need to meet him, but I think he'll be good for you if these early signs are anything to go by. I like Hot Stuff, but you have no future with him, Ky, you know this. And I'm still waiting to be fun Uncle Ash."

I laughed. "I think we're a long way yet from fun Uncle Ash." I let out a big sigh. "I just feel like a complete slut having had Paul in my bed an hour ago, and now going out for a date with Scott."

Ash chuckled. "Oh, sweetie. Do you think men contemplate things like this? What happened to embracing the power of being a woman?"

"It's my morals, Ashley," I said, rolling my eyes.

"Ok, ok, I get it. Just from the fact you called me Ashley. Let me ask you this—if Scott had had another woman in his bed last night, what would you think?"

I snorted. "That he was a man whore and just looking for the next conquest."

Ash laughed. "Trust you to be awkward. Not quite where I was going with that. My point is that people have needs. You and Scott have met once. Whatever sense of loyalty you feel, you need to firstly recognise as a good thing that you are ready for commitment. Secondly, you are not obligated to be loyal until he officially asks you to be exclusive."

"I know, I know...I just..."

"My sole piece of advice to you is this—do what feels right for you."

I nodded. "Yes. That I can work with. Thank you."

"Let me know how lunch goes," he said, before hanging up.

What felt right for me would be severing things with Paul for Scott. But would I be doing that too soon just because of one coffee date?

I picked up my phone and typed a reply to Scott:

Good morning, Scott, great to hear from you. I'm good thanks, hope you are too. Coffee sounds great. I have my lunch at 12:30. Do you know where my office is? Xx

Instantly, he replied:

Scott: I'm even better now I've heard from you. I know where your office is. I will meet you outside at 12:30. See you soon xx

My heart leapt a thousand feet and did a backflip. My body tingled with nervous anticipation, and it suddenly dawned on me that this was how dating was supposed to be. The butterfly effect lasting for weeks as you both navigate a whole course of 'firsts' that are only specific to you two. The joy of receiving a text and hoping it's them, the indecisiveness over what to wear, the stolen glances with the lingering sexual tension underneath.

I wanted all of that, and I wanted it with someone who wanted it with me. Yes, I loved the blind passion and the raw lust that me and Paul had, but what did we have outside of the sheets? Nothing. And he wouldn't even give it a chance to be nothing.

Yet someone new potentially wanted to see if things could develop. He liked me, and I liked him. For my own sake, and for fun Uncle Ash's sake, I had to give this a shot.

On my way in to work, apprehension filled me as I debated whether to tell Paul or not. Was it really any of his business? We weren't a couple after all. I kept thinking and thinking over this, right up until the moment I sat at my desk and looked at Paul's open office door.

He strolled out, flashing me a cheeky wink, and headed into the kitchen. I wondered for a brief moment if he wanted me to follow him, but I stopped myself there. I couldn't keep going down this path and being the lost little puppy whimpering for his attention.

Several minutes later, he reappeared at my desk, an eyebrow quirked up as a question, and asked, "Everything ok?"

I nodded. "Yes. Just busy."

He stared at me for a minute or two before heading back into his office. I busied myself in my pile of jobs to do and didn't look up once.

The next thing I knew, Paul stood in front of my desk, his sapphire eyes twinkling like glittering gems. "I'm nipping out. Did you want your usual from the sandwich shop?"

I smiled at him. "Thanks, but I'm good."

He raised an eyebrow. "But you'll only be going there in half an hour anyway."

My cheeks burned with heat. "No...not today."

"Oh, ok. Where are you going then? Having something different?"

I glanced away for a brief second before looking back at him and replying, "I have a coffee date."

He folded his arms across his chest. "With Ash?"

I wanted a hole to open up in the ground and swallow me. "No...Scott."

"Scott?"

"Molly's brother-in-law."

The twinkle in his eyes hardened over with a glassy stare. A muscle in his cheek twitched before he then said, "Don't be late," and stormed out without so much of a backwards glance.

The next half hour passed by at a torturously slow place. It felt like every minute dragged itself out five times longer than necessary. Paul, who usually only took fifteen minutes to go to the shop, didn't come back by the time I left my desk at half past.

My heart missing every other beat and my body trembling with excitement, I headed down the stairs and outside to see Scott waiting for me. His soulful brown eyes captivated me instantly, drowning me in thoughts of smooth Galaxy chocolate. His tight white t-shirt and dark denim jeans highlighted his body and his bronzed skin, giving him the real edge to a casual, sexy look. Seeing his broad shoulders, ripped biceps, and tight waist hugged by a tight top made it almost impossible not to stare.

"Hey," he said, giving me a dazzling smile. "You look great today. That dress really suits you."

I blushed, looking down at the floor for a moment. "Thank you."

"I see there's a café over the road. Is that ok? Or would you prefer somewhere else?"

"No, that's fine."

Placing a lower hand on my back, he guided us across the road and opened the door to the café for me. A young brunette girl behind the counter asked us if we were eating in or taking away, to which Scott replied eating in.

She showed us to a table next to the window and handed us two menus. Her porcelain skin flushed as red as a tomato when Scott took the menus from her and accidentally touched her hand. Poor girl. I knew exactly how she felt.

We made small talk about the kinds of foods we both liked, before ordering a pot of tea and a toasted sandwich each. As we were left alone now our orders had been placed, I couldn't help but ask him questions.

"What do you do for a living?"

"I'm a personal trainer. I've spent the last two years travelling around different countries, picking up tips, and learning from the best of the best. I decided I like England the best, so I've come here to set up on my own."

"That's amazing. Have you got any clients lined up yet?"

He rolled his eyes and chuckled. "I've had Molly begging me to get her in shape for her wedding day. She is a persistent woman for sure, isn't she?"

I laughed. "You have no idea. If she wants something, she gets it."

He grinned. "Looks like I may as well just do it then and save myself the earache."

I laughed and agreed with him.

We continued chatting to the point of which I nearly made myself late for work and ended up taking half of my sandwich with me. We'd been too busy talking to completely eat our meal.

Escorting me back to my building, ever the gentleman, he said his goodbyes and pecked my cheek before he left. As he leaned in, I couldn't help but inhale a deep breath of his invigorating aftershave, clouding my mind with vanilla, sandalwood, and a slight tinge of orange which I presumed to be shower gel.

When his soft lips brushed against my cheek, my imagination ran wild with what it would be like to kiss him. My belly filled with fluttering butterflies and my heart raced to a hundred miles an hour. Grinning like a Cheshire cat all the way up the stairs to my office, I had to wonder if this guy was in fact the full package.

All but skipping back to my desk, my grin soon evaporated into a deep frown as Paul appeared from his office, his face set like thunder. He dumped a huge stack of notes on my desk with a resounding thud.

"I want them typed up before you go home," he said, his tone of voice nothing short of rude and demanding.

"You are kidding me?"

He crossed his arms over his chest and glared at me. "Do I look like I'm kidding?"

I raised my eyebrows and lost the filter on my mouth. "What the fuck crawled up your ass in the last hour?"

"Kyra!"

I turned to see Mr. Tate walking up from the meeting room, his podgy face flushed red with anger. Paul flashed me a smug smirk before disappearing back inside his office, slamming the door shut.

Mr. Tate stood in front of his office door. "In my office. Now."

My heart pounded as I dragged myself over to his open door. I kept myself preoccupied by cursing Paul. Arrogant, good-looking bastard.

Mr. Tate slammed his door shut behind me. He wiped his plump, sweaty face with his wishy-washy white handkerchief. "You can take this as an official warning that if you speak to a director like that again, you will be instantly dismissed. Do you understand?"

I nodded, not saying anything in my defence because of my fuming rage at Paul.

"Good. This is going on your record. Let this be a warning. Watch your tongue. You are here to do a job without questioning what is asked of you. That is what you are paid for."

I nodded again, feeling like nothing but a slave.

"I'm glad that is understood. Out."

I scowled as I headed back to my desk, glaring at Paul's closed door, imagining the glee on his annoyingly handsome face at my telling off. However, my moment would soon come.

As per usual on Thursday afternoons, three or four of the directors left early to play golf. Once they'd all gone, Mr. Tate included, I stormed into Paul's office.

"You're a fucking dick," I said, my hands on my hips and glaring at him for all I was worth.

He leaned back in his black leather chair, making a temple figure with his hands. An amused smile crossed his face as he stared back at me, his features completely impassive.

"I thought Mr. Tate made it quite clear what would happen if you spoke to one of us like that again?"

"Seriously? Is that really how we're going to play this?"

He kicked his feet up on his desk, crossing them at his ankles, and leaned back in his chair. He shrugged his shoulders, exuding nothing but sheer arrogance.

"Fine. I'll save you the fucking bother, you arrogant tosser."

I stomped back to my desk and grabbed his pile of notes. Marching back into him, I threw them on his desk. The majority of them thudded against his wooden desk whilst a few scattered through the air, floating their way down to several different resting places.

"Do the fuckers yourself." I marched out, but not before stopping in his doorway and fixing him one last killer stare. "Just in case I'd not made it clear—I quit."

Chapter Twenty-Three

Emotions running high, I went to the one place I could relax and absorb myself in my thoughts—the riverbank where Scotch and I had our last ride. Edging quiet country lanes with ruins of an old monastery in the background, it was the one place where he and I could truly lose ourselves.

In the summer, I would often pack a sandwich and a bunch of carrots, ride down to the quiet spot under the shade of the picturesque old bridge here and sit and have lunch with him munching happily next to me.

I parked my car on the grass verge, climbing my way up the steep embankment barefoot. Leaning back against the cool grey bricks of the bridge, I closed my eyes, revelling in the heat from the afternoon sun.

Nothing but the sounds of buzzing insects surrounded me and that's all I needed—sheer bliss. I gazed out over the still, green waters, watching a pair of swans gliding through the water in all their grace.

Thoughts of my father began to surface, guilt nibbling at me once again for not visiting his grave more often. I had never been able to visit it without thinking of a rotting skeleton beneath my feet. The morbid silence that hung over the entire cemetery sent chills down my spine. Scotch had been my living memory of him in a way, my small sliver of reality that really, he was still around.

I sighed, resting my head back against the rough surface of the bricks. Losing myself in thoughts, I didn't even register the fact my body was slowly coaxing me into a deep sleep. My mind embraced the darkness, shutting off the jumbled mix of emotions tumbling around inside me...

"Kyra. Kyra. Kyra."

I startled awake, opening my eyes to see Ash stood over me. A vibrant night sky littered with stars served as a background for his looming figure, jumping me to my feet.

"What the...?"

He chuckled. "You've been asleep. And err..." He pointed at my face before picking bits of grass from my cheek.

I rubbed at my face, looking down to see an imprint of my body in the long grass where I must have slid onto my side. I blushed.

"You okay?" he asked.

I nodded. "What are you doing here?"

"Your charming boss rang me. He was worried about you."

A dawning realisation hit me square in the face. "Oh shit..."

"Yeah, he told me about your lovers' tiff."

"It wasn't a lovers' tiff, Ash. He was being a first-class dickhead."

"Well, he told me to tell you he won't be accepting your resignation."

I snorted. "About right. I can't even do what I want to do."

He raised an eyebrow at me. "Really? And just how are you going to survive without a job?"

I glared at him, narrowing my eyes. "Shut up. Just let me have my moment."

He chuckled as he picked up my shoes, taking my hand to help me back down the riverbank. "Can I trust you to get home okay, or do I need to escort you?"

"I'm fine."

As I sat in the driver's seat, he knelt down next to me, his eyes filling with concern. "I know you're emotional, Ky, but I'm worried about you lately. You sure you're okay?"

"Yes. Honestly, I'm fine. Stop fussing."

He fell silent for a few seconds. "You know he went everywhere looking for you—Paul. He does care."

I reached for my car door. "Good night, Ash."

He grinned and walked away, melting into the depths of the night.

I woke the next morning, my stomach churning as I made my way to work. When I pushed open the office door, Paul was sat on the edge of my desk.

He broke out into a huge smile, his eyes gleaming. "Are you okay?"

I walked straight past him, putting my bag down on my desk with a definitive slam. "Fine, thank you."

"Listen, I'm sorry about yesterday—"

"I don't want to hear it." I stole a glance at his handsome face as I crossed my arms over my chest.

"Okay," he said, frowning slightly.

"Is that all?"

"Yes. I mean, no." He paused and scratched his head. "Well, yes, I suppose, seeing as you don't want to hear what I have to say."

"Okay."

"Can I take you out tonight as an apology?"

"No."

"Oh. What about tomorrow?"

"No."

"Next week?"

"No."

"Is any day I ask for going to be a no?"

"Yes."

A strained silence fell between us for a minute or two before he switched tactics. "I've had your warning taken off your record and I've told Tate it was my fault. I've told him to back off with you."

I shrugged my shoulders. "Ok."

He sighed and crossed his arms over his chest. "I'm trying here, Kyra. Work with me. Please."

"Why should I? All you caused me yesterday was a shitty afternoon and a hell of a headache."

"I know. I'm sorry. I acted like a complete dick."

I snorted. "Yeah. You can say that again."

He pouted, batting his eyelashes. "Forgive me? Please?"

My body betrayed me as I looked into those dangerous blue eyes of his. Before I could even think, my head was nodding, agreeing to his demands. I was utterly useless when it came to resisting him. He surged forwards, scooping me up in his strong arms and planting a delicious kiss on my reddening cheek.

"So can I take you out tonight?"

I shook my head.

"Why not?"

"You think because you apologised I'm going to let you off that easy?"

He was silent.

I rolled my eyes. "Figured as much."

"Have you got plans?"

"And what if I have?"

He scanned across my face for a few seconds before admitting defeat and retreating back into his office. As much as I wanted to jump at his offer of dinner, my stubborn side refused to allow it. He needed to learn a lesson.

Chapter Twenty-Four

P AUL HIBERNATED IN HIS office for the rest of the day. Just before lunch I received a text from Scott, asking me if I would like to have dinner with him tonight. I smiled, texting my acceptance before even thinking of Paul. All afternoon I repeated his words about relationships to myself. I had to focus on the fact that no matter how much I wanted him, I couldn't have him how I wanted. I had now accepted my want for a proper family life and I sure as hell needed it.

The day went by without a hitch and Paul didn't try and push his luck with me any further, thankfully. Later that evening, as I got myself ready for my date with Scott, I found myself wondering about my future, places I could go, things I might see, people I would meet. And every scenario involved Scott at my side, not Paul.

Just as I slipped my shoes on, Scott knocked on my front door. My heart leapt into a new rhythm, pounding against my ribcage as nerves tingled through my veins. I opened the door, taking great delight in seeing the handsome man smiling back at me. Wearing a baby blue checked shirt that clung to his body, perfectly highlighting his bronzed skin, and black denim jeans, he looked good enough to eat.

"You look beautiful," he said, offering me a bouquet of a dozen red roses.

I blushed and took the flowers from him. "Thank you. You look really good yourself."

"Thank you." He took a step forward and lowered his voice, saying, "I feel a little guilty, seeing how incredible you look, but instead of taking you out to dinner, I wanted to cook for you. Is that ok?"

My jaw dropped. I'd never had a man cook for me, unless you included ringing a takeaway in the loose term of 'cooking'.

"I'm sorry," he said, pulling his lips into a thin line. "I didn't mean to upset you. I'm sure we can still go out somewhere. Let me make some calls."

I snapped out of my dumbfounded state and shook my head. "No, no. It's fine. I'm just gobsmacked to be honest. I've never had anyone offer such a sweet thing."

A broad smile folded over his face, his eyes glowing with warmth. "Don't worry about anything. I trained as a chef in my younger days. It'll be more than beans on toast, I promise."

"Ok. I look forward to it. Let me just put these in some water quickly. I'll be 1 minute."

"Of course," he said.

I ran to the kitchen and threw the flowers in the sink, stuck the plug in, and filled the bottom two centimetres with water. That would do until I returned home later. Rushing back to the door, I opened it and stepped outside, noticing this time he had a bright white Mercedes Coupe.

"New car?" I asked, allowing him to lead me towards the passenger side.

"Yes. Bought it today. I'm planning on sticking around for a while and I didn't want to inconvenience Chris and Molly, so I decided to treat myself."

"It's lovely."

"Thank you."

He opened the door for me and settled me inside, giving me time to make sure I had all the trailing pieces from my soft pink dress inside the car. Once he sat next to me and started the engine, the conversation started flowing again, easing my jumble of nerves.

Assuring me that Molly and Chris had gone out for the evening to give us some privacy, my stomach churned at the thought of being alone with him in a house. The temptation to peek beneath his clothes only heightened every time I saw him.

Once we arrived at the house, he led me through the kitchen and out into the back garden. I gasped, and very nearly choked up at the marvellous sight laid out before me. Molly's huge dark green marquee stood proud in the centre of the grass. The front opening had been draped back to show off the beautiful candle lit table for two inside. Fairy lights hung all around the insides, bathing the scene in a romantic setting.

"Wow, just wow. I really don't know what to say. It's incredible." I lifted a hand to push back a stray piece of hair, only to realise my hand was shaking.

He brushed a hand over my lower back and ushered me inside. He gave me the full gentleman treatment by pulling my chair out for me, pushing me in, and then pouring me some wine. He excused himself as he went to fetch the starters and I couldn't help but grin at this unexpected treat. This was, hands down, the best first date I'd ever had.

He returned after a couple of minutes with two plates. "How adventurous are you feeling?"

"Depends on what sort of adventure you're talking about."

He chuckled as he produced a red silk blindfold with a cheeky grin. "For the food."

I nodded, more than eager to accept his little game. This was such a novel, thoughtful idea, I wanted to play it to its fullest. He scooted around behind me, his hands skimming against my head as he tied the smooth fabric over my eyes.

"Ok. Open wide."

I giggled but did as I was told. Within seconds, a small amount of hot food settled on my tongue. Delicious flavours spread throughout my mouth, my taste buds jumping for joy at the glorious mix of zesty food.

"What do you taste?"

I chewed, definitely tasting meat but I couldn't quite place what. Apple puree was a definite along with some walnuts and something else. I gave him my known answers, asking for more to decide on the rest.

A minute or so later, he pulled the blindfold from me, showing me an empty plate. I blushed as I wondered just how much I'd eaten.

"That was fantastic. What was it?"

"Seared Scottish scallops with apple puree, walnut, and chicory."

"Chicory. Of course it was." I rolled my eyes at myself. "It was absolutely delicious. Thank you."

He nodded before leaving with two empty plates. I presumed he must have eaten his whilst I was busy chewing. Returning with two more plates, he lifted up the blindfold from the table, my grin returning as I nodded. We played the same game, my senses on high alert as I concentrated on the amazing food he served me.

After getting lost at fish and potatoes, he removed the blindfold to allow me to see my food.

"Poached seabass with seaweed and confit new potatoes."

I looked at him, my eyes widened in surprise. "It's fantastic. You should be a chef."

"Thanks, but I would be like a hippo if I was a chef."

I laughed, totally understanding.

After that mouth-watering course, he gifted me with dessert—lemon soufflé topped with a dollop of cream and sliced strawberries. I was floating on cloud nine with this exquisite treatment. What a guy and what a way to impress me for sure. He definitely ticked all the right boxes so far.

We chatted constantly after the meal. He was so easy to get along with and his eyes so easy to become lost in. He left me breathless with his chivalrous manners.

When Chris and Molly finally came home, we realised the time—near midnight.

"I'd best take Cinderella home," he said, taking my hand and leading me through the house.

I laughed, my pink floaty dress definitely suited for Cinderella. He drove me home, the entire time stealing glances at me and flashing me heart stopping smiles. Like a teenage girl, I could do nothing but giggle and blush as my heart raced to new dimensions. My mind wandered off into unknown futures, imagining us together.

As he pulled into my drive, he hopped out of the driver's side, making his way to my door to help me out of his low car. He grasped my hand, helping me out of the car before escorting me to my front door.

"I've had a lovely time tonight," he said, closing the gap between us. "I hope I can see you again?"

My cheeks burned as I nodded, too excited for words.

"Can I call you tomorrow?"

"Definitely."

He settled a hand on my waist and lifted the other to my cheek, stroking my face with the back of his hand. "May I kiss you?" he whispered.

Every cell inside me melted at hearing those words. I smiled and nodded.

He bumped his nose against mine, giving me an eskimo kiss before sweeping his rosy pink lips over mine. He turned his hand around, cupping my cheek as he slid his other hand from my waist, wrapping his arm around my back. Pressed in close against his body, feeling his solid warmth underneath me, I was done for.

When he teased my lips open with his tongue, entwining us together in a slow embrace, I couldn't help the small moan that escaped me. This guy was the epitome of romance. My imagination ran wild with what he might be like between the sheets.

Finally breaking his hold on me, leaving me breathless and wanting more, he wished me a good night.

Chapter Twenty-Five

SATURDAY MORNING, MY PEACEFUL slumber was interrupted by Molly ringing me at seven a.m . wanting all the gossip from last night.

"Scott will tell you," I said, yawning.

"No. I'll get a guy's version which will be 'it went well, we had food'. That'll be it. Besides, they've gone suit shopping and won't be back until later. Come over and tell me everything."

I groaned. "All I wanted today was a lay in, Molly."

"Come on," she said. "Or I'll come over to you."

I sat up in bed. "Ok. I'm getting up."

She laughed and then hung up.

An hour later, I was showered, dressed, and walking into Molly's kitchen.

"Oh my God, tell me everything," she said, grabbing my wrists and dragging me to the breakfast bar.

"Only for bacon," I said, pointing at the George Forman warming up on the side.

She rolled her eyes but headed to the fridge and picked out four pieces of bacon to lay on the grill.

"There," she said. "So, the gossip. He's so romantic, isn't he?"

I nodded, a stupid grin spreading across my face as I thought of the previous evening. "He definitely is."

"Are you going to see him again?"

"I'd be stupid not to."

An ear-piercing shriek erupted from her before she threw her arms around my neck, squeezing the life from me. Her excited state led to her chatting about the wedding for the next hour or so as she informed me of the colour choice, which, thankfully, wasn't anything exuberant. Luckily, my bacon gave me the energy I needed to survive her endless chatter.

We wandered outside to settle ourselves on the sun loungers under the warming rays of the sun. Considering the early morning hour and the thirty-degree heat already, we knew today would be a hot one. I pulled my vest top up to just under my bra so I could brown my midriff along with my legs, which were all out in my shorts.

I closed my eyes and let the sound of Molly's voice wash over me, not really caring much for what she was saying. Talking about flowers wasn't really my scene. The next thing I knew, a soft hand took mine, startling me awake.

"Hey, sleeping beauty."

I opened my eyes to see Scott sat next to me, his chocolate eyes dancing with amusement. I blushed as I realised my state of near undress and yanked my top down.

"I'm guessing this is why you've not texted me back?" he said, chuckling.

"I don't even know where it is," I said, sitting up and looking for my phone.

Molly woke up next to me, Chris shaking her awake. I stifled a giggle as I wondered if she'd talked herself to sleep.

"I was wondering," Scott said, stroking his thumb over the back of my hand. "What your plans are for this evening?"

I bit my lip to curb my growing smile and put a hand to my aching stomach. "Possibly drowning in after sun."

He chuckled. "I think we're getting a Chinese and having a film night. I'd be really pleased if you could stay."

I gave him my best smile. "I'd be really pleased to stay."

He lifted my hand to his mouth, brushing his lips across the back of it. My heart soared a hundred feet as I sat staring at him, totally bewitched. How could two guys have the same effect on me?

Molly gave a little squeal from next to me. "Ky," she said, her voice sounding alarmed. "It's after four. We've been out here nearly six hours." She grabbed my hand and dragged me up. "Come on. Enough sun. Let's get tea ordered."

No wonder my stomach was aching. I hoped it was hunger and not just sun burn. Heading into Molly's bathroom, I rummaged around in her cupboard for her aloe vera gel and applied some to my stomach and legs, just in case. By the time I returned back downstairs, tea had already been ordered.

"I ordered your usual—special chow mein with prawn toast."

I nodded. "Perfect, thanks."

Molly plonked herself down on one end of the sofa, Chris sitting next to her. Scott sat next to his brother, leaving a gap for me at the other end of the sofa. I slid into my spot, my heart pounding at being so close to him. Our legs were pressed together and I couldn't help but feel like a giddy teenager on a bus trip, sitting next to my crush.

Molly picked up the remote. "Right. Me and Ky will pick a film, then you two can pick a film. Deal?"

The guys agreed, no doubt because it was easier to agree with Molly than not. Of course, I didn't get a say in the film choice, the girl's choice was of course Molly's choice. Predictably, as I'm sure Chris knew, she picked a rom-com—Bridesmaids. I had seen it before and didn't mind re-watching it. Melissa and Kristen were brilliant actresses, always making me laugh.

Halfway through, the food turned up and we all tucked in. Maybe it was because I was hungry enough to eat a horse, but Chinese food had never tasted so good. I cleared my plate and still wanted more but restrained myself to letting my food settle for half an hour before digging around for second helpings.

By the time we'd finished eating, the film finished, which meant we were now to be subjected to the guy's choice. Chris loved gory horrors and of course, that's what he put on. To make it worse, of all the horrors, it had to be the last installment of the Saw franchise. I hated those movies with a passion. They really freaked me out because I knew that somewhere, someone would try recreating them.

I huddled into the sofa cushion, digging my fingers into the soft lilac surface. I kept my head pointing in the general direction of the TV, but actually picked out a spot in the wallpaper just to the right of it and focused on it, trying to make shapes from the weird abstract patterns.

As tortured screams and cracking bones blared at us from the TV, I hid my face into the cushion and sucked in a deep breath. Seconds later, an arm slid around my shoulders, pulling me into a strong, sturdy body. The familiar fragrance of sandalwood and vanilla enveloped me, relaxing me as I nestled into him. He pressed a kiss to the side of my head, sending my heart into overdrive.

Thoughts of Paul appeared from nowhere, wondering why he couldn't do this with me. I liked Scott and he seemed to be captivating me just as much as Paul, but Paul always seemed to be popping back into my mind for some reason. Forcing myself to remember that I would never have this with Paul, I pushed him out of my mind.

I stayed in Scott's embrace for the duration of the film, enjoying the warmth and the way he kept kissing the side of my head. I loved being close to him and knowing that he wanted this, that he initiated it, filled me with a deep satisfaction I'd never yet felt.

The movie finally finished, and I gladly announced it was my time to leave before I was subjected to any more blood and guts. It wasn't late, being near ten p.m., but I wanted my bed.

Molly grinned at me, her green eyes twinkling with mischief. "Why don't you stay?"

I narrowed my eyes at her. "No, Molly. I think its best I go home."

She pouted but thankfully didn't argue. We hugged good night before Scott offered to walk me out to my car. I slipped my shoes on and opened the door, shivering as the cool night air sent a chill down my spine, covering me in goosebumps. Seconds later, a thick suede coat settled on my shoulders as Scott smiled at me.

He led me to my car, closing the front door behind us and separating us from Molly and Chris. I appreciated the peace and quiet of just the two of us.

Like the true gent he was, he opened my car door for me. "Thank you for staying tonight. I really enjoy spending time with you."

"I'm glad I stayed, thank you for asking." My heart backflipped as I then said, "I love spending time with you."

"I'll speak to you tomorrow. Is that ok?"

I nodded. "Definitely."

He cupped my face in his hands and closed the distance between us. Brushing his nose against mine briefly, my stomach filled with butterflies as I waited for him to kiss me. He touched my lips with such a tender kiss, my entire body exploded with tingles. As he opened my mouth with his tongue, tangling our tongues together into a slow dance, my grip on reality completely evaporated, leaving me soaring towards heaven.

I found myself wondering, and almost desperate to feel his touch on my body. I wanted to feel his hands on me as he kissed me like this. The desire to have us together body to body, skin to skin, became almost too much to bear.

Before my cravings took control of me, he broke the kiss, leaving me somewhat dazed as he wished me goodnight.

I drove home in a complete trance, tracing my index finger over my lips as I relived his kiss over and over again.

Chapter Twenty-Six

SUNDAY, I HAD HOPED I would see Scott again. As soon as I realised I was eager and hoping to spend time with someone, I grinned and mentally patted myself on the back. I had never felt like this about anyone before. Sure, I had looked forward to seeing Paul, and hoped he would come over for our fuck buddy arrangement, but this, this was something different. That was when I knew where my heart truly lay.

Unfortunately, Scott was busy most of the day Sunday as he was house hunting. I appreciated a pyjama day of doing nothing anyway before work resumed tomorrow morning. However, as promised, Scott did text and we spent most of the day talking, albeit with small gaps in replies.

By Monday morning, I realised I hadn't heard from Paul all weekend and began to wonder if he had expected to hear from me. Was he still angry that I'd had a date? He only had himself to blame. I had no sympathy.

I arrived at work and sat at my desk, watching time tick by as Paul still hadn't arrived. Just after ten, he marched through the door, his face creased into a deep frown and barely muttering a greeting before shutting himself in his office.

Several tension filled minutes later, he opened his door. "Have you got a minute?"

I nodded, my heart pounding against my ribs as I scrambled up from my desk and hurried towards him.

He shut the door behind me, the definitive click cutting through our silence. He turned to me, his head cocked to one side, shoulders square and set, and then asked, "Why didn't you call me over the weekend?"

My mouth dropped open. I hadn't expected that. "I didn't want to demand your time when I know you're...otherwise engaged."

He let out a sigh and ran a hand through his hair, seeming to deflate some of his tension. "Sorry. I'm a bit stressed. It's been a long weekend."

"Oh. Ok."

An uncomfortable feeling began to flourish inside me before he strode towards me, cupping my face and planting his lips on mine. Such passion flowed from him it took my breath away. So shocked and taken aback by his sudden assault on me, I didn't know what to think or do. My brain became paralysed, completely preventing me from doing anything other than letting him kiss me.

He broke our embrace after a minute or so and rested his forehead against mine. "That was all I needed all weekend."

His words surged hot tingling hope through me. Once again, I became lost in the complications of us. Optimism started rising inside me again that maybe we could go somewhere.

"Why didn't you call me, then?" I asked.

"I wanted to, I really did."

"But you still didn't."

He closed his eyes. "It's complicated, Ky..."

I sighed, stepping back from him. "Isn't it always with you?"

"Don't be like that," he said, reaching for me. He grabbed my hand and pulled me into him, lifting a hand to my cheek and stroking it. "I've given you everything I can of me."

"Is Paul in?"

I froze at the sound of Mr. Collins's voice coming from outside. Fear coursed through me at the realisation of being caught.

Paul leaned into me, his lips brushing against my ear as he whispered, "We'll be fine. Trust me."

Just as I debated my options, the door burst open.

Mr. Collins took one look at us before closing the door and announcing, "Paul isn't in yet."

I shot Paul a confused look. "What the...?"

"He has an announcement to make."

Adrenaline surged through me as I wondered what it could be. "What?"

"I'm no longer a director."

I gasped, horror and panic filling me at the thought of not seeing him every day. "What? Why?"

He chuckled. "I'm now co-owner. Majority shareholder to be exact. My parents and I bought out seventy per cent of his business and I'm now at the helm."

My jaw dropped. "Oh my God."

He grinned. "I know. Come on. We'd best make an appearance."

Peeking out of the closed blinds, he waited for the directors to filter into the meeting room before ushering us both out of his office and into the meeting room with the others.

Mr. Collins and Paul made the announcement together to the other directors before heading downstairs to tell the rest of the staff. An agonising hour passed before he came back upstairs. As soon as he walked into his office, I followed him, intent on interrogation. Unfortunately, as I dashed through his door, Mr. Collins followed.

He shot me a distasteful glare before settling a hardened stare on Paul. "May I suggest you refrain from fraternising with the staff, Paul."

Paul cleared his throat. "Mick, I suggest you be very careful before treading along this road."

"Considering I'm still an owner of this company, I suggest you listen to me. I built this company up with my bare hands. Getting involved with staff is not a clever idea. Especially staff like her."

Paul glared at Mr. Collins, he clenched his jaw, a muscle twitching in his cheek. Anger oozed from every pore. Several seconds ticked by. I wanted to cringe with the growing tension between them both.

"May I point out," Paul said. "That you entered my office without consent or even knocking first. May I also remind you I now own the majority of this company and I have the final say. As for the staff, Kyra is technically now my employee and will be cared for as such. With regards to your comment regarding 'staff like her,' it is wholly unappreciated, and it will serve you well to remember in the future to address her with respect."

Mr. Collins fell silent for a moment whilst I stared at the floor, not daring to look at either of them. I couldn't help but feel a burst of pride and happiness at Paul's words. Comfort and warmth flooded me as I wrapped myself in the protective essence he'd shown towards me.

"Don't expect me to pick up the pieces when it blows up in your face," Mr. Collins said.

"It won't but thank you for your concern."

"How long has this been going on?"

Paul narrowed his eyes at him. "I don't see how that is relevant."

"I think I deserve to know considering we're co-owners."

"I think you deserve to remember you are privy to some of my extra-curricular activities. Whilst I cannot help the information you know about that, I can help the information you know about Kyra. As such, Kyra is strictly off limits to anyone except myself. Do I make myself clear?"

Struggling to contain my growing smile at Mr. Collins being put in his place, a creeping smugness climbed over me. A few seconds passed before I realised Paul had intimated Mr. Collins knew about the swingers' club. I hadn't expected that.

"Yes, perfectly," Mr. Collins said.

Paul nodded. "Good. One more word about Kyra and you're out of the club, understood?"

Mr. Collins nodded, giving me one final glare before storming out.

I met Paul's handsome face with a big grin. "Quite the speech, Mr. Connors. Thank you."

"No need to thank me. I won't tolerate disrespect from anyone towards you."

For the second time in one day, I found optimism rising that maybe, just maybe, this might mean he had feelings for me buried somewhere inside him.

Chapter Twenty-Seven

"Look, Kyra, I really don't want to keep going over this point but why would I tell you? It's not like we're together."

My interrogation soon faltered and fell flat on its face, along with any optimism I'd felt rising. Once again, he only served to reiterate his previous point about our 'arrangement'. All that did was reassure me that Scott was the better option. No, not just the better option, the only option. Paul was no longer an option. I had to drill that home to myself.

His words still cut me, but nowhere near as deep as before. That was my tell-tale sign that his hold on me was lessening. Not that he needed to know that.

"Ok," I said, shrugging my shoulders. "Fair point."

He opened his mouth and then closed it again, impersonating a dying fish. After a minute or so, he said, "Are you ok?"

I nodded. "Perfectly. Why?"

"You normally get upset when I say that. About where we stand."

I smiled. "No point anymore. It doesn't change anything."

Shock and confusion spread through his sapphire eyes as he took a step back, as if my words had caused him to stumble. "No, that's true. Ok, so long as you are fine."

I smiled. "Yep," I replied, before walking out of his office and returning to my desk.

For the rest of the day, we were nothing more than civil to one another. At four p.m., as I readied myself to go home, Paul came rushing out of his office with a pale face and his phone glued to his ear.

I guessed it was something to do with his home life and thought no more of it. His life outside of this office didn't concern me, nor did mine concern him. Just as I arrived home, my phone beeped with a text from Scott asking how my day had been.

Once inside the house, I couldn't help but smile as I replied and engaged in conversation with him. This only served to remind me that this was what dating was all about—taking an interest in each other's lives, caring about the little things, paying attention. The only attention I received from Paul revolved around my vagina. Nothing more.

The next morning at work, Paul never showed in the office. I heard nothing from him—not a text, not a call, not even an email. None of the other directors said a word and I didn't dare ask.

Wednesday was a repeat of Tuesday—nada from Paul. No mention of altering the movements diary, nothing. I tried not to think about it, satisfying my curiosity with it being something about the business and the recent acquisition on his part.

In the meantime, Paul's sudden absence had allowed the situation between me and Scott to bloom. We now texted from sun rise to sun set. The way my heart fluttered every time I saw his name in my inbox, I knew I had developed feelings for him.

We were arranging to see each other Friday night and I couldn't wait. The weeklong wait only heightened the anticipation and made me keener to see him.

Thursday midday, Paul reappeared at work. He said nothing as he sauntered past my desk and into his office.

A little annoyed he hadn't even bothered to say good morning, I debated going after him to remind him about his manners.

Minutes later, he appeared at his open door and said, "Can I have a word?"

I stood up and walked towards him, already debating giving him a sarcastic good morning greeting once inside.

He closed the door behind me and said, "Take a seat," before heading to his chair and sitting down.

Very aware of the fact he hadn't made eye contact with me once, I made my way to the black leather chair opposite his desk and sat down, looking at him.

His blissful blue eyes were nothing but flat, emotionless windows. Leaning his forearms on the desk, he glared at me as if I were the most annoying thing he had to deal with. "Kyra, I think we need to call it a day with our little...arrangement." He waved his hand in the air as if swatting at a fly.

I was stunned into silence, struggling to ignore the instant stabbing pain of someone twisting a knife in my heart. Blinded by my own stupidity and romantic fantasies, I now sat here with a deep ache resounding through me as his words hit home. What had I thought would happen? Right from day one, I knew this would come to an end, and now it was here, I didn't like it. Was it because it was him officially calling it quits? Or was it because he was now cementing the fact we would never have a future?

I looked at the floor, my heart hammering against my ribs. "What? Why?"

He drummed his fingers on his desk. "I can't explain my reasons. Well, I can, I just don't want to. I think it's for the best."

"Is it because I started dating Scott?"

He rolled his eyes and let out a snort of disdain. "Kyra, don't flatter yourself."

Ouch. That stung worse than a thousand bees. Tears pricked at my eyes. I couldn't comprehend this complete turnaround of events. What the hell was going on? I dared to look at his gorgeous face to see he was looking past me, staring at the wall behind me as if I bored him.

I stood up, speechless, and ambled over to the door.

"Do you not want to say anything?" he asked.

I shook my head, still facing the door so he couldn't see the tears brimming in my eyes. I shot out, heading straight to the toilet, and locked myself in. I attempted to compose myself, taking deep breaths and mouthfuls of cold water. It wasn't losing him that bothered me, it was how he'd treated me. Had I allowed it though? Had I put myself in the position of being dispensable and nothing more than something to throw away once he got bored?

Sending a quick text to Ash, I soon had a comforting phone call, reassuring me I would be okay.

"Just concentrate on the one guy who can give you what you want and need, Ky. As much as I hate to say it, it's not him."

I nodded, numb. "I know. He was just so...cold, Ash. Like you wouldn't believe. I can't get my head around how he's done a complete one-eighty."

"No guy is worth crying over, Kyra, but when you find one who is, he won't make you cry."

"That doesn't make sense. It's a total contradiction of itself."

He chuckled. "So is life."

Friday morning at work was awkward to say the least. We both ignored each other all morning. When I went out for lunch as normal, he headed out at the same time.

When I noticed him heading for the stairwell, I made a point of taking the lift. He knew I never took the lift, so I felt my point was well made.

I'd been back at work barely twenty minutes before I had a phone call from the receptionist downstairs telling me I had a package delivered.

"What is it, Kelly? I'm a bit busy."

"No worries. I'll bring it up to you."

A couple of minutes later, Kelly walked through the door with a massive bouquet of roses and lilies covering her petite face.

She settled them on the edge of my desk, her brown eyes glowing with the promise of gossip. "Secret admirer?"

I blushed and pulled the card from the side of the wrapper.

Beautiful flowers for a beautiful lady, love Scott XXX

My cheeks exploded with heat. I had never had flowers sent to me anywhere, let alone work. A mixture of embarrassment and excitement flooded through my veins, sending me almost dizzy.

"Thank you for bringing these up, Kelly, I really appreciate it."

"No problem. Enjoy," she said, giving me a big grin before disappearing back downstairs.

Paul emerged from his office just as I stuck my head in the bouquet and sucked in a deep breath.

"This is not a florist shop," he said.

The stern tone of his voice jolted me upright and I turned to see him glaring at me from the other side of my desk.

"I didn't know I was getting them," I said, feeling like I had to defend myself.

He pointed at the card and said, "You know who they're from, don't you?"

"Yes." I almost said 'Scott' but stopped myself.

"Good. Then make sure he understands not to do it again."

It took me a few seconds to realise he said 'make sure he understands'. He guessed who they were from and didn't like it. I doubted a bunch of flowers would be enough to irritate him, it was most likely the sender.

"Fine," I said, narrowing my eyes at him.

His sudden behaviour change towards me still baffled me but he didn't deserve my energy thinking about it. He stalked out of the office and returned a few minutes later, bursting through the door like a tornado.

"Alter my movements diary, please." He tapped his foot as I scrambled around my desk for his diary. "I'm out in Germany for the next three weeks. I will be back in the office on the thirtieth of August."

My automatic reaction had been to want to ask questions, but I made a point of saying nothing.

His tone of voice softened a little as he said, "It is work related, not personal, so I will be reachable on email and my phone."

I nodded, still saying nothing.

He paused for a second before marching into his office. Shortly after, he left the office, muttering a pathetic good-bye. He didn't even bother to look at me as he left for the next three weeks.

Chapter Twenty-Eight

I THOUGHT LITTLE MORE of Paul after he left. His behaviour bothered me, but not enough to keep going over it. I had been starting to realise before he officially cut things off that we weren't going to go anywhere anyway. I was just trying to make the adjustment my way. Perhaps the fact that he'd forced it along quicker than I was ready for is what bothered me, but either way, I'd gotten the desired result.

Friday night, I had my hot date with Scott. He told me to dress up casually and bring something warm for later. I couldn't help but wonder what on earth he had planned.

I settled on a pair of jeans, my white converse, a golden yellow t-shirt and a black cardigan, with a puffa jacket as my something warm.

He picked me up, as punctual as ever, at eight p.m., just as twilight started setting in. He greeted me at my door, looking delicious in his faded denim jeans and long-sleeved black t-shirt.

Giving me a kiss on the lips as a greeting, he led me to the car door and indulged me in his usual ritual of opening my door for me.

"Where are we going?" I asked, curiosity killing me.

He threw me a cheeky wink. "You'll see."

Waiting until I'd sat down, he closed my door and then jogged around to his side. Once seated and seatbelt on, he struck the engine up and reversed off the drive.

He glanced over at me, his chocolate eyes twinkling, and said, "Have you had a good day?"

I couldn't help but grin. "As I said in my text, you really don't know how much you made me smile with those flowers. Thank you so much."

"No need to thank me," he said. "It was my pleasure."

He headed out of town and towards the countryside, out into the middle of nowhere. As we rolled past fields and old barns and the odd farmhouse, I couldn't help but feel a slight sense of recognition as to where we were.

Looking straight ahead out of the front windscreen, I almost choked on my own breath when I spotted Paul's mansion in the distance. My heart did a backflip before stopping and restarting at a thousand miles an hour.

"How much further are we going?" I asked, trying to keep my voice calm and collected.

He reached over and grabbed my hand, giving me a reassuring squeeze. "Not much, I promise. You see that big house down there at the corner?" I nodded. I hadn't taken my eyes off it. "We're going to a little place just behind it."

"Ok," I said, smiling at him.

"Are you too hot? Your hand feels clammy."

I shook my head. "No, I'm ok."

I resisted the urge to faceplant myself. My goodness. This couldn't be coincidence, could it? Had Molly told him about me and Paul and this was his little way of telling me he knew? Or was this a genuine coincidence?

My heart pounding and my palms sweating, I focused on my breathing, counting to ten on the breath in, and counting to ten on the breath out. By the time we rounded the corner where Paul's house sat, I'd managed to calm my racing heart and dried my sweaty palms on my jeans. I forced myself not to stare at the house, but then wondered if Scott would find it odd that I didn't look because of the sheer size of it and how impressive it was to look at.

Still, I resisted the urge to stare and carried on looking straight ahead. Sure enough, just as he'd promised, the road curved back around the side of Paul's property, and then around the back. A small little farmyard sat here with an old red brick-built barn, an ancient looking tractor nestled inside.

Scott pulled up alongside the barn and switched the car off. He jumped out of the car and came around to my side, opening the door for me.

"I have so many questions," I said, letting out a nervous giggle as I stepped out of the car.

"I think I can guess one of them," he said, grinning at me. "Chris is the IT specialist for the people who live in the massive house we just passed."

"Oh," I said to myself, whilst secretly thinking *Of course he is.* "It's a small world."

Scott smiled. "He told me about this little farmyard being here. He spent months installing their system and their CCTV. Apparently, they don't use this for anything, it's just wasted space. So, I figured it would be the perfect spot for us to do what I had in mind this evening."

I followed him to the boot of the car and watched him take out a blanket and a wicker basket. "Oh my," I said, my hand flying to my mouth in surprise. "Are we having an evening picnic?"

He shut the boot and took my hand with a smile, not saying anything. He led me around the back of the barn and as we rounded the corner, I almost fell in love. Behind the barn sat an L shaped stable block, four red brick stables with white painted wooden doors and old-fashioned black iron hinges. My heart melted. What an absolutely perfect little stable yard.

Glancing around me at the rest of the land, my mind ran wild with how I could turn this into my own private stable yard, where the hay would go, how I would fence off the giant field laid out before us, where the exercise arena would go, where my tack room would go.

Then reality slapped me in the face and reminded me whose land I was on. And that my momentary fantasy would never take shape.

In front of us sat acres of ankle length green grass. Bordered by evergreen hedges, and with several giant oak trees dotted around, it was a picture-perfect meadow for any horse enthusiast. For the first time in a long time, my heart started to ache for the familiarity of a horse again.

"Over here," Scott said, leading me towards the closest tree.

We approached the majestic old oak, its lowest branches a good ten feet above my head. They reached out for a good twelve feet all around, providing the perfect cover with its thick leaves should the weather turn.

Letting go of my hand, Scott laid the blanket out just in front of the furthest reaching branch. He sat down and patted the ground next to him. "Come on," he said, opening the wicker basket. "It's a perfect clear night sky."

I looked up to see the hues of blues, reds, and oranges from the day blending into velvet darkness. "It's beautiful," I said, sitting down next to him.

He slid an arm around my waist and said, "Would it be too cheesy if I said it wasn't as beautiful as you?"

I laughed. "It's cheesy but it's sweet, so I'll let it go."

He brushed a stray hair back from my face and said, "There's supposed to be a meteor shower tonight so I thought we could watch that and do a bit of star gazing as well."

My whole body flushed with warmth and joy. He was so romantic he literally took my breath away. How could he be such a perfect package of everything I've ever wanted?

I nodded. "Another first for me."

He lifted a hand to my face and stroked my cheek, the intensity in his chocolate eyes making my heart race. "Am I giving you many firsts?"

"Yes," I whispered.

"Am I succeeding in the challenge of changing your mind about men?"

"Definitely."

He gave me an eskimo kiss before pressing his lips to mine, making my heart soar higher than the birds above us. When he slipped his tongue inside my mouth and caressed my tongue with his, I let out a small moan as an intense bundle of tingles settled straight between my legs.

After a minute or so, he pulled away, only enough to break our kiss, leaving our noses still touching. He then whispered, "I really like you, Kyra. If it's too soon then tell me no, but I would really like us to make this official. I want to be with you." He rubbed his nose against mine and then said, "Would you like to be with me?"

I couldn't help the broad grin that spread over my face. "Yes. I would love to be with you."

His eyes glowered with happiness as he leaned in and kissed me. This kiss was different to all the previous kisses, his touch became firmer, more confident, more demanding as he swept our tongues together into a passionate dance. My core ignited as I felt his desire for me.

We kissed until our lips became swollen and our restraint started slipping away. With darkness enveloping us and crickets filling the sound of the air, we laid back on the blanket and watched the skies above us.

"I brought some wine for you," he said. "Would you like some?"

"Yes, please, but I do feel a little guilty that I get alcohol and you don't."

He rummaged around in the wicker basket and pulled out a bottle. "Alcohol free beer. It'll do me."

I laughed. "Not quite the same but if you're happy then that's good."

He handed me my glass of white wine and said, "I'm more than happy."

We laid back on the blanket, only sitting up to sip our drinks, and made small talk about stars, horoscopes, and all things astronomical as we pointed at different shapes and watched the meteor shower.

It was a perfect, romantic night and I couldn't have asked for anything more. Until my phone rang. Wondering who one earth could be calling me at nine p.m. on a Friday, I pulled my phone from my jacket pocket to see **Paul** flashing across the screen.

My stomach churned as my heart dropped to my feet. I jumped up and said to Scott, "It's my boss."

He frowned. "At this time of night?"

I walked away a few feet and answered. "Hello?"

"Hi."

"Is something wrong?"

"I was looking for something and couldn't find it...but I've just found it now. Sorry to disturb you. I should have looked harder before I called."

"Ok, no problem."

An agonising second ticked past that felt like an eternity. Then he said, "Are you ok?"

"Yes."

"Ok, good." He cleared his throat and then said, "Ky?"

"Yeah?"

"I miss you."

It took a good few seconds for my ears to register the beeps of the line being cut, the following silence deafening me after his words.

Chapter Twenty-Nine

S COTT ASKED ONE QUESTION about my phone call from Paul, which my answer of "He found what he was looking for just as I answered the phone," served him well and he never asked anything more.

Close to midnight, we decided it was time to head back seeing as we were both cold and tired. Scott's flash new car had the luxury of heated seats, and I grinned like anything as I flicked it on and revelled in having a warm ass.

As we pulled up on my driveway, I turned to him and said, "I'm not suggesting anything at all, because I think for me it's too soon, but would you like to stay?"

I couldn't help but bite my lip in anticipation of his answer. I'd invited him to stay but pretty much told him no funny business. What possible incentive could he have to stay?

"I would love to stay," he said. "Lucky for me I have a change of clothes in the boot."

I raised an eyebrow and smirked. "Were you hoping I'd ask you to stay?"

He chuckled. "No. I always have an emergency kit of clean clothes in case I ever forget something in a hurry at the gym."

I laughed. "Of course, I forgot. You have the ability to think ahead more than a few hours."

He laughed with me. "Yes, yes I do."

Several minutes later, we were inside my house and I was giving Scott the grand tour of my humble abode. I left my bedroom until last so that once we were in it, we could stay in it.

A brief thought of Paul popped into my mind from nowhere as I realised that the last man in here had been him. Thankfully, I had changed the sheets since he had been in my bed so that made me feel slightly less worse.

I scratched my head and blushed as I said, "I didn't really think about this, did I?" My cheeks flushed with heat. "I probably should have told you that I sleep naked, but I can wear something tonight if it's a problem."

He looked at me from the other side of the bed and laughed. "Ky, come on. I'm a grown ass man. I think I can sleep in a bed with a naked woman and keep my hands to myself."

I laughed. "Kind of really making this a challenge, aren't I?"

He chuckled. "Like I told you, I love a challenge."

He pulled his t-shirt over his head and dropped it onto the floor. My eyes nearly bulged out of their sockets. I thought Paul had a good body, but jeeze, he had nothing on this guy. Every single muscle was clearly defined, not an ounce of fat clung to him. His abs were like a washboard, a perfect eight-pack that surrounded the delicious V down into his jeans.

"Forget your challenge. I think this is going to be my challenge," I said, not taking my eyes off him once.

He laughed. "Well, then let me tell you that there will be no funny business tonight. I'm putting my foot down."

I grinned. "A man who tells me what to do...hmmm, I like it," I said, quirking an eyebrow up.

He crawled onto the bed and over to my side, kneeling in front of me, making us now the same height.

He held my eye contact as he skimmed a hand along my left arm and whispered, "Let me undress you."

My breath caught in my throat, and I could do nothing but nod in agreement.

He moved both hands to the bottom of my top and inched it up my body, revealing my stomach to him inch by inch. When he reached my waist, I lifted my arms up, and as he pulled it over my breasts, revealing my white silk bra, I sucked in a deep breath and squeezed my eyes shut.

"Hey," he said, his voice low and quiet as he took my top over my head. "Look at me."

I opened my eyes to see him drop my t-shirt to the floor. When I met his eye contact, heat burned through my veins at a thousand degrees in an instant. Full of warmth and care, I knew I had nothing to worry about whatsoever.

"Don't be embarrassed," he said. "You have a great figure."

My cheeks reddened and it took all my will power not to hide my face in my hands. "Nothing like the gym bunnies though."

He slipped an arm around my back and pulled me against his chest. The feel of his skin against mine, soft and smooth and radiating heat, made me want to cry with joy. I'd missed this intimacy with someone so much. Not sex, intimacy, where both of you take time with each other and make each other feel safe and secure. The kind of intimacy I'd shared with Paul had been purely raw animal desire, both of us fulfilling carnal needs.

He pressed his nose to mine and said, "Gym bunnies aren't real people. They're skin deep and that's it. I don't want to share my bed with an ironing board that has the personality depth of a drop of water. I want a real woman with a real personality and a real body." He rubbed our noses together and then whispered, "You are absolutely perfect just the way you are. Don't ever let anyone tell you different."

"Ok," I breathed.

Drawing little circles on my back with his fingertips, he lowered his hand to my jeans before working his way round to the button and undoing it. He unzipped them and slowly pushed them down my legs until I had to step out of them, using his broad, muscled shoulders as a support.

Now standing in front of him in just my underwear, I smiled at him and said, "Come on. Time to lose your jeans."

He moved off the bed, resuming his full height as he stood in front of me. He popped the button on his jeans and with a gentle push let them fall to his feet, revealing his tight, black boxers and his beautifully toned legs.

Stepping out of his jeans, he looked down at me and grinned. "So..."

I giggled and blushed. "So..."

"I usually sleep in my boxers," he said. "But if you want to feel normal and have me as naked as you, I don't mind."

My eyes were dying to look down and size up what he was hiding in there. But I couldn't let myself be that obvious. Not yet anyway.

"Keep them on, it's fine," I said. "I'm thinking I might put a t-shirt on and keep my underwear on."

He wiggled his eyebrows up and down. "Don't you trust me?"

I smiled. "Of course I do...it's me I don't trust."

He tipped his head back and laughed. "Will you trust me to trust yourself?"

"That's an interesting one," I said, laughing. "Sure, why not?"

He reached out and settled his hands on my white silk thong. "May I?"

I nodded, biting my lip to curb the nervous smile that wanted to break out. As he eased my underwear down my legs, my breathing became shorter and shallower as I anticipated he might make a move.

But true to his word, he didn't.

When he reached around my back and undid my bra with one flick of his wrist, I let it fall from my shoulders, so I stood completely naked in front of him.

He still didn't make a move.

Instead, he stripped his own underwear off so we were stood, toe to toe, completely naked.

"Now we're even," he said, settling his hand on my waist. "You feel ok?"

I nodded, grinning like a little girl. "I feel perfect."

He pressed a kiss to my forehead and then reached behind him and lifted up the covers. "Bedtime," he said.

I climbed in first, scooting over to the other side to give him some room. He slid in after me and huddled up to me, wrapping his arms around me. Cuddling us together, skin to skin, I closed my eyes as I revelled in my perfect heaven. Having a pair of strong arms around me and a warm body next to mine was the most perfect thing I could have ever wished for at that moment in time.

As Scott dozed off into a peaceful slumber, I found myself wide awake, staring at his handsome face. A tiny voice in the back of my mind whispered that it should have been Paul, but Paul would never be so loving or affectionate because it just wasn't him.

My connection with Paul was physical, but the bond I was building with Scott was so much more than that. This right here proved it more than anything else.

Out of nowhere, three words from earlier returned to haunt me, ensuring a night of no sleep.

I miss you...

Chapter Thirty

I MANAGED TO FALL asleep and woke the next morning to find Scott wide awake, watching me.

"Please don't tell me you were watching me sleep," I said, laughing.

He grinned. "But then I'd be lying."

"It's really creepy you know."

He shrugged his shoulders. "That just means that I'm your creep."

I grinned back at him at the reminder of our official status as of last night. "Yes, you are. And a creep who managed to keep his hands to himself."

"So did you," he said, giving me a wink. "Seems we both passed our challenges."

He leaned in for a kiss, and just as our lips met, my phone burst into life, singing Molly's personal ring tone—Barbie Girl.

Scott burst out laughing. "Have you seriously got that as your ring tone for Molly?"

I laughed. "Yes. She gets a new one every week."

He chuckled to himself as I answered the phone.

"Scott didn't come home last night," she said, all but shrieking in my ear. "So how was it?"

"Nothing happened, Molls."

"What?" she yelled. "You had a hot as hell man in your bed and did nothing? Pffft. Are you turning lesbian?"

I laughed. "No. I'm just not quite ready for that stage yet."

She sighed. "Is this because of—"

"Why do you sound like you're in the car?" I had to cut her off before she said Paul's name.

"Because I'm on my way to yours. Please don't tell me you forgot."

My heart stilled. Fuck. I'd forgotten about her dress fitting today. "Ok, ok. I'm getting up now."

"Honestly, Ky. I hope you're not this forgetful when it comes to your own wedding."

"I just don't understand why you're having a dress fitting already. We only picked it out two weeks ago."

"Three, actually. And you're my best friend. It's another excuse for a girly day out."

"See you soon," I said, hanging up.

I turned to Scott and opened my mouth but he just grinned. "I heard. It's fine, no problem." Climbing out of bed, I looked through my draws for underwear. "I have to ask though...I heard her ask if you're not ready for sex because of someone. Is that right?"

My heart froze in my chest. Fuck. I hoped to high heaven he hadn't heard it. God obviously didn't love me today.

"My ex," I said, quickly. "I was very into him, but he wasn't so much into me."

Scott raised an eyebrow and looked me up and down. "Was he gay?"

I couldn't help but laugh, but most of it was nervous laughter. "No, no, definitely not gay. Let's just say he was emotionally unavailable."

He nodded. "Ok, I got it. No further explanation needed."

I threw some clothes on and tied my hair up into a quick ponytail. "You are more than welcome to stay whilst I'm gone. Of course, no offence if you decide to go either."

"What would you like me to do?"

I stopped for a moment. I hadn't even thought that far, I just presumed he'd take one of the two options and I'd find out which one when I got back.

"I don't know...I think my obvious preference would be for you to stay."

He gave me a warm smile. "Then that's what I'll do. I'll see you later."

I walked around to his side of the bed and gave him a quick kiss on the lips. "See you later." I turned to walk out, and as I reached the doorway, I turned back and said, "Thank you for staying. I appreciate it."

"No need to thank me. Go and have fun. I'll see you later."

I hurried into the bathroom to clean my teeth and put some deodorant on, literally just finishing as Molly rolled onto the driveway and beeped her horn. I ran down the stairs, slipped my shoes on, and headed out, sucking in a deep breath as I prepared myself for the death trap driving.

It seemed God loved me again as we made it into town in one piece and with little bother. Parking in the same place as before, Molly all but frog-marched us to the dress shop with an impish grin on her face.

As soon as we entered the shop, Edith scurried out, a bundle of joy and fake excitement like before.

"Come, dear," she said, beckoning Molly back to the changing room. "I have everything ready. Let's get you dressed."

Molly disappeared, leaving me to flick through the dresses once more, losing myself in fantasies of my own wedding day. My problem was picturing the groom. He didn't have a face yet and deep down, I was torn as to whose face I should imagine.

I nearly made my way around the whole shop before I heard Molly say, "Ta-dah!"

I turned around, my jaw dropping and my entire body filling with a heady mix of shock and rage. Molly twirled around in front of me in the very same dress I had tried on and fell in love with.

"What do you think?" she asked, her green eyes gleaming with joy.

"What the fuck, Molly?" I breathed, my chest starting to feel tight. I couldn't believe she would do this to me.

"What?" She shrugged her shoulders. "I told you to buy it before someone else does and you didn't." She twirled around again and said, "You snooze, you lose."

I could barely formulate a sentence other than, "When?"

"The next day after we first came. I was only joking when I said you were like a real-life model to try dresses on but then I realised we are a similar shape and if it looked good on you then it would look great on me."

Her words cut me to the core. Every single one of them was like a little barb of poison piercing my heart. How could she be so cruel?

"I'm out, Molly. I'm done," I said, heading for the door. "I'll find my own way home."

She stood still, her mouth wide open. "I beg your pardon?"

"You heard."

"Don't be such a diva, Kyra. The dress was never yours. Yes, it looked good on you, and you liked it, but you didn't like it enough to buy it, did you? So, what's the problem?"

"The problem is my so-called best friend buying something that she knew I loved but couldn't justify buying."

"And why is that my problem? If a Jane Doe from the street had come in and bought it, would you get mad with her?"

"No because I don't know her. She would have no idea how I felt about that dress."

"Surely it's better that you see it's gone to a good home?"

I waved my hand through the air at her. "I need some space, Molly. I'll call you when I'm ready to talk."

With that, I headed outside, already thinking of ways to get home. The obvious solution I really didn't want to take because it would mean a thirty-minute journey home with a lecture on how much of a shitty person Molly was.

Nonetheless, I called him anyway.

"Hello, little baby sister," Ash said, answering my call. "To what do I owe the pleasure?"

I sighed. "No questions, Ash, but can you come pick me up from town please?"

"Luckily for you I'm about ten minutes away so yes, I can. What's up?"

"I'll wait outside the Quayside car park entrance. I'll tell you when I see you."

I hung up before he had chance to interrogate me further and made my way towards the car park—a different car park to where Molly had parked her car.

Sure enough, ten minutes later, Ash rocked up, a stupid grin on his face. As soon as I opened the door, he started.

"Come on then. Details."

I sighed and indulged him in the latest developments, sulking like a little girl who'd lost her last sweet.

He chuckled at me. "Seriously, how many times do I have to tell you that I do not like that girl. There is always a reason why gay men don't like people, babes, take notice of me for once, hey?"

"Ash, she's my best friend."

"Really? Would a best friend really do that to you?"

I fell silent, realising I was fighting a losing battle.

"Look, I know it's not what you want to hear but I'm not going to sugar coat anything for you. There's no point."

"I know. Can we talk about something else now please? Tell me about house hunting with Ben."

Not fighting me, he did as I asked and told me of all the different houses and the astronomical prices of the houses he and Ben had been viewing in London. By the time we pulled up on my driveway, I felt marginally better. When I saw Scott's car, I felt one hundred percent better. The feeling of having someone wait for me at home lifted my spirits tenfold.

"You can fill me on this visitor later," Ash said, giving me a cheeky wink. "Are you going to be okay?" he asked.

"Aren't I always?"

I wandered into the house, feeling a mixture of elation at seeing Scott and also disappointed in Molly and what had just happened.

"Chris just called me," Scott said, coming out of the living room. "Are you ok?"

I nodded. "I just can't believe she'd be so selfish."

"I know," he said, stretching his arms out and wrapping me up in a big hug. "Why didn't you call me? I'd have come and fetched you."

"If Ash hadn't have been so close then I would have, but he was only ten minutes away."

"Ok," he said, pressing a kiss to the side of my head. "But next time you call me first, ok?"

I nodded and sighed, grateful I had such an amazing man to fall back on.

Chapter Thirty-One

THE NEXT THREE WEEKS were a blur. I didn't speak to Molly. The more I thought about what she'd done, the angrier I felt. I didn't want to speak with her until my anger had subsided and I could think clearly.

Scott started spending more and more time with me, more specifically at my house. He was tired of getting the Spanish Inquisition from Molly every time he went back to theirs regarding me and if I was ready to speak to her yet.

We still hadn't had sex as of yet. I was more than happy spending time with him, focusing on building our emotional connection before anything more physical happened. We had spent several nights naked in bed together, little more than hugging and kissing going on. Each night that passed with no sex only reassured me that he wanted me for more than sex and was as committed to this relationship going the right way as much as I was.

Tonight, though, I felt like I was ready for that to change. Taking things to the next level felt like the right thing to do to solidify our bond further and bring us closer together.

Molly and Chris had gone out for the afternoon, so Scott jumped at the opportunity to go back to theirs and fetch some clean clothes. When he came back, we decided to order pizza and indulge in some crappy TV.

Cuddled up on the sofa with him, watching Impractical Jokers and eating my body weight in pizza had me happier than a pig in mud. I briefly wondered why I hadn't ever wanted this before and instantly answered my own question—because I'd never had the right person to make me want it.

That dawning reality made me then question the depth of my feelings for Scott. Was I admitting that he was potentially the right one for me? If so, what did that mean exactly? Was I in love with him? Was it time to tell him?

I couldn't bring myself to think about that too much and potentially ruin the night for both of us. Thinking too deeply made me anxious and being anxious had done me no good up to this point in my life.

When Impractical Jokers finished at ten p.m., Scott suggested us going to bed and I readily agreed. We headed upstairs and stripped off before jumping into bed, snuggling up to each other.

My head resting on his shoulder as he laid on his back, I started drawing circles with my index finger all over his chest and then said, "Are you tired?"

He kissed the side of my head and said, "Not overly. Are you?"

"Definitely not," I said, turning my head to look up at him.

He glanced down at me and said, "I don't want to get things wrong and screw this up. Are you hinting at something?"

I giggled and nodded. "I think I'm ready."

My heart soared as I watched a broad grin sweep over his handsome face. "Are you sure?"

I bit my bottom lip and nodded. "Definitely."

He lifted a hand and touched the bottom of my chin with his index finger, tilting my face up slightly. "You've no idea how happy I am to hear that."

I grinned. "I bet."

He chuckled and moved onto his side, hovering over me with a pleasurable threat. "Just relax and let me love you." The sound of the dreaded 'L' word sent my heart rate through the roof. I don't know what my eyes said but he then said, "Don't worry. I'm not telling you I love you, I'm just saying let me make love to you."

A shy smile folded over my lips as I calmed down a little and succumbed to his words. He rolled me onto my back and told me to close my eyes. I did as I was told and shut my eyes, my whole body suddenly on alert as I awaited his touch.

He touched my stomach with his fingertips, gently drawing patterns over my skin as he made his way up to my breasts. Circling around my nipples but not quite touching them, he then trailed his hand back down to my hip bone, tracing a line right across my lower stomach.

Brushing his lips over mine, I laid my arms around his neck and kept him planted to my mouth as he slipped his tongue inside, gently lapping at my tongue with a slow, tantalising tease.

I could feel my core starting to heat up, flushing my body with heat as bundle after bundle of excited tingles built between my legs. He brought his hand back up my body, settling it in my cleavage as he deepened our kiss and entwined our tongues together.

Taking one of my hands from around his neck and running it down the length of his body, I reached out, needing to feel him and his desire for me. As I wrapped my hand around his erection, I let out a small moan of pleasure. He had such a girth my fingers could barely meet. I just knew he'd feel amazing inside me.

He moved his hand from between my cleavage and slid it over my left breast, letting the palm of his hand skim over my sensitive nipple. I gasped and shuddered from the unexpected touch but silently begged him to do it again.

Cupping my breast with his hand, he rolled his thumb around on my nipple sending potent throbs straight between legs. I began moving my hand up and down his length, eager to feel him and pleasure him as he was already doing me.

He broke our kiss after a couple of minutes and put his hand on mine. "Careful," he said. "It's been a while. I don't want to get too excited."

I smiled. "Ok, I understand."

He inched down the bed so I could no longer reach him, leaving me feeling a little frustrated that I couldn't return the favour to him at the moment. Kissing his way from my neck to my right breast, he gently took my nipple into his mouth, licking it with such a soft touch, I felt nothing except heat and excitement pooling between my legs.

As he continued teasing my left nipple with his thumb whilst caressing my right nipple with his tongue, I closed my eyes and allowed myself to fall back into heaven. I could feel my core tightening already and I knew if he carried on in this lazy, torturous rhythm I would find my release before he even touched me down there.

Minutes passed as he drove me to the point of insanity, to the edge of begging him to touch between my legs. When he finally moved his hand to my clit, I moaned with relief. He slipped a finger inside me, letting out a groan as he felt how excited I was.

He glided his finger back up to my clit, massaging me with a leisurely tempo as I edged closer to my sweet release. He flicked his tongue over my nipple with a little more pressure just as he picked up the pace massaging my clit. Within seconds I was gone, falling over my edge to float on cloud nine.

As I revelled in all the tension leaving my body and the fire in my core being dowsed slightly, he moved over the top of me and nestled between my legs.

Bumping our noses together, he looked at me with those chocolate brown eyes of his and said, "Can I?"

I nodded and smiled.

He positioned himself at my entrance and then pushed inside me at the same time he slid his tongue inside my mouth. We both moaned as he moved through me and as he reached his limit, he paused for a second. I could already feel him twitching inside me.

Keeping our tongues dancing together in a lingering embrace, he started moving his hips again, each stroke in and out hitting my G-spot. The more I focused on how amazing he felt, the more turned on I became and the closer my promise of a second orgasm.

I lifted my legs and curled them around his body, giving him deeper access. He shifted himself up slightly and carried on with his relaxed rhythm, reaching me at depths I'd only ever felt with one other person.

My core started tightening as his persistent, languid moves pushed me gently to my edge. As he started twitching inside me, I found my second release, breaking off our kiss to gasp for breath. Seconds later I felt him pulsing as he stilled and then gasped for his own air.

"Don't worry," he whispered, pressing a kiss to the side of my head. "I can do round two."

I smiled. "I'm already looking forward to that."

"Give me five minutes and I'll be good to go."

I couldn't help but grin like the cat who'd got the cream.

Waking the next morning with Scott next to me, after such an amazing night, felt absolutely out of this world. I knew instantly that I'd made the right call in making us both wait to be physically intimate, and it had been wholly worth it.

I felt closer to him this morning than I ever had, and I just knew that each time we had sex, it would reaffirm us as a couple and make us stronger.

Scott woke up and upon seeing me already awake, reached for me and pulled me into his arms. "Last night was incredible," he whispered. "I can't wait to do that all over again."

I kissed his chest and nodded in agreement. "Me neither."

"I'm hungry," he said. "Let's make breakfast."

We got up and headed downstairs, making bacon and egg rolls for breakfast. Just as we sat down and started eating them, Scott's phone rang. He gave a slight frown before dashing into the kitchen to grab it.

I heard him speaking in a quiet voice but couldn't really make out what he was saying. I knew he would tell me though when he came back.

"I'm really sorry," he said, coming back into the dining room a minute or so later. "But my dad has just called. He's just landed at Heathrow and wants to see me. I need to finish breakfast and go."

A swell of disappointment rose inside me, but I nodded and smiled. "Of course."

"I'll get some clean clothes whilst I'm out and come back around later. Is that ok?"

I grinned at him. "Did you even need to ask?"

We finished breakfast before Scott ran upstairs and made himself presentable. Giving me a quick peck on the lips before he ran out, I closed the door behind him and felt an empty space next to me already.

How weird was it that I was missing him already? I couldn't help but grin to myself as I headed upstairs for a shower that this was the beginning of me finally settling into a normal relationship and feeling all the things I should have been feeling before now. It just took the right person to bring it all out of me.

After my shower, I got myself dressed and set about cleaning the house. By lunchtime, everything was sparkling clean. I made myself a cheese and onion toasted sandwich and sat on the sofa, flicking through the TV channels mindlessly.

My phone beeped with a text and I grabbed at it eagerly, expecting to see Scott's name. When I picked my phone up and saw a notification from **Paul,** my heart somersaulted before leaping into a galloping rhythm inside my chest.

Paul: I meant what I said. X

I read those words over and over again, each time making my heart skip a beat. His words came back to haunt me all over again *I miss you...*, and I couldn't ignore the little tug at my heart whenever I thought about that phone call.

Regardless, I was with Scott now and I could not, and would not, jeopardise our relationship. The future I wanted was now finally here and nothing would make me let go of it. Not even that damn hot Greek sex God, Paul Connors.

I sucked in a deep breath and decided to reply.

Me: And you also meant what you said when you reconfirmed the status of our 'arrangement' repeatedly.

He replied instantly.

Paul: I had to. You have no idea how much I didn't want to. X

Me: What on earth is that supposed to mean?

I stared at my phone waiting for a reply, but nothing came. My light mood now darkened, I decided my answer to that was junk food. Raiding my kitchen cupboards, I found a half-eaten pack of peanuts, a packet of unopened Jaffa Cakes, and a share bag of cheesy Doritos.

Pouring myself an afternoon glass of wine, I sat back down on the sofa and stuffed myself silly. My phone didn't beep anymore, and I wondered what he was now thinking.

Twenty minutes later, as I peeled myself off the sofa to refill my glass of wine, a knock on the door scared the life out of me, making me jump. I was expecting no visitors today.

My stomach churned as thoughts of who it could be all pointed to one answer. My heart rate trebling, I walked to the door and opened it.

Sure enough, Paul stared back at me, his sapphire blue eyes tinged with a sadness I'd never seen before.

"Hi," he said. He flicked his eyes to my empty wine glass and then said, "Bad day?"

I snorted. "It is now."

"Don't be like that, Ky."

I glared at him. "What do you want?"

"I wanted to see you."

I snorted. "Didn't your mum teach you I want never gets?"

"Kyra—"

"No." My voice came out a little louder than I expected. "Don't 'Kyra' me. You treated me like a piece of shit on the bottom of your shoe before pissing off for three weeks without a single word."

"I called and said I missed you."

"And that's supposed to make up for it, is it?"

He sighed. "I know it doesn't. I just...I'm sorry. For everything."

"No, you're not."

"I am."

"Prove it."

He frowned. "How do you expect me to prove it? I wouldn't be here if I wasn't bothered, would I? I would have waited until Monday to see you otherwise. My plane landed three hours ago, and I came straight here."

I could feel my heart melting at being so near to him again, but this was not the time to be letting my heart rule my head. My heart is what got me into this mess in the first place.

My mind decided to betray me at that point, serving me with memories of his arms wrapped around me and his lips grazing over my skin. I couldn't help the shiver that ran down my spine. How could he affect me so much?

I pushed the thoughts away and said, "Ah, I see. You thought you'd come apologise and I'd hump your brains out in some idealistic view of make-up sex."

He shook his head. "Not at all. My life isn't black and white and simple. I need to explain a few things to you."

"For what reason? What are you going to gain from doing so?"

He hesitated before he replied, "I just thought if you understood a few things, our situation might be different."

"Different how? You finished this. Deal with it. You made your bed now go lie in it."

"Can I come in?" he said, his brilliant blue eyes imploring me to agree.

"Why?"

"So we can talk."

I shook my head. "No, it's not a good idea."

"Why not?"

I took a deep breath and then said, "Because I'm with Scott now."

Shock spread across his handsome face like wildfire. His eyes clouded over with confusion. "Since when?"

"Since you left."

"Oh." He took a step back, his voice barely audible. "Have you...?"

I raised an eyebrow. "I don't see how that's any of your business."

He nodded, staring down at his shoes. He glanced up at me, a slight glisten hazing over his eyes. "I think I should go."

I nodded, my own tears threatening to spill.

He walked back to his car, shoulders sagging and head down. I couldn't help that a little piece of me went with him.

Chapter Thirty-Two

M Y DAY ONLY PROCEEDED to go downhill from that point when later in the afternoon Scott called me and explained that he was joining his dad for a business dinner this evening and would be staying with him at his hotel in Birmingham. He likely wouldn't be back until tomorrow afternoon.

I didn't fuss or complain and instead exhausted Netflix for the evening. When I woke up Sunday morning, I found myself thinking about Molly and perhaps it was time to clear the air.

Picking up my phone, I sent her a quick text that literally said I was ready to talk. Minutes later, as I expected, she called me.

"Can I come over?" she asked, putting on her whiny voice.

"Sure," I said. "See you when you get here."

I threw some clothes on and trudged downstairs, trying to ignore how empty the house felt without Scott here. I had gotten so used to him being around I had all but forgotten what it felt like to live alone.

Making myself some toast and a cup of tea, I sat in the dining room and waited for Molly to arrive. Within an hour, I heard a car on the driveway and prayed to God it was her and not Paul again.

As soon as I heard the front door open, I knew it was her. Paul wouldn't dream of letting himself in, especially not after yesterday.

"Ky?" she called out.

"In here," I said, sipping at my cup of tea.

She walked in, her eyes full of sadness like a lost little puppy. "I've missed you," she said.

I flickered my eyes to the chair opposite me, indicating for her to sit down.

She pulled out the chair and sat down, clasping her hands together in front of her. "I'm really sorry for what happened in the dress shop. I was completely out of order."

I nodded. "Yes, you were."

"I'm sorry, Ky, I never meant to hurt you. I just saw how amazing you looked in it and I wanted to look like that. Does that make me so bad?"

I sighed and shook my head. "No, Molls, it makes you human. But you should have spoken to me about it beforehand, not just sprung it on me like you did. If you'd sat me down and said you really liked the dress, would I mind if you tried it on, I'd have been totally cool with that, you know I would."

She nodded, tears brimming in her green eyes. "I know, I'm sorry. I messed up. What else can I say?"

I shrugged my shoulders. "Nothing else to say, really."

"Well," she said, grinning. "If you still want the dress for your wedding, I'll give it to you for nothing."

I smirked. "Don't push it. Maybe we can joke about it in ten years."

Laughing, she said, "Ok, ok. What are you doing today?"

I shrugged my shoulders. "Nothing much. I'm waiting for Scott to tell me when he's coming back."

She frowned. "He hasn't called you yet?"

I frowned back at her. "Not today, no. Why? Has he you?"

She cleared her throat and said, "He spoke to Chris when you texted me. Chris is going over to Birmingham today. Apparently, these new clients of Scott's dad's are looking for help with their internal systems or something. I don't understand the technicalities of it."

My heart dropped a little. I realised then that our ritual good morning and good night texts had stopped. In one way, it was a good sign that our relationship was moving forwards, but it also made me feel sad that we were missing those elements that drew us together so much in the very beginning.

"Oh," I said, trying not to show my disappointment. "I guess he won't be back tonight either then."

Molly shook her head. "I don't think either of them will be."

"Lunch date then?"

She nodded. "For sure. And some retail therapy. But first, you need to tell me all about your hot sex."

I narrowed my eyes at her. "How do you know we had sex?"

She grinned. "He told Chris. He was so happy about it. Chris said that Scott now feels like you completely trust him, and he feels so great knowing that."

I couldn't help but smile as I realised that his analysis of it was one hundred percent correct. "He's right. I do."

"Put some proper clothes on then and we can head into town. You can tell me all about it on the way," she said, giving me a wink.

I headed upstairs, smiling to myself and feeling rather relieved that I'd managed to fix things with my best friend. Everything seemed to be falling into place.

Scott didn't come back Sunday night, just as Molly predicted. We spoke around four p.m. and he explained everything to me, along with many apologies. He said he would be back Monday evening, for sure.

Having had a busy day with Molly, I was more than pleased to have the bed to myself to stretch out in and get a good nights sleep with no smoking hot body distracting me.

Monday morning, I awoke to a text from Molly saying she was off sick today. She suspected the chicken curry she ate for lunch yesterday. Thankful I'd had nothing more adventurous than an onion bhaji and a salad, I got up and readied myself for another day in the office.

I arrived in the office before the directors, as per usual. Ten minutes later, Paul breezed in, my heart backflipping at the mere sight of him again. When would my body stop reacting to him like this? It was distracting at best and made me question everything at worst.

Flashing me a dazzling smile, he stood in his open doorway and said, "Have you got a few minutes please?"

My heart started pounding against my ribs as my mind raced with possibilities of what he might want. Would he try and kiss me? What did he want to say?

Thankfully, he retreated straight to his desk, perching himself on the end of it. My anxiety lessened a little now I knew he wasn't going to try anything physical.

"Hi," he said. He looked at ease, the usual cool, calm, and collected man I'd first been so taken with.

I smiled back but said nothing as I took a seat in the chair in front of his desk.

He scratched his head, as he looked at the floor. A minute or so passed before he said, "How are you?"

"Fine, thanks. What do you want?"

"I wanted to explain my behaviour to you."

I glanced away. "I don't want to hear it."

"Please, Kyra. Just listen."

I sighed, clicking my tongue as I crossed my arms over my chest. I stared at my shoes, noticing the little scuffs on the sides. I'd have to get some boot polish on them to cover them up. After a minute's silence, I glanced up at him. "Are you getting on with it or what?"

He cleared his throat, pursing his lips before speaking. "On the Monday evening when I left here, before I...cut things off between us, I received a phone call."

I nodded, remembering that night. He had marched out of the office with an ashen face and his phone stuck to his ear.

"Well, the purpose for that phone call was my father telling me there was someone of importance waiting to see me at the house." He faltered before starting his next sentence. "The person who was waiting for me is a good friend of my father's, and also happens to be in the club."

I raised my eyebrows, my mouth running dry at the thought of where this was going.

"My father called in a favour from him many years ago, for me. As a result, he insists I meet this man every time he comes over to show my gratitude to him."

Taking slight relief in the fact he said this was a man, I let out my breath, not realising I'd been holding it until now. I swallowed the lump that had formed in my throat as he continued.

"This man, Mr. Peters, has a wife."

My heart rate spiked in an instant. A ball of nausea began brewing in my stomach. I closed my eyes, as tears sprung up from nowhere. "Please, stop. I get the picture."

"Just listen." He paused, taking a sip of water. I dared to open my eyes, watching his face crease into sadness as he spoke. "Mrs. Peters has quite a liking for me and when she comes over, she requests my...presence."

I opened my mouth to speak but instead found myself choking back a sob, realising this was going where I thought it was.

"Mrs. Peters requested me on Monday evening when she arrived at the house—"

I stood up, my hands shaking, and turned towards the door. "I don't need to hear this."

He stood up with me, and moved around me, blocking my path to the door. "But I refused."

A wave of relief hit me. I sat back down, forcing myself to listen to the rest.

"My father was not amused in the slightest, nor were Mr. and Mrs. Peters. After much arguing, Mr. Peters announced unless I did as his wife wished, he would find a way to...undo what he'd helped me with years ago."

My jaw dropped open. His statement left me speechless. The ball of nausea returned to my stomach, only ten times more potent. The tears in my eyes threatened to spill overboard.

"So I had to...go ahead with their wishes."

I cringed, squeezing my eyes shut in an attempt to force unwanted images out of my mind.

"My father knew why I refused Mrs. Peters and was livid. I had no choice but to do what I did to you. My hands were tied from all sides. I did what I thought was best for you."

I let out a long breath, my mind reeling from this information overload. I didn't know what to say or do.

He bent down, placing his hands on my arms. I flicked my eyes to his, getting lost in his beautiful sapphire eyes once again. Now I understood why he had been such an arsehole to me and I couldn't be more grateful that he'd had the decency to end things instead of carrying on sleeping with me after that.

"I'm sorry, Kyra." He lifted a hand to my chin and tilted my face up to meet his. "I couldn't...be with you after I'd had to do that. I spent two days convincing myself I was doing the right thing. The only way I could make it happen was to be cruel to you. I'm so sorry."

Hot tears slid down my cheek as everything that had happened between us replayed over and over in my mind.

"But that's what you do," I said, my voice sounding weak and pathetic. "You go with other people and all of that. I don't understand."

He gave me a wry smile. "Don't you remember Tessa?"

I blushed as I let out a half sob, half laugh, nodding.

"Didn't you wonder why I didn't touch her?"

I thought about the situation again and shook my head. Then I remembered Tessa's last words to me "*Well, let's just say that's the first ménage a trois I've had where the guy makes his singular interest rather clear.*"

"Because I didn't want to touch anyone else." He moved his hands to my knees, my skin heating to new degrees under his touch. "I may have said I don't do relationships, but that was one to me. I wasn't having sex with anyone else. That was my commitment—I just didn't want to admit it."

My tears sprung free as I attempted a nervous laugh. "What kind of fucked up relationship is that?"

He gave me a cheeky smile and wiped my tears away. "I've not had a relationship for a long time, I've told you that before. Give me a break, it's been a while."

I smiled, finding myself silently begging for him to wrap me up in his arms. Why hadn't he just told me this before? So much heartache, and for what?

"So what's the deal with this Mr. Peters? What did he do?" I asked.

His smile faded as he raked a hand through his hair. "Mr. Peters is a judge."

"What? Why would you need a favour from a judge?"

He drew in a deep breath. "Remember my ex I told you about? The one who cheated on me?"

I nodded, dread filtering through me at what was going to be said next.

"Well, I caught her in bed with my best friend. To cut a long story short, I chased them across a road whereby they were hit by an oncoming lorry. I was up for manslaughter. Mr. Peters made it all go away."

My head spinning in a million different directions, I fell against the sturdy back of the chair as I listened to the confession of my boss, my ex-lover, being a killer.

Chapter Thirty-Three

PAUL'S ENTIRE CONFESSION OF the events that occurred that day left my mind boggling at his parents' ridiculous logic. The exact details turned out to be rather tragic.

Cassie, his ex, had been his first love, hence his strong emotions of finding her with his best friend, Daniel.

After running down the street away from Paul, Daniel had turned around to talk to him as they reached the road end. The talk hadn't gone well, which had resulted in Paul punching Daniel in the face. His sudden hit sent Daniel sprawling back into the road where Cassie ran after him. Unfortunately, in this moment, a lorry came over the slight hill they were on. The driver had no time to brake, his fully loaded truck obliterating both of them in an instant.

Nightmares haunted him for years, along with the phantom feeling of their matter splattering onto his face as he could do nothing but watch in horror. His parents felt it was jealousy issues that had been the primary cause of the situation. As such, they then demanded he join their lifestyle. Wracked with guilt, he could do nothing but follow their wishes after they made the entire situation disappear.

As the years passed him by, seeing married couples sharing each other with strangers had left him with little doubt it wasn't a lifestyle he wanted for himself and a partner. Therefore, he'd kept himself single with the firm belief his jealousy issues were too deep to even start a relationship. The psychological damage his parents had unwittingly caused was unreal.

I glanced into his captivating eyes, my heart melting already. "So, what are you saying?"

"I can't not have you in my life." My heart soared like a helium balloon being left to float sky high. Why hadn't we had this conversation weeks ago? "But I can't offer you what you want."

My balloon popped, reality hitting me once again. "Ok."

"I can't give you what you want from a relationship, Kyra. It's so complicated with my parents...and over my dead body would I let you become a part of that club. I can just about deal with you being with one guy but not—"

"I get it."

He traced a finger down my cheek, sending shivers through me. "You have no idea how badly I want you."

Before I knew it, he pressed his lips to mine with such tenderness, my heart physically ached. Tears fell from my eyes and as I thought of Scott and lifted my hand to push Paul away, he pulled back and said, "Can you promise me something?"

"What?"

"Please don't make that one guy Scott."

My jaw dropped. "What?"

Paul shook his head. "He's not right for you. You deserve someone good and decent. If I can't make you happy, then I want to see you with someone who can make you happy. Someone who deserves you and appreciates how special you are."

Anger boiled inside me in an instant. "I beg your pardon? So you tell me you want me but can't give me what I want. Then you demand I don't be with a guy who can give me what I want and does actually make me happy?"

"Sorry. I just...I don't like him."

"Well, I do." I stood up so quickly the chair fell to the floor behind me. "He's charming, kind, gentle, and considerate. He makes me laugh and looks after me. And he wants a future and isn't scared of commitment."

"Oh."

"Yes. Oh."

He reached out and touched my arm. "Does he make you feel raw passion though? Does he make your temperature rise from just a touch?"

My breath hitched in my throat as my skin sizzled from his touch. Scott was hot and we had amazing sex, but it wasn't full of the raw animal hunger me and Paul had shared but maybe that was because we had an emotional connection that ran so much deeper than that.

"Does he turn you on like I did?"

I swallowed the lump in my throat. "That has nothing to do with you." I broke away from his touch, backing away from him and all of the memories trying to flood my mind. "He's the complete opposite of you and I think that's a good thing."

"Ok. Whatever makes you happy."

"I need to go," I said, standing up and forcing him away from me.

He nodded. "Just remember I'm always here for you if you need something."

I didn't acknowledge his words as I walked out of his office and back to my desk.

Weeks later, little had changed from that point. We were civil to one another and kept our relationship strictly professional. He didn't text or call after hours, and I finally felt happy and settled that things were done between us.

Perhaps if we'd had this conversation before I met Scott, things could have been different, but we didn't, so things were as they were and that was the end of it.

My relationship with Scott had developed to the point that we were seeing each other most nights and talking about trips away next year. We were planning to go to Scotland as our first trip and I couldn't be more excited.

Today, however, was Molly's wedding day. All day I'd done nothing but be the good bridesmaid and do exactly what she wanted, when she wanted. Seeing her in my dress still caused a pang of hurt in my heart, but she looked beautiful, and she'd had the perfect day she wanted so far.

Now her and Chris were having their first dance to Savage Garden's 'Truly Madly Deeply', I was free from my bridesmaid duties to enjoy the day how I wanted. Or rather, night.

Sat with Scott at the head table, he touched my arm and pressed a kiss to my cheek. "How do you feel about stepping this up a notch?"

"Stepping what up?"

"Us," he said, giving me a brilliant smile.

"Ok...what did you have in mind?"

He grabbed my hand and gave me a reassuring squeeze. "How do you feel about living together?"

My heart began racing like a herd of wild horses. Then, as I thought about things, I couldn't help but smile. "I suppose really you are all but living at mine anyway. You're with me most nights, most of your stuff is there, I even do your washing," I said, laughing. "Sure, if you want to be an official label on it, let's do it."

He grinned and leaned over, giving me a proper kiss. "I'm so glad I met you."

"Me too," I said. "You are the best thing that's ever happened to me."

He nodded and bumped our noses together. "You know I'm falling for you?"

A lump formed in my throat as I stared into his chocolate eyes and nodded. "I know...and I think I am you."

A surreal fog enveloped my mind as the reality of our conversation sunk in. Not only had I agreed to make it official that we were living together, I'd nearly said the dreaded 'L' word and admitted my feelings for him.

As our lips met to seal the deal, I couldn't believe I was one step closer to my happy ending.

Chapter Thirty-Four

MOLLY AND CHRIS HAD a glorious honeymoon booked in the Seychelles for four weeks. Whilst they were away, Scott moved the remainder of his stuff into mine. With his PT business picking up as well as dabbling into new ventures with his dad, I didn't really see him much more than before, so nothing really changed.

In one way I was relieved we weren't clinging to each other twenty-four seven, but in another way, I often sat at home thinking I should surely see more of someone I lived with than this.

At work, mine and Paul's relationship hadn't changed. The Monday after the wedding, I had been so excited about Scott moving in with me that I'd told Paul, hoping he'd be happy for me.

He frowned and sighed, then said, "He really isn't the one for you, Ky."

My elation popped in an instant. "Why can't you just be happy for me? You didn't want me but quite clearly you don't want anyone else to have me either." I folded my arms over my chest and then said, "The next step from here is that you kill me. Do I need to be worried?" I asked, with a smirk.

He rolled his eyes. "I'm not playing games, Kyra. The man is bad news. Will you just trust me on that?"

"Tell me how you know he's bad news."

He ran a hand through his hair and sighed. "I...I can't. You just need to trust me. You need to end it with him and move on."

I shrugged my shoulders. "I'm sorry but unless I see undeniable proof, I'm staying with him."

"He's cheating on you, Kyra." The second the words left his mouth he came towards me with his hands reached out. "I'm sorry. I shouldn't have said that."

I shook my head, trembling with shock and fury. "Wow. Even that is a new low for you. What is wrong with you? You told me you couldn't give me what I wanted, and now I'm with someone else, you're trying to do everything you can to screw it up. It's your fault this mess is like this. Deal with it."

"I'm sorry, Ky. Please forgive me."

I snorted. "I think we just need to not share anything of our personal lives. You're my boss, I'm you're employee. That's it. Nothing more."

"Ok," he said. "Whatever you need to do, I won't argue."

I buried myself in my work and pushed all thoughts of Paul and what he'd just said to the back of my mind. I refused to even indulge Paul's accusation and investigate. I knew for a fact Scott wasn't and wouldn't cheat on me. For one, he was far too busy getting his business going, and for two, he was far too attentive to me when we were together for his mind and affections to be shared elsewhere.

Later that night, I made the mistake of telling him what Paul accused him of. He was livid. He seethed to himself quietly for the rest of the night, leaving me regretting mentioning anything to him. We went to bed in silence. I knew he'd be upset but I hadn't quite expected an extreme reaction like this.

As I sat at my desk the next morning, Scott burst through my office door. "Where is he?" His voice came out in a low growl, fury creasing over his face.

Panic swamped me in a split second. "What are you doing?"

The last thing I needed was Scott shouting at my boss and finding out we used to be involved. I hadn't ever told Scott that my emotionally unavailable ex was my boss. I didn't think that was a piece of information he needed to know.

"He is here." Paul said, standing in his open doorway. "I know why you're here. Shall we?"

Scott marched towards his open door with a thunderous look on his face.

I glared at Paul. "Are you crazy?"

He gave me a look of sorrow before closing the door, leaving me biting my nails for the next twenty minutes.

Scott finally emerged with a relieved look on his face. He gave me a peck on the cheek before saying his goodbyes.

"Don't panic," Paul said, walking over to me when the door closed behind Scott. "He doesn't know anything about us."

"What happened? What took so long?"

"We talked through some things." He shrugged his shoulders. "All sorted now. No worries." He gave me a warm smile before disappearing back inside his cocoon.

I didn't question him any further, figuring I would get the rest from Scott. However, when I questioned Scott later that night, he repeated almost word for word what Paul told me earlier. I felt uneasy but breathed a sigh of relief that the two of them smoothed out their issues.

After that day, Paul never mentioned another word about Scott. I couldn't say I wasn't intrigued as to why, but I also respected that he was respecting my wishes and keeping out of things.

Day to day life ambled on for the next couple of weeks until the works Christmas party, the week before Christmas. It also coincided with being the anniversary dinner for twenty-five years of the company, so it was a pretty big event.

I organised most of the event along with Paul and the other directors and I already had my perfect dress in mind that I couldn't wait to wear.

The hotel we'd booked for the party and for people to stay in after was rather swanky to say the least. Being a Hilton hotel down in London, the rooms weren't the cheapest, nor the food and drinks, but all the directors agreed on a big 'splash out' to treat all the staff.

Booking thirty-five rooms, arranging seventy meals, music, decorations, and the bar tab took a lot of juggling given the three-week deadline I'd been given at the end of November. Somehow, a miracle happened and we managed to pull it off. A few phone calls from the directors pulling in favours helped as well.

I was privileged enough to get the Friday before the main event off work and an extra paid for night in the hotel, with Scott by my side of course. Saturday morning I ran around the events hall in the hotel like a headless chicken making a few last minute alterations to the decorations and making sure everything was perfect.

Starting at seven p.m., I had to make sure I was in the room by six thirty at the latest. Myself and the directors all wanted to be there first to greet all of the staff. At six fifteen, I slipped into my peach and white lace dress, revelling in my reflection as it clung to me like a second skin. Sitting just off my shoulders and trailing down to my ankles, it was almost as beautiful as my wedding dress.

Almost.

Finishing the outfit off with a pair of nude high heels, I then fluffed my curls and attacked them with hairspray, turning around in the mirror to see my back and how they tumbled down past my waist. Even I would admit I looked good.

"You look stunning," Scott said, wrapping his arm around my middle. He nuzzled his face into my neck and took a deep breath. "You smell as gorgeous as you look too."

"Thank you," I said, kissing the side of his head. "You look really handsome in your suit."

He took a step back and looked down at himself in his tux. "Been a while since I wore one of these. And I definitely didn't have a beautiful woman on my arm last time."

I giggled. "Come on, let's go."

We headed to the lift, arm in arm, and took the quick ride downstairs. Wandering into the main room minutes later, my eyes immediately fell on Paul who stood at the far end of the room talking to the DJ.

He looked incredible. Dressed in a black suit with a crisp white shirt underneath, the top two buttons undone to reveal the top of his chest, I couldn't help but stare. He carried off the casual sexy vibe to perfection. I knew what he was hiding under that shirt and my traitorous mind decided to give me a visual memory of him shirtless in my bed.

Shaking the image from my mind, I focused on the man holding my hand and let him lead me to our table. We were sharing a table with Molly, Chris, Kelly and another admin girl.

By seven thirty, everyone was in the room and seated, eagerly awaiting their food and drinks. The waiters and waitresses soon bustled about the tables, filling people's glasses and serving the delicious food.

Good music and good conversation accompanied us through our meal and by nine p.m., all the food had been eaten and everyone was halfway drunk. At nine fifteen, the music stopped briefly so that Paul and Mr. Collins could give their Christmas speech and their anniversary speech, as well as remind everyone of Paul's new status of majority shareholder.

Ten minutes later and everything done, the music returned, and everyone crowded to the dance floor. Just as I grabbed Scott's hand to go dance, his phone rang.

"It's my Dad," he said, looking at the display. "I need to take this."

"Ok," I said, kissing his cheek. "I'll be waiting."

He chuckled as he headed outside the room to take his call.

I sidled over to sit next to Molly whilst I waited for Scott to come back. Chris had also gone for a loo break.

"Hold that thought," she said. "I'll be back in a minute. I'm going to wee myself."

She dashed off to the toilet, leaving me wondering if her and Chris were going to have a quick rendezvous in the toilet. Nothing would surprise me with Molly.

"Care to dance?"

A shiver ran down my spine as Paul's familiar voice surrounded me. I looked up, my breath hitching in my throat when I saw his sapphire eyes gleaming back at me.

I blushed and nodded. After everything we'd both been through, it would have been rude not to.

Holding his hand out for me to take, I put my hand in his and stood up, trying to ignore the fire igniting in my body the instant we touched skin to skin again. My heart pounding and doing the occasional somersault, I let him lead me to the dance floor just as the tempo of the music switched to something more soft and mellow.

Curling his arms around my waist, he pulled me into him, making my head and my heart fight with each other once more. I couldn't help an idealistic fantasy slip into my mind that we were here tonight as a couple and that I would be going to bed with him tonight.

Within a minute though, reality hit home, and the thought evaporated like a mirage in a desert. That scenario would never happen because of his past. Everyone had 'the one who got away' and Paul would always be mine. I just needed to finally accept that and stop these ridiculous fantasies from arising, no matter how infrequent they were.

Leaning into me, he pressed his face to the side of my head, his lips tickling my ear as he whispered, "You look beautiful tonight."

I blushed and whispered, "Thank you."

"I mean it," he said. "You look sensational."

Tingles ran through my whole body sending goosebumps all over me. My memories of us flooded me and for just a minute, I couldn't help myself.

"That could have been you sat next to me tonight," I whispered back.

"You don't know how much I would have loved that," he replied, holding me closer to him.

"I shouldn't say this...but I miss you."

He nuzzled into my hair and breathed, "Kyra..."

"I'm sorry. That's it, I'm done. I won't cross the line again. I've said what I've wanted to say."

He pulled his head back and looked at me, sadness swimming through his eyes. "I wasn't complaining. I miss you, too."

Tears pricked at my eyes and I had to close them to stop them from escaping. How did he have such an effect on my emotions? Especially after so long apart?

"Do you love him?" he asked

I opened my eyes to see him watching me, waiting for my answer. My stomach turned over. "I think so."

"If you think so, then you don't. You will know love when you find it."

My heart jumped up and down like a mad man as my mind shouted, *It's you! It's you!*

He twirled us around in time to the music, really sweeping me off my feet, and in true to me style, I tripped over my own feet and nearly fell flat on my face. Paul caught me just before I hit the floor and as I looked up into his eyes, one singular thought ran through my mind, *If only you'd been there to catch me when I fell for you.*

As I realised I was indulging myself in romantic fantasies that were totally inappropriate considering I was attending this event with my boyfriend, I decided it was time to go.

"I need to go," I said, pulling away from him, even though it pained me to do so.

"You ok?"

I nodded and took my shoes off, thinking fast for an excuse. "I think for the sake of my ankles I need to change these."

"Don't be silly," he said. "The floor is clean. Just go barefoot."

I gave him a withering glance as I tiptoed across the wooden floor towards the doors. I glanced back at my table to see no one had returned yet.

"Honestly," he said, chasing after me. "It'll be fine. There's no point in going up four floors just for a pair of shoes for a couple of hours."

I sighed. "I'm not attending a fancy anniversary dinner barefoot, Paul. I'll be back in a minute."

I made my way towards the lift, shaking my head at his ridiculous suggestion of going barefoot. Once in the lift, I fumbled my room key out of my bra as I waited to reach my floor. The metal floor inside the lift was cold on my feet, and I desperately wanted the warmth of the corridor carpet.

Finally, the doors sprung open, allowing me some respite as I savoured the feeling of the short, warm carpet underneath my feet. Room 408—on my right-hand side. I slid my shoes under my arm and pushed the key in the lock.

Swinging the door wide open and thinking over what had just happened with Paul, I stepped inside.

My brain didn't quite register what my eyes reported back, not for a few seconds anyway.

Then, a blood-curdling scream filled the air.

I collapsed on the floor at the sight in front of me—Molly and Scott naked on our bed.

Chapter Thirty-Five

THE SOLID WOODEN DOOR was my only support at this moment but even that failed to help me. My entire body turned to jelly, and I crumpled into a heap on the floor. I heaved for breath as I started to hyperventilate.

"Shit." Scott's voice floated around the outer edge of my consciousness, not really registering in this surreal haze.

It wasn't until his familiar hands wrapped around me that I snapped out of my swirling fog. "Get off me," I yelled, scrabbling backwards across the soft carpet and out into the corridor. I kicked my legs out at him, desperate to keep distance between us.

"Kyra, I'm so sorry. You were never meant to see this..."

I attempted to push myself to my feet, but my legs gave way. Huge, racking sobs grasped me as I tried to get some oxygen into my body, but the more I tried, the more I seemed to fail. I couldn't even manage basic functions. My entire being was consumed with the burning image of my best friend and my boyfriend, together.

Scott reached for my hand as I tried to stand again, but hysteria took over me and I screamed at him to stay away. My vision blurred as streams of tears poured from me, soaking into my chest. All I wanted to do was run from this twisted scene, but my body couldn't even grace me that reprieve. I felt completely and utterly helpless.

A shrill ping sounded through the air, silencing Scott's pleas with me. As I sat with a spinning mind, a pair of strong, muscled arms wrapped around me, lifting me into a much needed, comforting embrace.

The familiarity of Paul's warm chest only pushed more tears from me as the reality of my comfort, my rock, hit home. He nestled me into his shoulder, stroking my hair in a soothing rhythm.

He pressed his lips to the side of my head and whispered, "Everything will be ok. I promise." He kissed my hair and then my ear. "No one will hurt you now. I've got you."

From somewhere behind me, I heard Scott say, "Don't kiss my girlfriend," his tone low and full of warning.

Rage began to burn through me at his statement. I turned around, still leaning against Paul for support. "I'm not your fucking girlfriend. I think you effectively ended that the second you stuck your dick in her."

Molly appeared in the doorway, arrogance swarming all over her face. With the bedsheet draped over her naked body, she folded her arms over chest and said, "Oh, didn't you know, Scott? Kyra and Paul were at it for months before you arrived."

Paul glared at her, and then pulled rank. "You, young lady, are fired."

"Nice try, handsome. You can't fire me for personal reasons outside of work. I'll take you to the Union if you do."

"No, but I can fire you for gross misconduct. Namely using company property to send explicit emails to your lover here." Her smirk fell from her face like a stone dropping through water. "And I think I'll also be calculating all the time you took to write and send over three thousand emails." He gave her his own conceited smirk. "And I will be removing the equivalent pay from your last wage packet."

My own confident smile appeared as my knight in shining armour saved me in spectacular fashion. The fact he had known about this cut me in two. I couldn't really be mad at him because he'd tried to tell me, but I'd ignored him, refusing to believe it.

A quiet voice spoke through the piercing silence. "I see it's all blown up in your faces finally."

We all turned to see Chris stood at the entrance to the stairwell. I had no idea how long he'd been stood there or how much he'd heard.

Molly struggled for breath as she stammered, "You...knew?"

"Of course I knew. It's hard not to hear your fiancée's lovemaking noises in the middle of the night coming from the room next door."

Molly's face turned a new shade of red before tears started to fall.

"Don't," he said. "I know what you're like, Molls. I know I'm nothing compared to him." He gave Scott a glare of disgust. "I told myself it was just a fling. I was grateful when he moved out whilst we were on honeymoon. I thought that was the end of it. Evidently not."

I stepped forwards, Paul's grip loosening on me as I spoke to Chris. "You knew? And you didn't tell me? How could you?"

The betrayal from Chris hurt more than I thought it would. I would have expected him to be an ally of mine, not theirs.

"I didn't know how to tell you, Kyra. I'm sorry. When he moved in with you I thought that was him finally getting serious with someone. I figured there was no point in upsetting the apple cart now he was playing happy families. I didn't realise they were still going to be at it once we got back from honeymoon."

He gave the pair of them a menacing stare before throwing his wedding ring at Molly.

"Chris..." she said, her voice trembling as she ran towards him.

"Fuck off." He disappeared back down the stairs, the slam of the door signifying his feelings.

I turned to my best friend and my now ex-boyfriend, wanting answers. "How long has this been going on?" I asked, trying to control the quiver in my voice. "When did it start?"

Molly glanced down at the floor.

Scott squirmed and shuffled from foot to foot. "I don't think we should do this now."

I turned to Paul, scanning across his face. "You know everything. Tell me."

"Are you sure you want to hear this?" he asked, rubbing his hands up and down my arms.

I nodded. "I have you, right?"

His sapphire eyes filled with warmth as he nodded. "Always." He then glared at the two of them and said, "They were emailing from when Molly returned from Barbados engaged. It evolved from there."

A stab of pain shot through my heart. I stared at Scott, my voice barely audible. "Why? Why get involved with me in the first place?"

He licked his lips, glancing up at me before looking at the carpet. "It was her idea. She thought if I got with you, it would stop it between us. It didn't. It got worse because she got jealous."

The brazenness of his words ripped a new hole inside me. Then I remembered his words that day we'd gone for coffee. *Looks like I may as well just do it then.*

I gasped and I clutched at my chest. Tears began to form once again as I couldn't help but ask the inevitable. "Did you...in my house...in our bed...?"

Their silence was enough of an answer for me. Weakness and defeat swamped me once more. Scooping me up in his arms, Paul took me back to his room. I buried my head in his chest and cried myself to sleep.

I woke the next morning curled inside a pair of strong, familiar arms. The heavenly scent of Paul's aftershave combed over me. I glanced up to see his handsome face inches away from mine. For a brief second, I questioned why I was inside his embrace.

Then it hit me like a freight train.

I peeled myself from his arms, careful not to disturb his sleep. I wanted my stuff, and I wanted my phone to call my brother, but of course, all of that had been left in that room.

Taking a deep breath, I took the apprehensive walk down the corridor. As I approached the door, I realised I didn't have my key. I swore under my breath before noticing the idiots hadn't removed my key from the lock the previous night.

Taking the same path I had done only hours ago, I pushed the key in and opened the door. Seeing them both cuddled up against each other left puncture wounds in my heart so deep, I may as well have been bitten by a lion.

Scott was awake, and carefully slid out from Molly's sleeping form. He shuffled over to me, his face full of hope. "Hi..."

I dropped my eye contact, not even wanting to look at him. "I came for my stuff."

"I just want to explain myself. I do have feelings for you—"

"Are you kidding me?"

He reached out to touch me. "Ky..."

I batted his hand away. "Don't touch me."

Hurt flashed through those chocolate eyes I'd loved staring into not less than twenty-four hours ago. He took a step towards me and said, "I meant it when I said I was falling for you."

I stood my ground, ready to punch him square in the face if he took another step. "That's nice."

"But you said you were falling for me too."

I shrugged my shoulders. "Yeah. Thinking about it, I don't think I ever really loved you. I think I just loved the idea of what I thought you could give me. We had a good time, but thoughts of him were always there, no matter how hard I tried. You could never be him."

He stepped back, tears springing to his eyes. "You mean your ex? The emotionally unavailable one?"

"Yes," I said, not caring that my words were hurting him. He deserved it after he'd just shattered my heart. "My heart always belonged with him. You were just a welcome distraction because I couldn't have him."

He flickered his eyes, watching someone behind me. I turned around to see Paul stood in the doorway, still in last night's clothes, dishevelled hair and streaks from my mascara staining his pristine white shirt.

My heart jumped at the sight of him. I knew in that moment that it had always been him and it would always be him. I could distract myself with twenty hot guys all offering me everything—none of them would match up to my Greek sex God. Not one.

Paul closed the distance between us and cupped my cheek with his hand. "What are you doing?"

"I wanted my stuff."

He pressed a gentle kiss to my forehead and said, "Why didn't you wake me up? I'd have got it for you."

I gazed into his beautiful sapphire eyes, hypnotised already. I couldn't believe how much I'd missed them. "I didn't want to disturb you."

Scott spoke from behind me. "What the fuck is this? It's him, isn't it? What you were just talking about. He's the emotionally unavailable ex."

I turned to him, anger rising. "That's nothing to do with you."

"Have you been sleeping with him whilst we were together?"

I laughed, not quite believing he had the cheek to ask. "Are you seriously asking me that right now? No, Scott. I haven't slept with him since we've been together, but being brutally honest, it was hard to resist temptation."

A blank expression passed over him for a few seconds before he smirked. "Well, I guess you can now say you fulfilled the complete role of a PA."

Before I knew it, Paul flew from behind me, punching Scott square in the face, a sickening crunch filling the air. He crumpled to the floor, crying and holding his hands to his face.

Molly jumped up from the bed, screaming as she scrambled down to Scott. She yelled at Paul, fighting Scott's hands from his face to reveal streams of blood and a broken nose.

"I'm going to have you done for assault," she said, sobbing.

Paul chuckled. "Good luck with that one, sweetheart."

He stepped over the mess on the floor, grabbing my things from around the room from my instructions. I collected a few bits from the bathroom to my left, not even trying to hide my beaming smile at Scott's broken nose. Satisfying didn't even cut it. Karma came a bit closer.

I emerged from the bathroom, grinning at Molly's tear ridden face. "Have a nice life, Molly."

"Oh, I will do now I've wrecked yours."

"That's where you're wrong. You've made it better."

She stood up, her eyes glistening with a dreamy haze. "Don't you see? He chose me over you. For once I'm not in your shadow, watching everyone kiss your feet. This time it was me. Someone wanted me and not you."

I frowned, the reality of her words leaving me dumb founded. "What about Chris? He loved you, you bimbo."

"Pffft. He had no backbone. He was getting boring."

I raised my eyebrows, shaking my head in disbelief. "You really are a piece of work. Whatever. I'm done."

Paul took my hand, leading me from the room without so much as a second glance.

Chapter Thirty-Six

WHEN I ARRIVED BACK home on Sunday afternoon, I couldn't quite face the reality of being in my house, alone, with reminders of Scott everywhere.

"I'll stay with you tonight," Paul said, "But tomorrow I have to go to work."

I nodded. "Thank you."

"I don't want you on your own though. Will Ash come be with you?"

I rolled my eyes. "I'm not a toddler. I don't need a babysitter."

He grabbed me by my shoulders and looked me square in the eyes. "I care about you. I won't have you on your own. You're banned from work until you're mentally in a better place. Understand?"

I giggled. "Did you just ban me from my own job?"

"Yes," he said, smiling. "And I mean it."

Paul lifted my bag and hauled it upstairs. I followed him, only to wish I hadn't. Scott's clothes were still here and seeing the bed, knowing they had sex on it, made me feel sick.

"I can't sleep here," I said, my eyes brimming with tears. "I just can't."

"Ok, ok," he said, coming to me and ushering me out of the room. "We'll go to a hotel for tonight and tomorrow we'll sort something else out, ok?"

I nodded and let out a sigh of relief.

Right at that moment, my phone rang. Half expecting it to be either Molly or Scott, I was pleasantly surprised to see **Ash** flashing across the screen.

Paul took the phone from my hand and answered it. "Hi, Ash, it's Paul...yeah, long story. Any chance you guys are up this way? Kyra kinda needs some support...yeah, yeah, we're here now...ok, see you soon."

Handing my phone back to me, Paul said, "Ash is coming over. They're living back up this way in Ash's house at the moment. Maybe you can go stay with them tonight?"

I don't know why but his suggestion made me feel rejected. Like he didn't want to spend anymore time with me. Tears sprung up from nowhere and I glanced away, hoping he hadn't seen them.

"Hey," Paul said, taking my hand and pulling me into him. "I will still stay with you tonight, ok? I was just thinking you might appreciate your big brother around you as well. That's all."

A wave of relief washed over me. "Thank you."

Thirty minutes later, Ash and Ben arrived, Ash bounding through the door with a big grin on his face. The instant he saw me, his beaming smile dropped, and he rushed over to me.

"What's up? What's happened?" he said, shoving Paul out of the way and hugging me.

"Scott was cheating on me with Molly. The whole time."

He stepped back and held me at arm's length. "Are you kidding me right now?"

"Do I look like I'm kidding?"

"Dirty, good for nothing, fake boobed, shit tanned, Barbie looking whore," he said. He fished his car keys from his pocket and marched towards the door. "You wait until I get a hold of her."

Ben stood in the doorway, blocking Ash's path. "Don't be ridiculous. The instant you lay a finger on her she'll be screaming bloody murder and will have you done for assault."

Ash snorted. "She won't live long enough to report an assault. Move, Ben."

Paul stepped forward and grabbed Ash's arm. "Ben is talking sense and you know it. Knowing Molly she'll pay every copper in town in kind and have you locked up for breathing in the wrong direction at her. Be smart, not reactive."

Visibly vibrating with rage, Ash turned to Paul and said, "Fine. Then I'll bury him instead. He even had me fooled."

"No need," Paul said, grinning. "I broke his nose yesterday."

321

"Just his nose?" Ash grinned. "I was thinking more along the lines of breaking his back."

"Stop it," I said. "This isn't helping anyone. Can we please just get out of here?"

All three of them looked at me before agreeing to my demands.

Paul took my keys from me and locked the house before walking me to his car and helping me in the passenger seat. I said nothing the entire ride over to Ash's, immersing myself in my own thoughts and what to do from here. I didn't even want my house anymore and I loved my house.

Once we reached Ash's house, I announced I was taking a long bubble bath and going to bed. Not one of them dared to argue with me. After a two-hour long soak, I climbed out and headed into Ash's guest bedroom, collapsing on the fluffy purple duvet, still wrapped in my towel.

At some point during the night, I became aware of a familiar pair of arms pulling me into a warm chest, but the lull of a peaceful sleep pushed me back into darkness.

I woke the next morning feeling determined. Once Paul had left for work, I begged Ash to take me to my house, which, when he saw what I had in mind, he would regret.

As I opened the front door, the reality of them being in here hit me square in the face. How would I ever get over this? How could I ever trust anyone again? I rummaged around in the kitchen draw for my shed keys, grinning to myself before marching outside to my little wooden shed.

Taking the full can of petrol from inside and a box of matches from the windowsill, I placed them in the middle of the garden. I then bounded up the stairs, scooping up Scott's clothes before starting myself a lovely warm fire.

As the flames licked at his expensive clothes, an overwhelming sense of glee washed through me, fuelling me further. Ash sat on the bonnet of his car, arms crossed, saying nothing. I darted back inside, grabbing anything Scott related to feed the roaring blaze outside.

My next move startled Ash into action as he watched me shove one of my sofas out the door. "What the hell are you doing?"

"What does it look like? I'm getting rid of anything they might have had sex on. I don't know what I could catch."

He pursed his lips, glancing at me with concern when I brought the second sofa outside and took it to its fate. I rushed upstairs and ripped the mattress from the bed. The duvet and pillows were next to be thrown to their death along with the rest of my sheets. I didn't care they were clean; they'd probably still suffered seeing Scott and Molly like I had.

The more things I burned, the more images I saw of them doing it in my house. It drove me crazy, and I battled furiously to force the unbendable mattress down the stairs.

I threw it onto the unforgiving fire and collapsed on the ground with huge, racking sobs. The heat burned my face, but I didn't care. I wanted the fire to consume all the pain inside me as well as everything I'd fed it.

Ash dragged me away from the fire. "Pull yourself together. What are you going to do now you've burned all your furniture?"

I snapped out of my wallowing self-pity, looking at my brother with renewed inspiration. I wrenched his grip from my arm. "Burn everything else."

The curtains throughout the house were next. I was upstairs attempting to rip up my carpets when I heard a stomping up the stairs.

"Leave me alone, Ash. I know what I'm doing. If you're not going to support me, then just leave. I didn't ask you to stay."

"Get your shoes on."

That wasn't Ash. It was Paul.

I whirled round, feeling like a rabbit in headlights as I looked up at him. "What are you doing here?"

"Get your shoes on."

Seeing him dressed in his black trousers and baby blue shirt made my heart race. I graced myself a few seconds to drink in his delicious body. I loved that look on him.

"Why?"

He said nothing. Instead, he strode towards me, picked me up, and carried me downstairs. He set me down after I hit his chest for the twentieth time.

"Shoes," he said, pointing to my low-heeled boots.

"Fine."

I stalked outside to see Ash smirking and I narrowed my eyes at him.

Paul placed his hands on my shoulders. "Car."

"Where are we going?"

"Get in the car, Kyra."

"When you tell me where we are going."

He said nothing, merely wrapping his arms around my waist and carrying me to the car. Opening the door, he stuffed me in the passenger seat despite my protests.

"Paul, stop it. Where are we going?"

He ignored me, settling himself in the driver's seat, still silent. I continued to demand to know where we were going but he remained wordless, his face shadowed with a serious edge. I knew not to push him too far.

He drove us deep into the countryside, and I stared out the window, sulking like a petulant child. Watching the green fields roll by did little to calm the jumble of emotions furling around my body.

The car crunched along a gravel driveway, switching my attention forwards. Apprehension rose within me when I realised we were heading towards a magnificent stable yard. Post and rail fencing edged acres as far as the eye could see, dozens of horses grazing their way through the lush grass. Cross-country fences spanned over all the fields, which surrounded the fabulous yard itself.

The long driveway led us closer, my heart pounding as I watched a couple of riders in one of the several arenas I'd managed to count. What a place. If Scotch was still here, this would have been paradise to me.

As he parked the car, fear rose up my throat with a taste of bile. "What are we doing here?"

He exited the car, making his way round to open my door. "Come with me."

"Paul, I'm not messing about now." My voice became high pitched as my fear took control of me. "What the hell are we doing here?"

He looked at me, his eyes edged with determination. "I'm not messing about either. Now get out of the car."

Taking a couple of seconds to debate my options, I thought better of arguing. I licked my dry lips and tried to swallow the ball of fear in my throat. He took my hand and led me through the fantastically, spotless yard. It was like something from a magazine.

Taking me through a small alleyway between two stables, my eyes almost bulged from my head when I noticed yet another arena out here, Olympic sized and covered with soft, expensive rubber as a surface. This place had some money invested in it, and then some.

A young blonde girl stood in the middle of the arena holding a huge dapple-grey warmblood mare. I could tell from this distance that this horse had a hell of a pedigree. Her confirmation perfect, groomed to perfection, and the expensive tack on her back—she was no common cob bought for a riding school.

My eyes widened. "If you're suggesting what I think you are..."

He glared at me, shoving me through the wooden gate into the arena before dragging me over to the young girl.

"This is my sister, Rebecca."

My jaw dropped open as I stared at him. "You never told me you had a sister."

"I believe I just did."

Rebecca giggled and held out her small hand to me. "Hi."

I smiled, noting how her facial features were so similar to Paul's. Her green eyes danced with glee as her pretty face creased into a broad smile.

We swapped pleasantries before she turned her attention to the horse. "This is Eloise."

I cast my eyes over the mare once more, my eyebrows raising at her expensive Stubben tack and pure wool lined boots. "She's lovely."

I held a hand out to her, offering for her to sniff me. She cocked an ear in my direction but other than that, didn't acknowledge me at all. Her majestic arrogance told me all I needed to know about her personality.

Rebecca smiled. "Don't take it personally. She thinks she's too good for people."

I pursed my lips. "Ah." I pointed to the hat in her hands. "And I'm guessing I'm supposed to ride her?"

Her eyes flitted over to Paul before she nodded.

I shook my head. "I'm sorry, but no. I haven't ridden for five years. I actually had no plans to ride again either." I settled a hardened stare on Paul. "You knew that."

His eyes blank and his face holding an impassive stare, he simply said, "Get on the horse."

"No."

"Get on the horse, Kyra."

"No. You've been a complete ass to me since you barged your way into my house twenty minutes ago and practically kidnapped me. Stop ordering me around like a damn army sergeant."

Rebecca spluttered with laughter.

Paul's face darkened. "Get on the damn horse or so help me God I'll put you up there myself."

I folded my arms over my chest. "No."

"Last chance, Kyra. Get on the horse yourself and keep your dignity or I'll put you up there. Either way, you are getting on that horse, and you are getting on it now."

I scowled and threw him a swear word or two, making my feelings rather clear. He held the same look until I caved in a couple of minutes later.

I sighed. "Fine."

Ignoring the fluttering in my stomach and my trembling hands, I put the hat on. As Rebecca sorted the stirrups and girth, I wiped my sweaty palms on my jeans, silently cursing Paul.

He carried over a wooden mounting block, my knees not far off knocking together when I climbed it and stood at the side of the big mare. I took a deep breath before swinging into the saddle and sitting on my first horse in over five years.

Having already noticed her special bit and noseband, I looked down at Rebecca, more than apprehensive. "Anything I should know?"

"You don't scare easily, do you?"

I shook my head. "I used to event."

"You should be ok, then."

'Should be ok'? What the hell did that mean?

Throwing one last dirty look at Paul, I pushed the mare forwards into a walk. She eased forwards with her ears pricked. We made our way around the outside of the arena, and I began to relax. Memories of Scotch began to replay, ushering me back into my quiet confidence, and even pushing a smile from me.

Asking Eloise forwards into a trot, I began finding my old rhythm, my body going into autopilot. Just as my nerves finally eased, I suddenly found myself hurtling at an insane speed towards the gate.

Before I could do anything, a massive buck threw me through the air, splattering me on the ground at Paul's feet.

Chapter Thirty-Seven

P AUL AMBLED OVER TO me, helping me to my feet.
"Are you ok?"

"Ok? I just got thrown from an apparent Lilith of
horses, and you're asking if I'm ok?" I brushed the dirt
from my jeans, trying to ignore the throbbing coursing
through my body. "I actually hurt all over if you must
know."

He tweaked his lips up into a victorious smirk. "So,
what are you going to do?"

The penny dropped and I realised what the whole
point of this was. A mixture of anger and irritation
began bubbling as I stared at the handsome, intelligent
man before me.

"I'm sure you could have taught me this lesson in a
much nicer way."

He shrugged his shoulders and grinned. "But this was more literal. And from where I'm standing, more entertaining."

I narrowed my eyes at him as Rebecca offered me a short whip. "I don't like using them."

She pushed it into my hand. "You will need it. Don't be afraid to use it."

I chewed my lip and remounted the awkward mare. Thinking over my options as I walked her around the edge of the arena, she strolled along like butter wouldn't melt. Curving her round onto a wide circle, I pushed her forwards into a trot, more than ready for her little trick. When the gate appeared in view, she tensed, resulting in a tap on the shoulder from me. She squealed, shaking her head from side to side as she tried to break the circle.

I sat deep in the saddle, preparing myself for whatever she may throw at me. We fought for nearly twenty minutes as she snatched at the bit, crabbed all over, and tried dropping her shoulder several times. Every time she misbehaved, she received a tap on the shoulder and was made to work on a smaller, tighter circle. When she did as I asked, the circle became wider and easier for her.

She finally gave in with a massive sigh, dropping her head and working into a beautiful outline like a pro. For the next half an hour, I had the ride of my life as I played with her, pressing her finely tuned buttons and seeing what she could do.

I rode back over to Rebecca and Paul, grinning like a Cheshire cat—I couldn't have been happier.

"Wow." I slid down from the saddle, my legs shaking. "What a horse."

Rebecca smiled, taking the reins from me. "She's a tricky little mare. She broke her owner's back."

I glared at Paul. "And you knew that?"

Rebecca stepped in, explaining the mare's history to me. It sounded mostly her owner's fault, and with her eventing career on hold whilst he recovered, Eloise needed exercising, but she always threw people off.

"She needs to be ridden and competed. She lives for it. She wants it, needs it. Now you've cracked her, she'll be like putty in your hands."

I smiled, blushing.

"She's here whenever you want to ride. I mean that."

I gave her my thanks for the offer and for today before Paul drove me home. He explained to me how his sister, who was two years younger than me, had left home at sixteen, disgusted by her parents' lifestyle and business venture. So desperate to leave them, she'd gone to live at a local riding school, living in a dirty, rotten caravan.

Outraged by this, his parents tried to bring her home, only for her refusals to continue. Eventually, they reached a compromise where she agreed to a distanced relationship with them and in return, they bought her that amazing yard complete with a house.

She had changed her surname to disassociate from them but as she knew the truth behind Paul's feelings regarding the club, she'd kept a close relationship with him.

A strange feeling of closeness washed over me as I revelled in the fact he'd introduced me to a 'secret' member of his family. A small sliver of hope started to climb inside me but I pushed it away. I couldn't afford to go there right now.

We pulled up on my driveway, Ash all but running over as I stepped out of the car to inform me Scott had been round, asking for my forgiveness.

Ash proudly told me he'd gifted him a black eye to match his broken nose before telling him where to go. I couldn't help but grin.

Until I walked inside my bare house and the reality hit home of what I'd done.

Paul chuckled next to me. "Did a proper job, didn't you?"

I nodded, sighing. How could a couple of hours change me from a desperate woman in the middle of a meltdown to one feeling empowered and in charge of her own life?

"Here." He pulled a card from his wallet. "Go to this place tomorrow. Tell them I sent you and to put it on my tab. Furnish your house and get yourself back on track."

"I can't do that."

"Yes, you can, and you will. Don't make me come down there with you." He grabbed my hand and lifted it to his mouth, brushing a kiss over the back of it. "This whole mess is my fault. This is my way of trying to make up for it."

I frowned. "How is this your fault?"

He hesitated for a second, softness seeping through his eyes. "Well, maybe if I'd been honest with you from the start, then things may have turned out differently." He shrugged his shoulders and said, "And I can afford to help you and I want to help you. Please just let me."

My heart warmed at his words. "I don't know what to say. Thank you."

He pressed his lips to my forehead, my heart crying for him to complete me. It was too soon and definitely not the right time to be reviving anything complicated with him, no matter how much my heart ached to be with him.

I closed my eyes and enjoyed the moment instead, just grateful that I had this right here, right now.

"Ky, I know it's soon, but I wanted to—"

The sound of my brother running whilst sobbing hysterically broke off Paul's sentence. I made a mental note to ask him to continue it until I saw my brother's pale face, tears streaming down his cheeks, and his hands shaking, his phone in one of them.

"What's wrong?" I said, my heart doing somersaults. My stomach churned with dread. It was something bad, I could feel it in my bones.

His chest heaving as he tried to rake in enough breath to speak, he finally said, "Mum's dead."

Chapter Thirty-Eight

M Y WHOLE REALITY SPUN on its head. I felt myself swaying as I took in his words. "What?"

He held a hand to his chest and let out a primal cry. Then he said, "Mum's been killed in an accident."

His words rattled around my head for a few seconds before I burst into tears. Paul stepped back, allowing Ash to stumble forwards and swallow me in a hug.

My legs gave way and I found myself clutching onto my brother for support as I looked for somewhere to sit. "Where's my damn sofa when I need it?"

He chuckled as he pulled me down to the floor, kissing my head. We sat in a daze for several minutes, just holding onto each other.

After a few minutes, I regained enough composure to ask the vital questions. "How? When?"

He sucked in a shaky breath. "Just before seven this morning, our time. It was just before one in the morning their time. I don't fully understand what happened myself. Something to do with one of the horses getting out during a thunderstorm. She went to catch it, but it spooked or something and kicked her in the head. It killed her outright."

I gasped. "What? Mum wouldn't be that stupid."

He shrugged his shoulders. "It seems she was."

I frowned, suspicion setting in right away. A shiver ran up and down my spine as I thought of that horrible man. "Tim told you, didn't he?"

Ash sighed, pushing me away as he stood up. "Don't start this again, Ky. Please. Not now."

"Why have you never believed me? I don't get it. He's a creep, Ash."

"Kyra—"

"Whoa, steady on guys," Paul said. He took my hand and pulled me to my feet, away from my brother. "Don't fall out now. This is where you're supposed to support each other."

Ash crossed his arms. "He's booked us onto the first flight out. We fly at seven, which means we have about two hours before we need to leave. We're flying back on Christmas Eve."

I snorted. "Typical Tim. Taking control of everything again. Why can't you see it?"

Ash rolled his eyes. "Kyra, he's just paid for our flights for goodness sake. Have some damn gratitude and respect."

I glared at him. "Why can't you respect me in the fact that what I said is true?"

He clenched his jaw, a muscle twitching in his cheeks as he glared at me. After a minute or so, he announced he was going home to pack some stuff and would come back for me shortly.

I trudged upstairs, feeling defeated, but focused on the task in hand of packing some stuff.

Paul followed me upstairs. "Can I ask what that was all about?"

A shudder ran down my spine as I thought about that fateful night again. "The guy came on to me at the wedding reception. The same reception where he'd just married my mum."

Paul raised an eyebrow. "He what?"

"Yep. It wasn't just a case of him trying a glancing kiss. He pinned me against a wall and practically forced his tongue down my throat." I shivered again as I remembered the vile taste he left in my mouth. "He was too strong, and his hands went places they shouldn't have..." Tears pricked at my eyes. "If I hadn't punched him in the face I dread to think what would have happened."

"Did you tell your mum?"

"Of course I did. She thought it was me overreacting to her remarrying. Ash agreed with her because he thinks Tim is the best thing since sliced bread. Before he went to Australia, he spent six months in America. Some of it with them. Of course, he and Tim became best buddies."

He came to me and enveloped me in a hug as he stroked my hair. "Do you want me to come with you?"

I took a minute to register his words. Had I heard him correctly? "You'd really do that?"

He pulled back and lifted a hand to my face, cupping my cheek and stroking it with his thumb. "Of course I would."

My heart cracked in two. Where was this side of him six months ago? "I...I really want to say yes but is it a good idea with how odd things are with us?"

His eyes softened as he smiled. "I'd do anything for you. You know I would. I want to talk to you about things but now is not the time."

My heart stopped for a second before soaring to a thousand feet in seconds. Was he suggesting what I thought he was? "I look forward to that, whenever it happens," I replied.

"Me too," he said, dropping his hand from my face. "I think for now, to keep things as uncomplicated as possible, it's best if I stay behind. If something happens with that slimeball, anything at all, and you need me, promise me you'll call?"

I nodded. "Of course."

Spending the next hour packing my life into a suitcase with the man of my dreams next to me was less than easy when I knew he was staying behind. Especially when I combined that thought with the reality of having to see Tim again in a few hours.

When Ash reappeared to drive us to the airport, tearing myself away from the safety of Paul's arms only made my heart ache even more.

The flight to Dallas took a little over ten hours. Silence encompassed us during the majority of the flight. What Ash had failed to tell me earlier was that good old Tim had also paid for Ben to come out with him. How charming. I was pleased Ben was with us but also fuming that I was seemingly now on my own as Ash turned to Ben for comfort.

We trundled our way through the airport towards the exit, my stomach turning into a complicated mixture of gnarled knots as I braced myself for meeting Tim once again. He was picking us up from the airport and the closer it came to seeing him, the more nauseous I felt.

My mind had replayed that night over and over again, refusing to let it go. Walking through the doors to the outside, there he stood, leaning up against his big black truck, legs crossed at the ankles as he chewed on gum. He looked far from the grief-stricken husband he should be.

His panther-like green eyes settled on me and a depraved smirk spread across his face. "Well, hello there."

Hearing his lazy Texan drawl once again sent shivers down my spine. Ash gave him a man hug before introducing Ben. I stayed well back, letting Ash steal the show. The less attention that man had on me, the better.

Ash turned to me, his eyes glowering. "Kyra?"

I nodded, sighing. "Hi."

Tim broke out into a huge smile. "Hello, dear. Good to see you again."

He took a step forwards, his arms outstretched. I glanced at Ash, who narrowed his eyes at me. I had little choice but to accept Tim wrapping his arms around me in a supposed hug. As I patted his back in my half-assed attempt at a hug back, he dropped his hands to my lower back.

"You look good," he whispered.

Chills covered me in an instant and I stepped back. He settled his hands on my hips for a few seconds before moving away and allowing us to get in the truck. I chewed on my lip and kept my thoughts to myself. I knew I wouldn't be sleeping well whilst I was out here.

Well aware Ash was watching my every move like I was a naughty child, I said nothing and looked at no one, just so I didn't get accused of anything.

The half an hour drive back to the ranch involved no interaction from me. Ash took pleasure in catching Tim up on all his adventures since they had last seen each other. As we turned down the dusty road to the ranch and then veered off track heading towards the guest quarters, my stomach turned itself inside out. Why was he putting us down here and not in the main house?

Part of Mum and Tim's business had been running a dude ranch. The log cabins for the guests were on the other side of the ranch to the main house. It was easily a mile long walk from one side of the grounds to the other.

Again, I kept my thoughts to myself, not wanting any more upset with Ash. Pulling up in front of the U-shaped collection of cabins, Tim informed Ash and Ben they would be sleeping in cabin number two whilst I would be in number eleven—the furthest point from them.

A horrid feeling of unease settled inside me. Brushing it aside, I took my luggage inside, making sure to shut the door behind me. I looked around the cosy setting, quite liking the rustic theme.

An open fire dominated half of the far wall, a grey stone fireplace surrounding it, whilst a king-size bed took the centre of the room. A black wrought iron chandelier hung from the ceiling, holding candle shaped light bulbs, and two chairs sat against the window with a small table between them giving exquisite views of the open landscape, including the lake and the wooden jetty leading down to it. It was beautiful.

Next to the edge of the fireplace was a door leading to a large, airy bathroom. With a sparkling white marble floor, a white sink with a wall length cupboard underneath and a huge mirror above, it was very modern considering the rustic theme in the main room. A free-standing white bathtub with gold taps sat in the middle of the room, a huge window on the outside facing wall, frosted over of course, but still allowing in plenty of natural light. Several LED spotlights in the ceiling were the light source in here. It fitted the theme of the room perfectly.

I smiled, thinking to myself how this could actually be really enjoyable if it wasn't for the letch who owned it. Starting to unpack my stuff, I jumped as Ash burst through the door.

"Stop being so damn rude," he said, staring at me.

I crossed my arms over my chest, glaring back at him. "I'm not being rude. I'm being civil."

"You're being rude, Kyra. Get over yourself already."

My jaw dropped. "You're unbelievable."

"No, you're unbelievable. The man just lost his wife for goodness sake."

I snorted. "I'm well aware of that. She was my mum, remember."

His dark eyes hardened over. "Not that you treated her like one for the past couple of years."

I gasped as he slammed the door shut behind him. I couldn't understand his behaviour at all. Starting to feel the effects of being alone, I crawled into bed and curled up into a ball.

I drifted off into a deep sleep, my dreams playing me scenes of Paul and me together. A gentle shoving startled me awake. I looked up to see Ash leaning over me.

"It's dinner time," he said. "Are you coming?"

I blinked my sleep away before nodding. Waking from sweet dreams of Paul to then walk outside to a living nightmare was quite a stark contrast. Still, if those dreams of Paul were to continue, at least I had some comfort.

Chapter Thirty-Nine

DINNER COULD ONLY BE described in one word—awkward. Tim and Ash dominated conversation whilst I sat quietly, mulling over my own thoughts. Ben joined in with their man talk now and then. He kept giving me sympathetic looks from across the table, smiling at my obvious discomfort.

"How are you feeling, Kyra? Tired?" Tim asked.

"Yes. I'm still a little tired."

"I hope you like the room."

I nodded.

"The beds are the best money can buy. Should give you an excellent night's sleep."

I nodded again, faking a smile.

A sharp kick in the ankle followed by a glare from Ash only worsened my mood. I decided to ask Tim a question.

"Where's all the Christmas decorations, Tim? Mum loved Christmas. She was like a kid in a candy shop when it came to Christmas."

Ben sucked in a sharp breath. Ash scowled at me, his eyes burning with hatred.

Tim faltered for a second before he sniffed and then wiped at his eyes, which had no tears anyway. "I just can't bear to celebrate Christmas now. I had to take them all down."

Ash patted Tim on the back and said, "It's ok, we understand." He stared at me, narrowing his eyes, and then mouthed, "Stop it."

I smirked back at him and then announced it was my bedtime.

Tim turned behind him and lifted up a crystal decanter. "Nightcap? Before I take you all back?"

"Just what I was thinking," said Ash.

I grumbled under my breath but involved myself in the ritual just to stop Ash from moaning at me. A couple of minutes later, the sharp tang of aged whiskey flooded my mouth. An awkward few-minute car ride after that and I was back in the safety of my room.

I peeled my clothes from my body, collapsing into the soft duvet before falling into a deep sleep. Sometime during the night, I awoke, the fire dwindling and barely giving off any light or heat.

Feeling a slight chill in the air, I climbed out of bed, still naked, and padded over to the fireplace, picking at the logs next to it and throwing them on the fire. I grabbed the poker and moved the burning embers around to get some air flow. After a minute or so, they reignited, taking hold of one of the fresh logs.

"Yes," I said to myself. "All I need is one of you to start burning."

I pulled one of the chairs from the window to the fire and sat in front of it, waiting for the heat to hit me.

"You should be careful of the spitting ash."

I screamed and jumped up, grabbing at the duvet to cover myself. Turning to face the front door, Tim emerged from the shadows, a sickly smile on his face.

"What the fuck are you doing?" I yelled. "Get out!"

He grinned at me and started walking towards me, step by step. With each step he took forwards, I took one back, eyeing up my escape into the bathroom.

"I figured it was about time we finished what we started that night."

I shook my head. "'We' didn't start anything. And I have no desire to finish whatever you think was started."

"Oh come on," he said, now halfway around the bottom of the bed. "I know you want me. I've seen it in your eyes from the first day we met."

"You're crazy. The only thing I want concerning you is you dead."

"You don't mean that."

"Yes," I said, nodding. "Yes, I do."

I glanced behind me quickly to see I only needed another two or three steps to be in the safety of the bathroom.

"You can run, Kyra, but you can't hide. Not forever."

I dropped the quilt and bolted into the bathroom, adrenaline surging through me to the point my shaky fingers almost didn't twist the lock in place. I heard a satisfying clunk just as he hurled himself against the door, making it bounce from his weight.

"Unlock the door, Kyra," he said, his voice deep and commanding.

"Fuck off, Tim," I shouted, my voice shaking.

I doubled myself over, really feeling the cold now I was sealed off in the bathroom. The cool marble floor in the middle of December insulated nothing at all. Grabbing a fluffy towel from the cupboard under the sink, I wrapped it around me and then sat on the side of the bath, my feet resting on the soft floor mat next to the bath.

"Kyra, unlock this door. Now."

"No. Nothing is going to make me unlock that door. Not even God himself. Unless he's coming to send you to hell."

A sadistic chuckle sounded from the other side of the door. "I expected you would be like that." He paused for a moment before he then said, "You're forgetting that I built these cabins with my own hands, piece by piece."

My heart stopped and my breath caught in my throat. My veins filled with dread. What was he insinuating?

The silence on the other side of the door worried me, but not enough to unlock it and peer out. I waited. A minute passed, then two, then three. Had he gone? Just as I started calming down and regaining some sense of reality, a scratching noise came from his side of the door.

I frowned, focusing as hard as I could on what I could hear. After a few seconds, I stood up and crept closer to the door. My eyes widened in horror as I heard the scratch of metal on metal and the rhythmic sound of a screwdriver undoing a screw. He was taking the hinges off the door.

Panic laced adrenaline flooded me in an instant. He'd be in here in less than two minutes. I glanced around me, desperate for a way out. The huge six foot long by four-foot-high frosted window was my only option but I needed something to break it.

As I looked around the room, nothing obvious stuck out. I ran to the cupboard under the sink and opened the doors, desperate to find anything with a bit of weight that would have enough momentum from a throw to break that window.

My eyes settled on a handheld metal mirror. The circular mirror couldn't have been much bigger than a side plate, but the metal pole that supported it was a good eight inches long and fairly thick. It wasn't big, but if I threw it hard enough and at the right spot, the glass would break. It had to. It was my only shot.

"Don't make me break the window," I yelled, my voice trembling. "Because if I do, I'll scream bloody murder and Ash and Ben will be over here quicker than a bullet leaves a gun."

The sound instantly stopped. Had I hit on something he hadn't expected?

"There's nothing in there that will break the window. Nice try." The sound of the screwdriver resumed.

"Wanna try me? How much are you willing to bet on that?"

The screwdriver stopped. "I checked that bathroom myself. I took anything out that could break that window."

I wanted to cry. The desperation filling me sent me into overdrive, panic completely taking hold. He had planned this. He had a plan B for plan A, and I bet he had a plan C for plan B. Just how sadistic was this man? In that instant, I knew he'd done this before. This wasn't his first rodeo, in any sense of the term.

In fear of my dignity, as well as my life, I screamed back, "But did you check the cupboard under the sink?"

Silence.

Seconds later, a primal roar sounded from the other side of the room. I heard something being smashed and then the door slamming shut.

I collapsed into a heap on the bathroom floor and cried my eyes out.

Chapter Forty

P OUNDING SOUNDED THROUGH MY head, waking me from my slumber.

"Kyra."

I gasped and sat up, looking around me.

"Kyra."

Ash's voice from outside as he hammered his fist on the bathroom door brought me to my senses.

"Yeah, one minute," I said.

My body aching and freezing from sleeping on a hard, cold floor, I pushed myself to my feet and stumbled towards the door, blinking the sleep from my eyes. My fingers unwilling to co-operate, it took a few seconds for me to turn the lock and open the door.

Ash and Ben stood staring at me, their eyes full of concern and confusion.

"What the hell happened out here?" Ash said, standing to the side and motioning his hand out into the room.

The duvet still lay on the floor where I'd dropped it when I ran into the bathroom. The top hinge on the bathroom door was hanging off, the screws missing, and as I peered around the corner of the fireplace, I saw the chair I'd sat on had been smashed to pieces and shoved in the fire. Half of it had been burned already, the other half still sticking out, its wooden legs in the air like a frozen corpse.

I looked my brother in the eyes and with a trembling bottom lip, I replied, "Tim."

Ash let out a long sigh and said, "I don't have time for this."

With that, he turned and left.

Ben looked at me and said, "I believe you, Ky. Let me talk to him. He's just really overwhelmed with everything at the minute."

Tears filled my eyes as I nodded. "I know, Ben, but I need him right now. I need him on my side, not fighting against me."

Ben stepped around the duvet and came to me, enveloping me in a big hug. "Just give him some time. The house hunting in London hasn't gone well, we had to pay his tenants in his house a severance package so we had somewhere to live. My work is getting busy, his work is swamping him, you and your problem with Scott, now this with your mum, and the ancient history with you and Tim..." He pulled back and put his hands on my shoulders "...I don't think he knows what to deal with first. He knows he needs to be a big brother to you regarding your mum, but he doesn't know what to do or how to do it."

My tears sprung free, sliding down my cheeks. "I just need him to believe me."

"I think he does, sweetie, deep down. I think the problem is he doesn't know what to do about it."

"Kill him. It's quite simple," I said, smiling.

He touched his index finger to the bottom of my chin and smiled. "There she is. That's the fighting spirit we know. Just bear with him, ok? Hang in there."

I nodded. "Not much else I can do."

"Are you ok? I'm going to go talk to Ash, ok?"

"I'm fine," I said, wiping my tears away.

"Ok. Tim is picking us up at nine to take us to the house for breakfast."

"Ok."

Ben gave me one last smile before running out of the door and over to his and Ash's cabin. I went to my door and locked it, not that it had served me much use last night, but now it was daylight, the chances of Tim making a sudden reappearance were slim to none.

I spotted my phone on the bedside table and grabbed it. I took photos of everything from all different angles. The duvet, the chair in the fire, the bathroom door hinge, and finally the bathroom itself. I put the mirror back in the cupboard where I'd found it and took a picture of it in there. For my own curiosity, I wanted to see if it would still be there tonight.

After taking the pictures, I found myself staring at Paul's name in my contact list. I had messaged him when we landed to say I was safe and sound, to which he had sent back a long line of kisses, but I'd heard nothing since.

If something happens with that slimeball, anything at all, and you need me, promise me you'll call replayed over and over in my mind. I did need him. I really needed him. The longer I debated calling him, the harder my heart pounded against my ribs.

I sucked in a deep breath and pressed the call button.

After two rings, he answered. "Hey, you ok?"

Just hearing his honey laden voice broke me completely. I burst into tears, managing to sob out, "I need you."

"I'm on my way," sounded like music to my ears before the line went dead.

I thought I'd been keeping it together quite well up until that point. That's when I realised that I trusted myself to be vulnerable with him. Not only that, I trusted him to see the side of me I allowed no one else to see, to see the other side to my 'fighting spirit'. I needed my rock, my comfort, and I needed him to wrap me up in his arms and tell me everything would be ok.

But most of all, I wanted him to do all of that too. And I knew he wanted to do it.

I pulled myself together just in time for Tim to pick us up for breakfast. I sat in the back of his truck, quiet and not saying a word. I made no effort to make eye contact with him at all.

Ben and Ash acted like nothing was wrong and that they knew nothing, making senseless chit chat with him all the way up to the house and all the way through breakfast.

I picked at my food, managing to swallow down one pancake. Every few minutes I would check my phone, desperate to see any communication from Paul as to when he would be there, but not a word as of yet. Given the length of the flight, plus travel times and everything else, I realistically didn't expect to see him for at least twenty-four hours.

"Kyra," Tim said. "Did you sleep well?"

I snapped my head up and looked at him. I could feel the burn from Ash's stare without even looking at him. I nodded.

"Good," he said, smiling. "I like to take care of my guests."

I said nothing back to him which earned me a hardened glare from Ash. I couldn't keep feeling under attack by own family and letting it get me down. Reaching across the table for another pancake, I forced it down me as things started whirring around my head.

Tim placed a glass of orange juice in front of me, and as he did, I looked up at him and in my most innocent voice, asked, "So are you going to tell us what exactly happened with Mum?"

Tim froze. His green eyes filled with surprise before he cleared his throat. Sitting back down on his side of the table, he said, "We had a thunderstorm. Your mum heard one of the horses getting upset so she went to check on them. It was Nelson, my big black stallion. He can be rather sensitive and temperamental at the best of times. All the horses were in the barn, so I thought nothing of it. But something spooked him, and he lashed out and caught your mum on the side of her head. I didn't find her for nearly half an hour. It wasn't until she'd been gone that long that I realised something was wrong." He broke down in tears and started sobbing. "If only I'd gone out instead of her. It would be me laying dead and not your beautiful mother."

I rolled my eyes at his crocodile tears. My gut niggled at me about his story. Something was up with it. Call it woman's intuition or whatever, but it just didn't sit quite right.

Ash scooted up next to Tim and threw an arm around his shoulders whilst staring at me.

Ignoring Ash, I looked at Tim and said, "That's a good question. Why didn't you go out to them instead of her?"

"Kyra!" Ash yelled. "Stop it. Now."

"No, Ash," I said. "I have questions I want answered and he has the answers."

"What?" Tim asked.

"Why didn't you go out to the horses? It was the middle of the night and pouring with rain, so why did Mum go?"

He faltered for a moment, wiping at his tearstained face. "She was already dressed as she hadn't come to bed yet. She grabbed her hat and coat and off she went."

I shrugged my shoulders. "Why didn't you follow her? Why would you leave your older wife to deal with spooked horses on her own in the middle of the night? Especially when there are stallions in there?"

I wasn't going to leave it alone. It didn't make sense to me. Unless he was just a coward of a man.

Ash kicked my shin under the table. "Kyra...," he said, his voice low and full of warning.

I glared at him. "No, Ash. I'm entitled to ask questions."

A sheepish look crossed Tim's face before he whispered, "The truth is..." He inhaled deeply. My heart rate spiked as I wondered if this would be the ultimate confession. He let his breath out and said, "I'm scared of thunderstorms."

I couldn't help but laugh at his pathetic admission and poor excuse. "Of course you are. A seasoned cowboy scared of storms."

"Are you happy now?" Ash said, the venom in his voice almost giving his words a life of their own.

I stood up and said, "I'm going out for some air."

"I'll come with you," Ben said.

Surprised but grateful for Ben's company, we wandered outside into the cool December air. We meandered our way over to the nearest paddock, leaning on the post and rail fencing as we gazed out across the rolling hills at the grazing horses. I'd always thought of Texas as being nothing but sandy desert until I'd actually visited it. It still amazed me seeing lush green grass somewhere so baking hot.

"I don't like that guy," Ben said.

I turned to him, trying to read the confused emotions swirling through his dark eyes. "Can I ask why?"

He shrugged his big shoulders. "I don't know. Just something a little—"

"Off?"

He nodded, smiling. "I can tell there's tension between you both."

"I presume Ash told you what had happened at the wedding?"

He nodded again. "Like I said earlier, I believe you. I know why Ash thinks you did it, freaking out about your dad and all, but I don't know, there's just something not right with him."

I grinned, glad I had at least one ally on my side. "I know exactly what you mean."

Chapter Forty-One

AN IDEA STARTED BREWING in my mind and I couldn't let it go. I knew of Nelson from before me and Mum had our fall out. She had bought him for Tim, but he took to her. She adored that horse, and they had an incredible bond. From what I understood, he would do anything for her. So why would he kick her and kill her?

Even if spooked, which from what I remembered he was more than storm proof, that was an extreme reaction to a horse being scared. If he was with his handler that he solely trusted, he wouldn't act like that.

"Will you back me up?" I asked Ben, as we continued staring at the horses in their fields.

"With what?"

"I have an idea. I just need you to encourage Ash to let it play out."

He raised a busy eyebrow. "Dare I ask?"

I grinned. "Probably best not to."

He chuckled. "Sure. Let's see what you've got."

We headed back inside the house to see Ash still comforting Tim.

I stood in front of the table and folded my arms over my chest. "Take me to the barn," I said, staring at Tim.

"What?" he said, his mouth falling wide open.

"I want to see where Mum died. Take me to the barn."

"Kyra, not today," Ash said, his voice soft and pleading. "Please."

"Ash, just let me do this, please."

Ben cleared his throat and said, "It's just a barn, right? No harm ever came from seeing a barn. Just indulge her, Ash, stop fighting with her. This is all hard enough."

Ash let out a big sigh. "Ok." He turned to Tim and said, "Can you do that for us please? Take us to the barn?"

Tim nodded his head and grabbed a tissue. "Yes, of course. Follow me."

He put on his boots before leading us down to the red and white traditional barn. As Ash stuck to Tim's side, I dropped back a few paces, pleased when Ben matched my strides.

"Thank you," I whispered. "I really needed that."

"You're welcome. I'm curious what you're planning."

I grinned. "I think Tim has forgotten that I know horses."

Ben frowned, his eyes filling with questions, but he said nothing more.

As we entered the barn, my eyes adjusted to the dim lighting, the familiar smell of horse manure, hay, and straw invaded my nostrils, taking me straight back to my fun filled horse days. My heart started aching for Scotch all over again and I pondered for a moment taking Rebecca up on her offer of riding Eloise.

On the left as we walked in were two wooden doors, one with a toilet sign, one with a sign that said 'Office'. Next to it and before the stables started, were bales and bales of hay, all stacked up right to the ceiling. Definitely plenty for several horses for the winter.

I could hear a horse pacing in its stable, the shuffle of the straw a constant noise. The horse blew through its nostrils, then started pawing at the floor, its hoof hitting the concrete.

"They all have rubber matting except for a foot space before the door," Tim explained. "They're not bedded down on pure concrete."

A concrete aisle split the barn in half, each side lined with a dozen stables. Every single stable was empty, save for the one unsettled horse at the bottom.

"Why is there one horse in on its own?" I asked, raising my voice.

The pacing in the stable stopped. Aside from the tragedy that happened in here, it was a picturesque barn and I knew Mum would have loved spending her days in here.

"That's your mum's horse, Nelson," Tim replied.

We carried on walking down the aisle. As we approached the last stables, a big black face with a white stripe pinged over the stable door. Bright, alert eyes and ears pricked, he started nodding his head up and down.

"Why is he in on his own?" I asked.

Tim cleared his throat, hesitating before replying, "I have mares in season."

"In December?"

Tim stopped one stable away from Nelson. The horse looked at the group of us, his interest in our presence more than evident. I brushed past Tim and Ash and went straight towards him.

As I came into his personal space outside his stable door, he stretched his neck forwards as far he could, blowing heavily through his nose as he tried in vain to reach me, desperate for some form of contact.

I held my hand out to him and let him sniff me. He nickered softly and banged his front leg against the door.

"Ah ah," I said, walking towards him so he didn't have to stretch so far to touch me. "Don't be naughty."

He lifted his nose to my head and snuffled through my hair, his top lip messing my hair up. I didn't care, I'd missed this aspect of horses with their funny little quirks. I peered over his stable door and recoiled back within a second.

"When did you last muck him out?" I said, turning to Tim.

"I...well, I've been a bit busy and haven't had chance since your mum died. Everything has just gotten on top of me."

I narrowed my eyes at him and looked into the stable next door to Nelson's. It was clean, the bed perfectly arranged, a mound of hay in the corner ready for the night-time occupant. I went to the stable on the opposite side of the aisle that faced Nelson's stable. It too was all clean and ready for the evening.

"Do I need to check each one of these stables before you tell me what's going on?"

Ash looked at Tim, questions forming in his eyes. If I could raise one bit of suspicion in Ash then I knew I was onto a winner.

Tim lifted his hand and ran it through his hair. The sudden movement of him lifting his hand made Nelson squeal and turn in Tim's direction. He pinned his ears back flat against his head and snaked his head up and down in an aggressive manner.

I'd only ever seen that behaviour in a herd of horses when a stallion would use this body language to move horses, primarily mares, in the direction he wanted them to go. It was a strong behaviour that only really occurred when dominance or order was threatened within the herd.

My gut churned and a voice in my head told me the obvious answer.

Nelson viewed Tim as a threat.

The million-dollar question was why?

Determined to dig further, I looked back at Tim who still hadn't answered my question and said, "Tim?"

"He doesn't like me. I can't do anything with him."

I raised my eyebrow. "So what were you planning to do? Leave him in here to rot?"

"He won't even let me get near him with hay so I can feed him. What am I supposed to do?"

Alarm bells started ringing then. All horses were food orientated. Some more than others, but their natural grazing behaviour meant that food was their primary concern in life. What could make a horse dislike a human so much that they wouldn't let them near them with one of the basic things they lived for?

"You get someone in to help," I said, my voice full of disdain. "That's what you do."

"How am I supposed to live the rest of my life paying someone to come feed a horse that hates me?" He shook his head. "It makes no sense."

"Give me his headcollar," I said.

Tim widened his eyes. "Are you insane?"

"Do I look insane? Give me his headcollar. I will take him outside so you can clean this mess up."

Tim sighed and reached over to the hook next to him, picking up a leather headcollar and leather lead rope. Had it not been for Ash and Ben, I knew he wouldn't be giving in so easily. He walked towards me which only elicited more aggressive behaviour from Nelson.

Banging his legs against the door, he stretched his neck towards, snapping his teeth as he tried his best to get a hold of Tim. I had little doubt that if let go, Nelson would take a chunk of Tim's flesh and then some.

Tim threw the headcollar at me and scuttled backwards, visibly breathing a sigh of relief. As soon as he returned to his previous spot, Nelson settled down but still kept an eye on him.

"Ky, are you sure you should be handling this horse?" Ash said, his voice shaking slightly.

"Ash, trust me. I'll be fine."

I positioned the headcollar in front of Nelson's nose, smiling as he thrust his head inside it. The poor boy wanted out so desperately.

"So what happened, Tim? Where did you find Mum?" I asked, doing up Nelson's headcollar.

He pointed at me. "Literally in front of his door, where you are now. Her head was facing that stall," he said, pointing at the stable opposite Nelson's. "It was like she'd opened the door and he'd just flattened her in his panic to get out."

"But you said he kicked her in the head."

He nodded. "Yes. The coroner said her injuries were consistent with the shape of a horseshoe." He shrugged his shoulders. "Like I said, I wasn't here. I can only guess what happened. I'm guessing he ran out, your mum tried to control him, and lashed out and caught her."

"So her injuries were consistent with being hit with a horseshoe but no one saw Nelson, or any other horse for that matter, kick her?"

Tim glared at me. I knew I'd hit a nerve.

"Ky," Ash said. "What are you trying to say?"

I shrugged my shoulders and smiled, trying to appear innocent. "Nothing at all. Just clarifying the situation." I undid Nelson's stable door and said, "I'm bringing him out now."

Stallions had been known to become protective over their female owners, and knowing how my mum was with her horses, I would bet my last penny that this was how their relationship would have been. I wondered, if he viewed Tim as a threat, if he would feel inclined to protect me as well. My mum and I were very similar in our looks, height, and build, and I hoped that something in me reminded Nelson of my mum. My entire plan hinged on that fact.

I opened the stable door and waited for him to barrel over the top of me but he didn't. Even with an open doorway, he stood and waited for me to say, "Walk on," before moving a muscle. I let him get his front legs out before saying, "Woah. Stand." He stopped immediately.

I glanced at Tim and said, "Considering this horse has been in his stable for..." I looked underneath Nelson and between his legs, looking at the state of his stable. "...I'm guessing three days, maybe four, and desperate to get out, he still seems to remember his manners perfectly, despite going crazy with hunger and pent up energy."

Without doing anything else with this horse, I knew Mum had trained him to perfection. Stallions were hard to handle and a good relationship was the basic foundation of stallion handling. Mum wouldn't have had it any other way—for her safety and everyone else's. There was no way this horse kicked her in the head, scared or not.

"Your mum was an exceptional horse woman," Tim said, his voice weak and pathetic. "I'm glad to see the horse remains that way without her being here."

"Walk on," I said, clicking my tongue to Nelson.

He followed me like a little puppy. Until he got within six feet of Tim. An ear-piercing squeal left the horse before he lunged himself at Tim, swinging his hind legs out and kicking at his head.

Tim screamed like a little girl, a look of horror on his face as he backed up and ran for his life. Ash and Ben jumped out of the way as Tim fled to the safety of the office. I let the lead rope go and watched as Nelson chased after him, snaking his head and neck with his ears pinned flat back against his head.

It was then that I noticed the other key part to Tim's story.

Nelson was barefoot—no shoes.

Chapter Forty-Two

A S SOON AS TIM shut himself away in the office, Nelson calmed down and wandered over to the massive pile of hay bales, greedily snatching at them as he filled his empty belly.

I walked over to him and picked up the lead rope.

Ash and Ben followed, keeping their distance from Nelson. "What the hell was that?" Ash said, his eyes wide with fear. "You're just proving that the psycho horse that killed Mum is in fact a psycho horse."

I rolled my eyes. "No, Ash. I'm proving that the psycho horse who adored Mum and protected her like a guard dog hates one person."

Ash rolled his eyes. "My goodness. You are unreal."

"Ben," I said, holding my hand out. "Will you come and touch the horse please?"

He widened his eyes, his eyebrows raising as shock settled in his dark eyes. "What?"

"Please? You'll be fine, I promise."

Ben glanced at Ash before sucking in a deep breath and coming over to me. I stood next to Nelson's head as he munched through the hay and took Ben's hand, placing it on Nelson's neck.

I could feel the tension in Ben, his arm rigid and his shoulders shaking as I did what I needed to do. As soon as his fingers touched Nelson's silky coat, he relaxed, realising that Nelson actually wasn't that bad.

I stared at Ash, waiting for him to catch on. Then I whispered to Ben, "Nelson has no shoes on." I pointed at his feet which showed no signs of recently removed shoes. His hooves were perfectly smooth and well-trimmed. "He hasn't worn shoes for at least six months."

Ben's face paled. He nodded. "I understand. You need to give me some time to talk to Ash," he whispered back.

"Thank you." I pointed to a hay bale and said, "Can you bring one of them outside please? Then prise Tim from the office to clean his stable."

"Sure."

I sat outside the barn, on the hay bale as Nelson tore chunks of hay from beneath me, filling with glee at how perfectly my idea had worked. Whatever happened, this horse would be coming back to England and living his life out with me. Even if I had to beg, steal, and borrow money, I would make it happen.

Minutes later I heard the office door creak open as Tim emerged. Now a good thirty feet away from him, Nelson didn't bother about him at all. I suspected the fact that Nelson being between me and Tim also helped Tim's situation.

An hour later, Nelson was back in a clean stable with a mountain of hay that would easily last him a day. We headed back into the house in silence, no one saying anything. As Ash and Ben took their shoes off near the door, I wandered into the kitchen, feeling somewhat victorious.

Tim glared at me as he flicked the kettle on and whispered, "You're going to regret that."

The rest of the day, unfortunately for us, was spent listening to Tim's sorrowful howls combined with lame excuses and his stories about Mum.

We were due to go to the funeral parlour tomorrow and pay our last respects. In all honesty, I didn't want to go. It had been difficult for me to see Dad laid out in his coffin. The nauseating smell of the embalming fluid hanging in the air was something I would never forget. It was definitely not something I wished to repeat.

I wanted Mum buried at home next to Dad, but she was being cremated and having a memorial stone here. I was not impressed to say the least.

That night, after food and drinks, Tim drove us back to the cabins. Being close to ten p.m., and after such a shitty day, I wanted nothing more than to curl up in bed and sleep, but I knew that was unlikely to happen.

As we jumped out of the truck, Tim announced he would leave the truck there for us to use ourselves in the morning to drive up to the house for breakfast. Immediately, I knew something dodgy was going on.

Ash offered to drive him back to his house, but he refused, saying the walk would help clear his head. I could do little but roll my eyes at his continued dramatics.

The boys disappeared back inside their cabin, and I knew I was on my own. I took a deep breath and opened my cabin door, skirting through it as quickly as possible and then locking it behind me.

I grabbed the remaining lone chair from the little table and jammed it underneath the doorknob. I knew if he really wanted in, it wouldn't stop him, but the noise would wake me up and give me a few precious seconds to escape into the bathroom.

My interest piqued about the mirror, I headed straight for the bathroom to see if it was still in the cupboard. I opened the door and stopped dead in my tracks as a gasp escaped me.

I hadn't turned on the bathroom light yet, but the dim glow from the main room behind me highlighted my knight in shining armour. Paul sat on the side of the bath, his legs crossed at the ankles and a broad grin on his handsome face.

He immediately put his index finger to his lips in a shush motion and I nodded my understanding. I rushed towards his open arms and threw myself inside them. The relief at knowing I would be safe, not just tonight, but always, let my tears free like a dam bursting its banks.

He wrapped his arms around me and hugged me so tight I could barely breathe, but I didn't care. I had so many questions, but they were not for now.

"You need to act like you would if I wasn't here," he whispered. "I brought a spy cam and set it up on the fireplace. I have so much to tell you, but not now."

My mind whirling at a million miles an hour, wondering what on earth he was up to, I nodded and did as he said. I headed back out into the main room, threw some logs on the fire, stripped off, and jumped in bed, really wishing he would come and join me.

I couldn't fall asleep knowing Paul sat feet away from me, waiting in the darkness, but I knew what I needed to do so I pretended as best I could.

We didn't have to wait long. Sure enough, the sound of the doorknob being turned ever so slowly filled the empty silence in the cabin. The noise was so quiet, it was no wonder I hadn't woken last night from it. The slow turning didn't upset the balance of the chair at all which made the whole thing even more sinister.

A gentle click then followed as he somehow undid the lock. When he pushed against the door, the chair scraped against the floor before toppling over. I sat up in bed and pulled the duvet up around my chin.

"We meet again," Tim said, kicking the chair out of the way as he turned to shut the door and then locked it from the inside. "I told you that you would regret your little trick with the horse today."

"It's not my fault that you forgot I know horses. You know what my mum was capable of. Her and Dad taught me everything I know. That's your undoing, not mine."

He grinned. "We'll soon see your undoing, don't you worry. Are we going to have theatrics like last night?"

I bit my lip to stop my smirk. Knowing he was on camera and had just admitted to what happened last night made my soul soar. I needed to keep him talking so he incriminated himself as much as possible.

"I think it'll be more like the theatrics from your wedding night with Mum if you carry on."

He grinned, showing his pearly white teeth like a dog baring its teeth. "You broke my nose that night. Did you know that?"

I smiled at him. "I didn't, but thanks for the clarification. They say once a nose has broken once, it's easier to break the next time. I have a feeling I wasn't the first person to break your nose, was I?"

"Now that would be telling."

"So how does this work then, Tim? Indulge me. I'm curious. Is it still as much fun if I lay here and let you get on with it, or can you only get hard if I'm screaming and begging you to stop?"

He wiped the grin from his face quicker than I could blink. His predatory eyes settled on me like a lion watching its prey, empty, soulless, and full of intent. "You're a mouthy little bitch, you know that? I often wonder if you hadn't punched me that night would I have carried on strangling you."

"I think the answer is no, Tim. Dead bodies can't scream, can they? Where's the excitement then for you?"

A sadistic smirk folded over his lips. "Believe me, watching the life drain from someone's eyes is much more satisfying than fucking them when they are begging you to stop."

My heart pounding as he edged closer to the bed, I wondered at what point Paul would emerge from the bathroom. I couldn't believe how easy it was to get Tim talking.

"Why are you telling me all this? You know I will tell people."

"Two things there," he said. "Number one, no one believed you about the wedding night, so why would they about this? Number two, you won't be alive to tell anyone, sweetheart."

His words rattled around my brain and fear climbed through me like ivy. If Paul wasn't here, I would be in real trouble. A cold sweat broke out all over me as I watched him sit on the end of the bed.

"And how would you explain another death on your property?"

He licked his lips and said, "There's only a death if there's a body. No body, no evidence."

In that instant, I knew why Mum was being cremated. "And what would you say to Ash?"

He shrugged his shoulders. "That you went home after we argued. He would believe that. If you vanish back in England, not my problem."

I frowned. "Do you really think something as weak as that would stick?"

"Like I said, sweetheart, no body, no evidence. You are going to be the accumulation of all my fantasies in one. You are worthy of something that grand. You should be honoured."

I managed to settle my mind into focusing on the fact that I was having first hand experience into the mind of a raving lunatic. I knew there was no point in trying to rationalise with him—a rational mind will never comprehend an irrational one.

But what I could do is try to understand him as best I could. If Paul wasn't here, I would be doing anything to make him see me as human. If a killer sees their prey as human, instead of something to 'play with', it makes their end goal so much harder to achieve.

Most survivor stories of murderers and rapists were because the victim made the offender realise they are a person, not a thing.

"Why me? What makes me different from all the other girls in the world?"

He shrugged his shoulders. "Why do women always ask that question? Do you realise how pathetic you sound?"

"I'm just trying to understand, Tim, nothing else."

"All you need to understand is you won't be seeing another sunrise. You don't need to worry your pretty head about the minor details."

I cleared my throat and said, "But Mum told you about my degree, surely?"

He grinned. "Yes, she did. Isn't this ironic?"

"So before I die, at least let me understand what makes you pick the people you do. It's not like I'm going to get to study any further to get inside one of your guy's minds."

He puffed his chest out like a peacock and let out a long sigh. "Fine, but this is the last question. Is that clear? I'm quite frankly getting a little bored of this chit chat, but I understand you wanting to prolong your life as much as possible."

I couldn't help but wonder how many people had been in my situation and not had help. How many people had asked him similar questions in an effort to save themselves?

"Ok," I said. "Understood."

"Are you familiar with Ed Kemper?"

I nodded. "The Co-ed Killer."

"His most famous quote that more or less sums up my thought pattern is that when he sees a pretty woman, one side of him wants to talk to her and date her but the other side of him wonders what her head would look like on a stick." He paused for breath. "I'm not into dismemberment. That isn't my scene. But I do wonder what it would be like to stare into her eyes as I squeeze the life from her body. As she stares up at me, the life draining from her, in that moment I am her God."

"And you want me to see you as my God?"

"Sweetheart, I hold your life in my hands. Don't you see how powerful that is? In your dying moments, you will be thinking of God and looking at me. What could possibly be more enlightening than that? What else does a soul need to ascend to heaven other than being the status of a God?"

His ramblings could be described as nothing more than a psychotic episode. The man was unstable, at best. Completely delusional and irrational.

"Why do you need to be a God to go to heaven?"

"Look where God is thought to be—in heaven. Millions of people pledge their lives to him, an invisible being, someone they've never met, and they trust this never seen man to take their soul to the afterlife and look after them. I am an actual living, breathing person who can take their soul to heaven with me. And because they have pledged their life to me, I am a God. I cannot be refused entry to heaven when I have good souls with me. I have to be let in by default. Don't you see?"

I nodded, still trying to grasp his twisted logic. I could only feel relieved that all of this would be on video. I would need to replay it over and over for the next decade just to get my head around it.

The click of a gun sounded from the bathroom. "I think it's time you see," Paul said, emerging from the shadows with a gun pointed straight at Tim's chest.

Tim jumped to his feet. His face started to redden as his body started vibrating. When he let out an animalistic roar, I knew he was filled with pure rage. Like a wild animal with nothing left to lose, he charged at Paul.

Paul pulled the trigger.

Chapter Forty-Three

T HE NOISE OF THE gun firing made me pull the duvet over my head. Shaking like a leaf in a storm, I let all the tension out of my body and started crying.

Tim rolled around on the floor, howling like a wolf.

"Shut up," Paul said.

I took the duvet from my face to see Paul hauling Tim up into a sitting position. Blood and bone were protruding from Tim's right knee. Just the sight of all the blood and dangling flesh made me feel sick.

Paul pulled cable ties from his back pocket and tied Tim's hands behind his back before then tying him to the leg of the bed.

The front door rattled as Ash pounded on the door. "Ky! KYRA!"

"She's ok," Paul said, walking to the door and unlocking it.

Ash and Ben rushed through the door, Ash letting out a breath when he saw me alive and well.

"What the fuck?" he breathed, taking in the scene. "What the actual fuck?"

Before me or Paul could answer, the sound of sirens cut through the midnight silence.

I looked at Paul, raising my eyebrow as my question.

"Yes," he said. "They're coming here."

Relief swallowed me to the point I collapsed into an exhausted heap on the bed. My nightmare was over. The worst thing was that Mum had unfortunately been a victim. Nothing we did now would bring her back, but we could serve justice. The fact that Paul had blown his kneecap out gave a tiny bit of karma.

Ash climbed onto the bed and hugged me for all he was worth. "I am so sorry," he said, bawling like a little girl. "I am so so sorry I didn't believe you."

I threw my arms around him and started crying. "It's ok. Better late than never."

He let out a small laugh. "I swear to God, I will never not believe you again. I promise."

I nodded and said nothing more. His words were all I needed to hear. I glanced at Ben and mouthed, "Thank you."

He smiled at me and gave me a thumbs up. "You need any help, Paul?"

Paul shook his head. "No. The police will be here soon."

Tim said nothing as he continued shouting out in pain.

"I need to get dressed," I said, as the sirens came closer.

Ash let me go as Paul passed me a towel to wrap around myself to head into the bathroom with. I grabbed some clothes from my suitcase and shut myself away in the bathroom.

I couldn't help but think how much things had changed in twenty-four hours. What a difference a day makes.

Needless to say, none of us got much rest that night. We were all taken down to the station and made to give statements, then told we would be contacted in due course if anything else was needed. Tim, naturally, had been taken to hospital but remained under the watchful eye of three policemen.

When Paul explained the situation and that we were due to fly back on Christmas Eve, the lead detective, a rather aging, slim man by the name of Jimmy North, asked if there was any chance someone could stay behind as a local point of contact until the investigation had been completed.

"We will," Ash said, without any hesitation. "Me and Ben."

My jaw dropped. I had been ready to volunteer based on the fact that someone needed to take care of the horses. "What? Are you sure?"

Ash nodded. "Why? Did you want to stay?"

"I was going to offer to, yes, because of the horses."

"Here's an idea," Paul said. "Why don't we all stay?"

"That suits me," said Detective North. "Leave me all of your numbers please. I have the address where you will be staying."

I couldn't help but grin at Paul when he said what he said. I had a million questions for him, and I didn't know where to start.

"Come on," Paul said. "Let's get some coffee and food."

We called an uber and headed to a diner on the outskirts of town, not far from the ranch. After the waitress took our orders, Paul took a long drink of his coffee before setting it back down on the table.

"Who's interrogating me first then?" he asked.

"I think," Ash said, taking a sip of his drink. "It would be easier for you to tell us what you've been doing, and we ask questions for any gaps."

"Ok. So, let's go back to the beginning. After hearing you and Kyra arguing about Tim the other day, I decided to do a bit of digging."

I raised an eyebrow, curious what he meant.

"Sometimes my parents' lifestyle has its up sides. It means we always know people," he said, giving me a cheeky wink. "What do you guys know about Tim?"

I shrugged my shoulders. "Mum met him three years ago whilst she was out here with work. She fell in love, decided to stay, and there we go. She married him two years ago."

"Well," he said, lowering his voice. "Mr. Tim Masters is also known as Mr. Tim Roker, and Mr. Tim Bycraft."

I gasped, not quite grasping what he'd just said. How could he have three identities? Why did he need them?

A feeling of dread began to unfurl inside me as endless possibilities swam through my mind.

He took a sip of his water and cleared his throat. "Mr. Tim Bycraft is originally from New York and was under suspicion for a series of rapes that happened in and around his apartment building. He vanished before the police could formally charge him."

"What? Are you being serious?"

He nodded, pulling his lips into a thin line. "Mr. Tim Roker suddenly appeared in Florida twelve years ago. He married a lady called Lisa a year later who happened to be worth a lot of money. She was found dead eighteen months later after a nasty fall down the stairs whilst Mr. Roker was out of town. Mr. Roker inherited all of her two-million-dollar fortune as she no longer spoke to her kids and had written them out of her will. Two years later, Mr. Roker remarried another wealthy widow who also ended up dead within two years from a nasty fall. She had also written her only child out of her will, leaving her six-million-pound fortune to Tim."

I leaned back, running my hands through my hair. How could someone get away with all of this so easily? My mind was whirling, spinning at a million miles an hour from this massive revelation.

"There's more," he continued, giving me a sympathetic smile. "Three years later, he married a divorced lady who ripped her plastic surgeon husband off for fifteen million dollars in the divorce courts. She died within months, and Mr. Tim Roker disappeared after her children and ex-husband contested her will in court. Mr. Tim Roker was awarded twenty-five per cent of her estate with the remainder being split between her three children. He then vanished before Mr. Tim Masters appeared in Texas a mere six months before your mum unfortunately met him."

"What? Is he some kind of black widow or something?"

Paul smiled. "He always goes for older women, and those who are on their own or divorced. They always have kids as well. Now, going back to the rapes back in New York. They were connected with a series of cash robberies as well. The police were putting a link together between the victims being raped and their bank accounts being emptied. They were getting close, and I suspect this is why he disappeared."

"I can't believe this," I said, leaning my head in my hands. "This happens in movies, not real life."

"Unfortunately," Ash said, sighing. "The movies get their ideas from somewhere, or rather the criminals get their ideas from somewhere."

"So what do you think this has to do with me and my mum? Mum didn't have any fortune to her name."

"That's where you're slightly wrong, sweetheart," Paul said. He reached over and grabbed my hand. "The compensation she received from your father's accident she invested in the stock market. And very cleverly. She pulled her shares three weeks ago and was worth nearly ten million. In sterling."

I balked at his words, my mouth hanging wide open. I couldn't even formulate thoughts let alone words. Thankfully, the waitress appeared with our food.

"There's something else," Paul said, after the waitress left.

I looked up at him, holding my breath in expectation. "What else?"

"Your mother changed her will the day after she pulled her shares."

I gulped, adrenaline now pumping around me at a rate of knots. What else was he going to surprise me with?

"After your row at their wedding, she had changed her will and cut both you and Ash out, leaving everything to Tim. Three weeks ago, she changed it so that Tim was left with nothing, and you and Ash were left with everything—split fifty-fifty."

Tears sprang from the corners of my eyes. Endless possibilities of what could have made her change her mind raced around my mind.

"She filed a report of assault against him ten days ago—after they rowed over his discovery of her changing her will."

I was speechless, stunned, frozen in time. I felt somehow guilty for not being able to do anything for her. Why hadn't I just patched things up with her? I picked at my food, not really hungry.

"Please eat," Paul said. "You need to keep your strength up."

"I can't eat after hearing all of that. How do you know all of this?"

"One of the guys in my dad's club is a private detective. A damn good one. He also advised me to do what I did with the spycam in your cabin. His brother works in the

FBI and he tipped him off and got the local police involved. The FBI will end up taking the case as it spans more than one state."

"What made her change her will?" I asked. "And how did he get away with all of this?"

"I managed to stumble across a couple of reports where women had stayed at Tim's ranch and reported a man in their cabin at night. No charges were ever brought against him as they couldn't be sure whether it was just a dream or if it was real. I can only assume he was planning on something rather sinister. My guess is that your mum discovered what he was up to."

"This is insane. I just can't believe it."

"He won't ever be getting out," Ash said, reaching over and patting my hand. "You're safe."

Paul nodded. "Definitely. He'll be lucky to escape death row."

I ate a chip and sighed. "Death row is too easy for him. He doesn't deserve a last meal of whatever he wants either. I hope he rots in hell."

Epilogue

THE NEXT FEW DAYS were a blur that I really couldn't have gotten through without Paul. We decorated the main house as best we could for Christmas and made the best of a bad deal. Waking up with him on Christmas day was the only present I ever needed.

Considering the short notice and unexpected stay, none of us had presents for one another, but that didn't matter. What mattered was the fact we were all together as a family, spending time together.

After lunch, Paul suggested we take a walk to help our massive lunch settle. He took my hand and led me outside. We wandered along the edge of the paddock, watching Nelson enjoying his own Christmas lunch of endless grass.

"So," he said, lifting my hand to his mouth and kissing the back of it. "It's been quite an eventful few days, don't you think?"

I nodded. "I think that's putting it mildly."

"Do you think now is a good time to have a conversation about us?"

My heart stilled before restarting and racing to a million miles an hour. "I think it's a perfect time," I said, smiling up at him.

He nodded and gave my hand a reassuring squeeze. "I'm just going to be honest," he said. "I absolutely adore you. I'm crazy about you. You have never left my mind for more than a minute since the day I first laid eyes on you. I know I messed up but if you'll let me, I want to spend the rest of my life making it up to you."

My soul felt like it was leaving my body, floating way up sky high somewhere in the clouds. My head whirled as this new reality took a hold of me. Having this conversation with Paul seemed even more surreal than everything that had just happened.

"I can't think of anything that I want more," I replied, my eyes filling with happy tears. "But what about your parents and everything else?"

He shrugged his shoulders. "I'll deal with it. I'm not letting anything jeopardise me and you. Ever." He pulled us to a stop and swung me round into his warm embrace. Lifting a hand to my cheek, he stroked the back of his hand across it and smiled down at me. "I love you, Kyra Wilson, more than life itself. And I don't want to spend a minute more of my life without you in it."

I let my happy tears spring free as I smiled back up at him. "I love you too, Paul Connors, and if you spend another minute of your life without me then I will hunt you down and kill you."

"You're not wondering what my head looks like on a stick are you?" he asked, grinning.

I grinned back at him. "Not yet."

As he leaned down and graced me with a tender kiss, I couldn't believe that I had finally, at long last, found my happy ending. The journey had been one hellish ride but the destination more than worth it.

The coming months after everything that happened were an eye opener to say the least. We found out that Tim had paid off the local coroner to agree with his version of events and upon having another autopsy done, it turned out that the kick to Mum's head had happened approximately six hours before her death and her actual cause of death was blunt force trauma from what appeared to be a shovel. We now knew why Tim wanted her cremated.

Paul and his father pulled lots of strings and dealt with all the red tape to get Mum flown back home so she could be buried next to Dad. That meant more to me than anything else ever would.

Tim had been formally charged with Mum's murder after our recording of the entire thing on the spycam. His admission to me not being his first victim made the FBI dig deeper and eventually, Tim cracked under the pressure and confessed to everything. I would have been his first murder victim that he hadn't married. I'm not sure if that made me special or just potentially the first of many. I suspected the latter.

Karma really served a boot to Tim as we discovered that his next of kin was my mum. Of course, with us being the beneficiaries to Mum, it meant everything of his was now ours. Given his situation, he signed over his rights to everything being relinquished to Mum's estate.

There were a lot of legal proceedings to get through as a lot of it was classed as evidence where it concerned Tim's money, but as it had been written into wills that it be left to Tim, it was a tricky area.

Ash and Paul went through all of his affairs and were immensely surprised to see he had twenty-four million dollars in the bank. Why someone would want more than that was beyond me. I couldn't understand it.

Paul had entered into negotiations with solicitors to see if he could return the stolen money to the children who had been left behind in Tim's past. It would still leave us with half of what he had but we planned to give that away to charity if we could. The money Mum had left us would easily set me and Ash up for life; we didn't need anymore, and we certainly didn't want Tim's blood money.

We arrived back home at the end of January. Paul had spoken with his parents in great detail whilst we were still in Texas. He ironed everything out with them concerning him and the club.

They eventually decided to split the businesses up—Paul took the nightclubs on, and his parents took the club. When he announced he was looking for somewhere to live, I was amazed to hear his parents immediately concede that they would be the ones to move, not him. They weren't comfortable with forcing him out of his childhood home. By the time we arrived back in the UK, they had bought a new estate and moved everything to it.

I moved in with Paul at his house and rented mine out. Rattling around such a big house seemed peculiar to me but I soon got used to it, and from recent discussions with Paul, I knew it wouldn't be much longer before we weren't alone in the massive house anymore.

The little barn and stables at the back of our house were freshened up and made usable again. We flew Nelson over along with his two favourite mares and decided to start introducing American Quarter Horses over here. Eloise's owner never made a full recovery and gladly sold her to me so she ended up occupying the fourth stable on the yard.

Molly and Chris had gotten divorced rather quickly. Chris pushed it all through, at an insane cost, and managed to get it finalised last week. We kept in touch loosely to see how each other were coping. He was in therapy, still trying to deal with the betrayal by his fiancée and his brother. I felt bad for him, but I knew he would, in time, heal.

Molly moved to Wales to get a fresh start. She never attempted any sort of contact with me and I was grateful for that.

Scott moved out to the States courtesy of his father. I was a little saddened to hear he had been shot and killed in a series of riots that took place in Boston where he was visiting for a few days. I knew he never intended me any harm and I felt that was a rather sticky end to meet. Paul and Ash, on the other hand, gave each other a high-five when they heard the news.

Whilst I continued on with my criminology degree, I found myself going into business with Rebecca training horses. Her and Paul's relationship flourished now he had cut his ties to the club and I couldn't be more pleased that things had turned around for both of them.

Ash and Ben announced they were getting married at the end of the year after they had now permanently relocated themselves out in Texas. Ash was teaching Ben about horses and they were making a good go at running a dude ranch along with some help from the locals.

Everything settled and made itself right. I couldn't have asked for anything more. Today, nearly a year on from where I had first started, had been the cherry on the cake, and as I lay in bed listening to the rhythmic breathing of my sleeping Greek god next to me, I couldn't help but grin.

I lifted my left hand up in the moonlight streaming through our window and twirled the sparkling diamond around my third finger with an aching smile spreading onto my face. He'd proposed to me only a few short hours previously.

I'd been competing at a one-day event with one of the up-and-coming youngsters. After a rather sticky situation at one of the fences out on the cross-country course, we came home, splattered in mud and me utterly overjoyed I was still alive after he refused a simple log fence and sent me flying into a puddle of mud.

I slid down from the saddle weak at the knees and gasping for breath. I'd turned to lead the horse back to the lorry when Paul greeted me with a stupid grin on his face. He hugged me in his designer clothes before bending down on one knee.

Opening a dark blue velvet box, he presented me with a stunning diamond ring and the words, "If this is the worst you'll ever look, which I think it is, then I'd still marry you right now if I could. Will you marry me?"

He'd been grinning like a Cheshire cat as he'd said it, full well knowing how I'd react to him doing that to me at such a horrifying moment.

I pushed him over into the squelching grass before jumping on him like a starfish on ecstasy and screaming my answer in delight. I then interrogated him as to why he couldn't have given me hearts and flowers and let me look my best.

His response, with a big grin, had simply been, "Because then it wouldn't have been a surprise."

I couldn't believe after the past year of insane highs and hitting real rock bottoms, that we had both given in to our want and need of each other, despite everything being against us.

We had finally found our happy ending.

A Note from the Author

I hope you enjoyed Kyra's story. If you did, I would be eternally grateful if you could leave a review to let others know how much you enjoyed it. Even one sentence is fine. Thank you so much!

If you want to follow me and keep up to date with all my latest goings on, visit www.cjlauthor.com and sign up for my newsletter, or look me up in the places below:

www.facebook.com/CJLaurenceAuthor
www.instagram.com/cjlauthor
https://www.bookbub.com/authors/c-j-laurence

I love hearing from my readers and will always reply to you!